SEXY FILTHY BOSS

PIPER RAYNE

Cover Design: Okay Creations

First Editor: Joy Editing

Second Editor: My Brother's Editor

Proofreader: Shawna Gavas, Behind The Writer

DEDICATION

With love to a real OG Unicorn:
Ceej Chargualaf
We miss you everyday.
Rest in peace.

About Sexy Filthy Boss

He's the sexy alpha male in the corner office who goes through assistants faster than free donuts in the breakroom.

I'm the assistant who was chosen to cover for his last fire.

The owner of the company is clear—hook the biggest client in our firm's history and there's a partnership for him and a promotion for me. Stipulation—we do it together.

It doesn't take a tarot card-reading psychic to figure out where our story is headed... late nights, trips out of town, and more than a few awkward moments filled with sexual tension.

No worries though. I pride myself on my willpower. I can totally ignore his sexy grin, his rock-hard body and his dreamy brown eyes. I will not become the woman other women hate.

But it turns out that Enzo Mancini has a lot of layers and if I don't stop peeling, I'm going to lose everything, including my dignity.

SEXY FILTHY BOSS

CHAPTER ONE

Annie

"I QUIT!" a woman's shout echoes through the office.

"Good. I was about to fire you anyway. You're saving me some paperwork." Enzo Mancini's office door opens, and his voice travels all the way to my desk.

Seconds later, the phone on my desk rings, and I pick it up.

"And... she's gone," my coworker and friend, Jake, says with a chuckle.

"I give her credit. She lasted two weeks longer than I gave her."

He sighs. "Damn it. That means Mae won the pool again. Put your drinking cap on, we're going out tonight."

From the corner of my eye, I spot my boss, Shelby, speed-walking through the open floor plan in her heels, ordering everyone back to work as though we're a bunch of fourth graders. She's officially the one in charge of all the admin staff, but we each work side-by-side with one of the senior advertising executives, so in essence, we all have two bosses. Lucky us.

"Shelby's on the move," I say in a low voice.

"She looks semi-frantic this time around," Jake comments, having more of a front row seat than I do at this end of the office. While I get the privilege of counting our coworker Milo's trips to the bathroom because of his weak bladder, Jake is blessed with staring at Enzo Mancini whenever he wants. Life is so unfair.

I lean back in my office chair, tapping my pen on the desk. "Sorry, you'll have to navigate Mae all by yourself. I've got plans." I glance at the time on my computer screen. "Damn, I better go if I'm going to make it."

"Where are you going?" he asks.

Mr. Mancini must have come out of his office because I can hear his now calmer voice more clearly. "Explain something to me, Shelby..." The door to his office must close then, because I can't hear anything else.

"I'll tell you after," I say.

He tsks. "Secrets won't win you any friends, Annie."

I open my bottom drawer, grabbing my purse.

"Oh, shit." Jake hangs up.

I look across the office to see a bunch of the assistants on the move, all disappearing in different directions. A few head to the break room, a few to the bathroom, and the rest sprinkle over to my side of the office. I double-check my desk to be sure I haven't left anything I'll need this weekend and look up to find Shelby and Mr. Mancini's former assistant walking toward me.

"Mr. Mancini is a difficult man to please. You're not the first one to quit. Don't feel too bad about it." Shelby walks by with her arm around the assistant's shoulders.

"I thought I was supposed to be learning. Shouldn't he have worked with me?" The poor girl has no idea how screwed she was when she was hired on as Lorenzo Mancini's assistant.

"Mr. Mancini does things differently than our other ad execs. If you need a reference, please have them contact me." Shelby shoots me a sympathetic smile as she walks by my desk.

I smile at her, hoisting my purse on my shoulder and grabbing my rain jacket from the coat hanger outside Mr. Beardsman's office. I'm hurrying because I'm scheduled to leave early today, and everyone knows that someone will have to cover now that Mr. Mancini's assistant is gone. It's not like Enzo Mancini can get his own coffee, let alone use the big, bad copy machine. Perish the thought.

The presentation for Coddle is this afternoon, and if he lands the account, he could very well be named partner by the end of the year. No way will he prepare alone for something so huge.

I knock on Mr. Beardsman's door.

"Come in." Mr. Beardsman hangs up the phone and swivels in my direction, his usual smile on his face.

"Do you need anything else before I leave?" I tie my rain jacket at my waist.

"No, I'm right behind you. Can you believe my Scarlett is in her first play?" He beams at the picture of his daughter on his desk.

"Tell her I said break a leg, though I know she'll do great. Oh, I should have gotten you flowers to give her for after." Damn it, I meant to run to the florist during my break this morning.

"You spoil me, Annie. They'll mean more if I do it

myself. Plus, you helped me with that Nectar ad. I should be thanking you."

Could my boss be any better? He's in at nine, out at five. Never expects me to work on weekends or after hours. Mr. Beardsman took me under his wing two years ago, enabling me to slowly gain the knowledge I'll need to one day become a full-fledged ad exec. Sure I haven't gotten to work on an actual campaign yet, but I'm involved in all the periphery stuff.

He stands, collecting his briefcase and his umbrella. He eyes the clock and glances at me. "Soon you'll probably get promoted over me."

He smiles as if the thought doesn't bother him in the least. Although, I don't think he's right about that.

I smile. "I'll see you Monday."

"Have a great weekend." He shrugs on his coat.

I walk out of his office and right into Shelby.

"Annie," she sighs, relief in her shoulders as though I'm her life preserver after treading water for hours.

"I'm off this afternoon. I can't do it."

"He needs someone." She chases me to the elevator.

I press the button to call the elevator. "Not me."

"It's just for one afternoon," she insists.

We wait by the elevator, Shelby at my side. I examine her sweater vest, complete with sporadic cat hairs poking out. Will I be her one day? No, I'm *choosing* to be alone. It's different.

"I have plans, otherwise you know I would," I say to fill the silence.

"Shelby!" Mr. Mancini bellows as he walks down the hallway.

I press the down button on the elevator again, harder this time, and glance to the stairwell sign. Tempting, but seventy-five floors isn't ideal in my heels. I'd be soaked in sweat before I made it onto the Manhattan street.

Shelby pales as her eyes flicker to Mr. Mancini walking toward us. "Please. I'll give you two days extra days of vacation. Name your price."

"I'm sorry."

The elevator doors ding open, and I step in as Mr. Mancini reaches Shelby. She throws herself between the elevator doors before they shut, and they pop back open. I catch Jake and Mae snickering as they watch, and I narrow my eyes, pressing the button for the ground level.

Mr. Mancini holds a stack of papers. "Who's mine for the rest of the day?"

Shelby shoots me pathetic and somewhat desperate eyes. She smiles at Mr. Mancini, putting up her finger. "One moment." She turns to me, tearing up. "I'd do it myself, but I have to get Pinkie to the vet later today. She's in awful pain. I think something is wrong with her."

I sigh. Using a sick cat is a low blow. But Shelby would never lie about that because she'd be worried about karma coming back to her or one of her precious cats.

I contemplate my choices. The pedicure I was getting before moving into my new place can wait. If I get out by four, I'll be good.

"I can only stay until four." I step out of the elevator.

The papers are still under Mr. Mancini's arm, and his thumbs move over the screen of his phone like a teenager.

"You know Annie Stewart, Ted Beardsman's assistant?" Shelby touches his upper arm.

I bet it's rock hard with muscle.

He nods without lifting his head, still entranced with his phone. A moment later, he takes a break from texting and hands me the pile of papers, not bothering to look at me. "I need this proposal copied and bound. There will be six people total." He turns on his heel and walks down the hallway.

"See you, Enzo," Mr. Beardsman says while walking toward us, his forehead crinkling the closer he gets.

"Ted?" Mr. Mancini stops him.

They talk about something I can't hear, but Ted laughs and slaps Enzo on the back.

"Just remember come Monday, she's back to being mine."

Mr. Mancini must say something else because Ted laughs again. Lorenzo Mancini, funny man. Yeah, right.

Mr. Beardsman joins us at the elevators, pressing the down button. "You're too nice, Annie. Should've run out of here."

He steps into the elevator while I stand here holding a stack of papers that came with instructions from a man who didn't bother to look me in the eye. "You so owe me, Shelby."

I stomp down the hallway and throw my purse and jacket onto my chair like a toddler having a fit. If I could, I'd jump up and down, screaming. After grabbing my cell phone from my purse, I text Jake and Mae and head to the copy room.

I'm not in there for more than a minute before they join me and shut the door. I blow out a breath, organizing the papers in my hand.

"Sorry," Jake says, sliding onto the table with a bag of Twizzlers. Obviously, he hid out in the break room.

"You could've taken one for the team." I shoot the papers through the color copier.

"I'm innocent. I'm in accounting." Mae holds up her

hands and joins Jake on the table, digging her hand into the bag of Twizzlers on his lap.

"I had somewhere to be," I whine, grabbing my own Twizzler from Jake's stash. I bite off the top of it with more ferocity than necessary.

Jake tilts his head. "And where is that?"

I roll my eyes.

Mae says nothing because she already knows.

"Nowhere, but if I don't get out of here by four o'clock, I'm going to make a little voodoo doll of you, Jake Hill, and prick you right between the legs."

Mae laughs.

Jake squeezes his thighs together. "Whoa. That's harsh."

The copies finish, and I shift my attention to the binding area. Jake stays put, but Mae hops down and puts her hand on my shoulder.

"I'll be over tonight to help," she whispers.

"What am I missing? I thought this was a three-way friendship?"

Mae and I look over our shoulders and laugh. I pop the rest of the licorice into my mouth.

"You wish it could be a three-way." Mae leans across the small room, grabs two more pieces of licorice, and hands one to me.

"We *are* alone and there's a lock on this door..."

I put my hand to my ear. "Ever heard of sexual harassment?"

"Relax, I see you both as sisters."

I wink and bind the third presentation together. There's silence except for the sound of each of us chewing.

"Come on, guys. I feel like that loser friend no one talks to," Jake whines.

Mae shakes her head, eyeing me to see if I'm willing to share my news. The only reason I've kept it from him is because I don't want him making a big deal of it. Though it *is* a big deal to me, it's not as though people don't buy condos every day.

I turn around, and Mae takes over binding the next presentation packet for me. "I'm moving. I bought a condo."

He jumps off the table and wraps his arms around me, dancing in the middle of the room.

"It's small. One-bedroom and in Inwood, so..."

He continues to sway us side to side with his arms around me, while Mae finishes my job for me.

"I have to call my dad to meet the movers now." I groan.

"Your dad loves doing stuff like that," Mae says.

"We need to celebrate." Jake spins me just as the door opens.

He loses his grip, and I twirl until I fall into a rock-hard body. One fleeting glance into his soft brown eyes and I slide down his body as though he's caked in Vaseline, landing in a heap at his feet.

"What the hell is going on in here?" Mr. Mancini's voice booms through the small room.

Did God curse him because he's so beautiful? When he was doling out attributes, did he check the box next to "ass-hole" to prove you can't have everything in life?

CHAPTER TWO

Enzo

I stare down at the replacement assistant. Ann, Erin, or something. She blows the dark hair falling down over her forehead from her eyes and glares at me.

She has a backbone, I'll give her that.

"Sorry, Annie," the male assistant whose desk is near my office says. He's always eavesdropping on my conversations and thinks I don't know.

"I'm sorry, Mr. Mancini, I'll be right in your office with your files," the replacement says.

I cross my arms. "I didn't mean to interrupt your party."

"Oh no, we were just, um… I was sharing some good news with my friends." Her cheeks redden. It's a cute look for her. Innocent and pleasing. I wouldn't mind seeing that same look on her face when she's on her knees, sucking me.

My forehead creases in irritation as I reprimand myself. My line of thinking isn't appropriate, and I've never thought anything like that about someone who works for me. Even when that blonde with the breast and butt implants was my assistant.

But this woman's not my assistant. I'm simply borrowing her from Ted Beardsman. I'm sure she doesn't get enough work from that guy to keep her busy anyway.

"That's what five o'clock down at Blarneys is for." I turn but stop at the door. "Three minutes, Erin."

The guy scoffs and I'm guessing I got her name wrong, but she's temporary, so what does it matter as long as she does what I need her to.

Heading into my office, I look at the assistant's desk. At least the girl I fired took her plant with her. Thank fuck. She kept going on and on about how it's aloe and if I wanted, I could rip a section off and run it along my skin. Did she not realize this is an ad company, not a massage parlor?

My phone vibrates on my desk, and I hurry to grab it, figuring out too late it's Carm. "What?"

"Nice way to answer the phone for your younger brother, dickwad."

I sit down, my attention on my computer screen, clicking through the slides. "I'm busy. I've got a presentation in about an hour and my assistant just quit."

He laughs. Of course he does. Carm would have to flick his assistants off like leeches because he treats them too nicely. Once, he gave an assistant a purse he'd noticed her admiring at an open house. 'Course, he was probably fucking her. He denied it, but everyone knows Carm lies about stupid shit like that.

"This the one you could make partner with?"

"Don't jinx it." I click through the rest of the slides. "Why are you calling me?"

"I set up a basketball game for tomorrow."

"Cool."

"We're playing at the rec center by Ma's."

"What? Why aren't we playing here in Manhattan?"

"Because the team we're playing is in Brooklyn. I figured I'd hear no complaints from the rest of you. We're going to get our championship back."

I rub my hands together. "Why didn't you start with that? How are you a successful real estate broker?"

"It's called closing the deal."

"Piss off."

A knock sounds on my glass door.

"Gotta go." I click off on the phone and wave in the temp.

"Here you go, Mr. Mancini. What else did you need?" She pulls out her pad and pen. "I don't know where Denise was with everything."

"Denise?"

Her jaw tenses but loosens immediately. Doesn't matter, I've already read her body language. "Your previous assistant."

"Oh yeah. My assumption is that her notes are on her desk, but I'm fairly sure she's done nothing." I stare at the screen in front of me. The words are perfect, and this presentation is the best I've done on something family related. How I got chosen for an ad campaign geared toward families who buy diapers, I haven't a clue, but if I can sign this client, I'm a shoo-in for partner.

"I'll go check and I, um..." She straightens her back. False bravado. "I have to leave at four." She swivels on her heels to leave.

"Nope. I need you in the room to take notes for me."

Her fake smile falters, and a look I'm used to getting

from my assistants transforms her face. No longer are those cheeks slightly pink with a flush. Her eyes are shooting red and her muscles tense. "I am doing this as a favor. I had planned to have the afternoon off since Mr. Beardsman is off too. I'm helping because you're in a bind. I don't sit in on Mr. Beardsman's meetings, so I don't see why I would sit in on yours."

If I didn't love Teddy, I'd tell his assistant she doesn't sit in because he keeps her at arm's length on purpose. I may not hold my assistant's hand through preparation of my presentations, or even allow any input from them, but they've all sat through pitches. They've seen the good, the bad—hell, one of them saw me practically beg once at the beginning of my career.

I sit up straighter. "I'm curious, Miss...?"

"Stewart. Annie Stewart." Her jaw tics.

"Miss Stewart, other than having dance parties in the break room, I assume you must value your job. My other assumption is you're not interested in being an assistant forever, otherwise you would have told Shelby to shove it and hopped on that elevator, to hell with the consequences."

Her eyes fixate on my steepled fingers.

"Watching me pitch to what could be our biggest client is a huge opportunity for your career. You're willing to let that go for some primping before your Friday night date?"

Her chest rises and falls, her gaze meeting mine. "Of course, you're right. I'd be happy to sit in on the pitch."

"Would you like to have dinner after?" I ask.

She huffs and turns around to leave.

I chuckle. "A celebratory dinner with the clients, of course."

She turns back to face me and swallows. I'm unsure

why I'm enjoying this. I shouldn't. She's right, she did me a favor by sticking around. Although since she's Teddy's assistant, I don't hold out hope she's worth much as far as talent. I'll probably be leading her the entire way this afternoon.

"That would be great. Thank you, Mr. Mancini."

"Enzo."

Her eyes widen a fraction of an inch, but I catch it.

"Call me Enzo."

"Then feel free to call me Annie, not Erin."

"We're not equals here, Miss Stewart. Better to remember that."

She blinks but doesn't say anything, leaving my office while probably wishing she could slam the door.

Once again, rather than annoying, I find her amusing for some reason.

I STEP into the boardroom at three thirty and color me impressed. Trays of refreshments have been set in the middle of the table. Each chair setting has a bottle of water from a brand we handle the advertising for. Each person's packet has been printed and set in front of each chair.

I straighten my suit jacket and smooth out my tie while I soak in the room. Maybe I was wrong about Miss Stewart. I straighten a few of the binders. "Nice."

"I already had the tech department come in, and everything is set for you when you're ready to present." She signals to my computer and the white screen in front of the oval table.

"Thank you."

A buzz rings from the phone in the room. "Annie, the

clients are here," Elise from reception says through the intercom.

She smiles at me, straightening her dress. "I'll be back."

I say nothing as she walks out of the room. I could compliment her on a job well done thus far, but right now, it's her plump ass in her tight pencil skirt I'd like to compliment.

Damn it. She needs to go back to work under Teddy, pronto.

I stare at the New York skyline, hands in my pockets, while I wait. *You got this. You're Lorenzo Mancini. The best in this biz.*

"Mr. Mancini," Annie interrupts my mental pep talk, the one I do before every pitch.

I straighten my tie and turn around. I make sure to make eye contact with each of them and give them a big, toothy smile with my newly whitened teeth. Holding my hand, I break the distance. "Nice to see you all again."

We all shake hands and say our hellos and Billy from the art department joins us before they each find a spot at the table.

"Miss Stewart will be assisting me today, so if you need anything, she'll be happy to help." I approach the head of the table as our owner, Mr. Jacobson, pulls out a chair for Annie and she smiles, sitting down.

"I can't wait to hear what you have for us, Enzo." Mr. Peterson, the President of Coddle, says.

I nod. This is the first time I've been nervous in years.

"First of all, we decided to go a more comedic than heartfelt route. We focused more on dads and the ease..." Once I start the spiel I've practiced for the past week, the tension lifts off my shoulders and I'm in the zone. I run my hands over one another, confident in the campaign I put together.

I don't even have to motion for Miss Stewart to turn off the lights. She must have read my proposal and knew just when to do it.

As I lean against the ledge along the window, watching the short film Billy in creative put together, I'm feeling good. It's funny and every dad will love it. The last line comes on along the bottom of the screen over an image of a sleeping father and an infant wearing only a diaper... Fatherproof.

The lights slowly come to life so that no one has to blink and see stars. Good thought on Miss Stewart's part.

Mr. Jacobson gives me a thumbs-up, but I turn my attention to Bill Peterson. He's the decision-maker.

"Well, it was okay... do you have anything else?" he asks, his attention going to the woman across from him.

I glance at Billy to my right. "We had a few other ideas, but none as great as this one."

Mr. Peterson's silence tells me I didn't hit this out of the park.

"Give us a few days to think it over." He grabs the binder from the table.

Mr. Jacobson widens his eyes because we both know that if Mr. Peterson leaves, he'll end up somewhere else.

"Mr. Peterson"—I slide the chair out next to him and take a seat—"clearly you don't love it."

He leans back in his seat, steepling his fingers in front of him. "We usually prefer to go the more emotional route, tug at the heartstrings."

"Isn't that what *all* diaper companies do? With something like this, you'll stand out." I glance at the woman who was introduced as his daughter earlier. I noticed Mr.

Peterson glancing over to her while the video was rolling, gauging her reaction so she must have some say.

"Blair, right?" I ask.

She nods.

Inching my hand up the table, I grab my pen and search for something to write on.

"Here you go." A pad of paper slides across the table.

I thank Miss Stewart with a nod. She doesn't smile.

"Give me five words," I say to Blair.

"What will that do?" she asks.

I wave. "Five words you want to see in your commercial. Not the actual word but the feelings or actions. For example, love, crying..."

She glances at her father. "Really, Enzo, I think we have enough information. Let us think this one over."

Mr. Jacobson shakes his head.

My blood pressure rises, and I feel the blood pulsing in my neck. I have no doubt that everyone at this table can probably see it.

"Are you looking for just a mother in the commercial?" Even I hear the panic in my voice. *Calm down.*

"Or are you looking for a shared moment between parents?" Annie chimes in.

I really don't need her input, but Blair's eyes light up and she grants Annie all her attention.

"Like how?" I ask, drawing her attention back my way.

"You figure babies bring people together. A couple doesn't have to be married or even like one another to smile at their baby with one another. Families come together when a baby is born. It's magical when a new life is brought into the world." I swear Annie's eyes are tearing up.

Blair points at her. "Exactly." She looks back my way. "That's what we want, what she just said."

"A family? You're in luck, I come from a big Italian family. I know all about family. Give us a couple weeks and we'll have a whole new campaign ready for you." I slide out from the table, offering my hand to Blair Peterson.

She stands and nods to her father, shaking my hand.

"Will she be on your team?" Bill Peterson asks.

Mr. Jacobson smiles at Annie and back at me. "I'll make certain of it," he answers before I can say that she's an assistant. And not even my own.

"Great. It's been a pleasure."

"I'll see you out." Annie walks Mr. Peterson, his daughter, and the rest of his people out of the room and Mr. Jacobson joins them.

I slump down in the chair, Billy across from me.

"I don't get it," I say.

"She kind of saved our asses." Billy stands.

She returns, standing in the doorway.

"Thanks, Annie." Billy pats her on the back on his way out.

"Have a great weekend, Mr. Mancini." She smiles and leaves the conference room.

I don't bother mentioning the celebratory dinner we were supposed to be having. There's not much to celebrate at the moment unless you count being upstaged by an assistant.

CHAPTER THREE

Annie

My mood is soaring by the time I reach my new condo. Coddle loved my idea. I want to run and tap my heels together when I hop out of my taxi and see a moving truck pulling away from the building.

I practically run through the lobby and into the elevator. When I reach my floor, my condo door is open, my dad, Mae, and Jake inside unpacking boxes.

"Dad, thank you," I say, dropping my purse and bag on the couch.

"What else did I have to do today?"

"And you guys were going to go out," I say to Mae and Jake. I hurry to help my dad unload my cups into the cabinet.

"The quicker we get you moved in, the quicker Mae buys us drinks." Jake winks. "Unless someone has to take your sister to the hospital."

"What?" I screech, abandoning my dad, but I don't have to go far.

Beth waddles down the hallway, holding her back. "Someone needs to call the toilet paper police. She had two boxes full of toilet paper."

"Beth, sit down." I move my coat and bag off the couch.

She waves me off. "I'm trying to induce the baby." She looks at her swollen belly. "You have two more days before I ground you for the rest of your life." She sits down and puts her feet up on my coffee table.

"What does Sam have to say about this?" I ask with a smile.

She waves me off again. "Ask him. Sam!"

"What?" A bunch of metal clanks down the hall. "Is it time?" He appears in the doorway, his forehead slick with sweat.

"No, because the baby is as stubborn as you."

Sam rolls his eyes at me, and I smile. "You're right, honey, *I'm* the stubborn one."

"Spoken like a trained husband." Mae joins Beth on the couch, her hand clutching a bag of chips, then places her ear on her belly. "Can I listen?"

"You guys are too much. I can get all this done on my own." Although the stacks of boxes lining the walls are a tad overwhelming.

"Who's going to put your bed together? Jake?" Beth grabs a chip from Mae's bag.

"I'm going to ignore that dig. I could've done it." Jake rips open a box with gusto.

Beth rolls her eyes. "Whoa, Hercules, don't make more work for us than necessary."

"Oh!" Mae's head shoots up off Beth's stomach. "Piss

her off some more, Jake, he's moving." She places her head back down.

I leave those two on the couch, knowing Mae's probably just doing her best to keep Beth seated. I unpack some pots and pans, tackling the kitchen first like my dad taught me.

"So?" Jake eyes me.

"What?" I hand a stack of pots to my dad and he puts them in a cabinet. I'll move them after he leaves.

"When I left, you were sitting in a dark room with Lorenzo Mancini."

"Who's he?" Beth asks Mae.

Mae dramatically sighs. "Only the hottest asshole you'd ever want in your bed."

"Asshole being the keyword." Jake's gaze falls on my dad's back. "Sorry, Mr. Stewart."

"Thanks, Jake, but I've heard the word before."

"Why was my baby sister in a dark room with him?" Beth digs her hand in Mae's bag of chips and pops one in her mouth. So much for her "I eat healthy for the baby" mantra.

"It was a presentation for a client and Mr. Jacobson was in the room too, as were a lot of other people," I say, pulling more kitchen items from the box.

"Kinky. I had no idea." Jake laughs.

"Tread carefully," my dad says.

I stick my tongue out at Jake and point at him as if we're ten and he got in trouble.

"I thought you worked for some Beard guy?" Beth asks.

"She does, but Mr. Mancini is famous for losing every assistant who works for him. Everyone knows to get the hell out of Dodge when it happens mid-day because the man can do nothing for himself." Jake tears open another box.

"I'd like him to make me a cup of coffee one day. Preferably naked." Mae looks up at the ceiling as though someone's going to answer her wish.

"He's so good-looking that it overrides his jerkiness?" Beth asks, reaching for a chip.

Mae hands her one then places her hands on my sister's belly. "Do you like the salt?" she baby-talks to my sister's belly.

"No. The fact that he can't manage to make one copy by himself or even remember my name brings his attractiveness down, believe me." Even I hear the lie in my tone.

"Huh. I think I need to come into the office."

I point at my sister. "You stay far away."

She laughs, and Mae sits up, crossing her ankles on the couch while pulling out her phone. "Here."

"How do you even have a picture of him?" I find myself leaving my dad's side to go check it out.

"It was an article some Manhattan business magazine did on him, and guess who his brother is?"

No one answers.

"Carmelo Mancini, the realtor guy."

"The half-naked guy on the billboards that say, 'You know you want it'?" Beth laughs while her finger scrolls down the screen.

I sit on the edge of the sofa. "I'm sure that was his brother's idea."

"He's just as good-looking as his brother though. If I was in the market to buy a place, I'd definitely call him."

I roll my eyes at Mae and stand up before drool actually falls from my mouth. The picture of Mr. Mancini in the article is definitely drool-worthy. He's seated on a couch with a drink in his hand, staring out over the New York skyline like he owns the city.

"Very eatable," Beth says and hands back the phone.

"You mean edible?" I ask, returning to my dad, who throws up his hands.

"I have a feeling Sam needs my help."

We laugh as my dad shakes his head, walking down the hallway.

"So you like him?" Beth asks.

"*No*!" I screech.

"She does," Jake deadpans. "Like, drool-down-her-chin and heart eyes every time he walks by. I give you props, today must have been so hard."

"Shut up!" I throw wadded-up newspaper at him. "I would never date a man like Enzo Mancini. Not that he'd ever look for a girlfriend. I mean, he's about as soulless as Ted Bundy."

"Oh, comparing him to a serial killer. Could you by chance be in denial?" Mae taps her lips.

I narrow my eyes.

"She's always liked unavailable men," Beth says, sliding to the edge of the couch. I pray she's going to have the baby so I can get out of this conversation.

"Beth..."

She laughs. Mae helps her to her feet when she sees my sister struggling. Seriously, I already secretly love my niece or nephew for putting my sister through this hell.

"You always love the ones who don't want love. Remember Timmy Gross, senior year?"

"Other than his name, what was wrong with him?" Jake asks, handing me a stack of plates.

"He was the quarterback of the football team and asked Annie to senior prom, but then ended up skipping it altogether to head to a college party. She had to go stag."

"Thanks for that trip down memory lane, sis. Any other horrible times you'd like to bring up to boost my self-esteem?" I break down a box, imagining it's Timmy's head.

"I keep telling you it's their loss, but this guy, he sounds like the kind of guy who will break your heart."

"Give me some credit. I'm twenty-seven now. I know a bad boy when I see one. Especially one who would never commit. Besides, you'll be happy to know he doesn't even know my name. So everyone can just stay out of my love life."

Beth takes a sip of water, one hand on her belly as she stares at me. "Just reminding you. Remember Sam has that cousin who really liked you at the wedding."

Mae cringes behind my sister's back because I told her all about the guy with the bad breath and a diamond stud who wouldn't leave me alone at my sister's wedding.

"Thanks, but I don't think he's my type."

Beth rolls her eyes. "I can see that. I mean, he's a nice guy looking for a wife and excited to have a family. Definitely not Annie Stewart's type."

I've never been so happy to see my sister waddle away.

Mae rushes over and sits on a stack of boxes. "So tell us for real. How was he to work with?"

"Well, after the striptease and asking me to lick whipped cream off his abs..."

Mae's eyes are practically lighting up.

"Snap out of it," I scold. "It was horrible, and now Mr. Jacobson wants me to work on the Coddle ad with him because I opened my big mouth in the meeting."

Jake stops and slides to the side of the box. "You get to work on the Coddle account?"

"Well, I mean, who knows. Mr. Mancini will probably squeeze me out."

"Do *not* let him. This is your big opportunity." Jake's

hands land on my shoulders. "You better let me ride your rainbow all the way to the top with you."

I laugh. "I'm pretty sure I'm going nowhere."

"It's the biggest account Jacobson and Earl have ever had a shot at. I heard the diapers account is only the beginning. That if we nail the diaper campaign, they'll shift everything over to us. A whole rebranding of all their product lines." Jake's way more excited than I am. "Pretty soon, you'll be out of Inwood and moving to the Upper East Side."

I roll my eyes. "Shut up. Honestly. Nothing is going to happen."

Jake raises his eyebrows and returns to unpacking boxes. Mae squeezes my forearm and gives me a smile.

I take a moment to let it sink in... what it might mean if I actually get to contribute to the Coddle campaign. It would do amazing things for my career. But working alongside Enzo Mancini presents its own challenges. Challenges I'm determined to meet.

CHAPTER FOUR

Enzo

"What are you so pissed off at?" Carm asks, shoving the basketball at my chest.

"Nothing. Let's just play."

"You ditched me last night. Wanna talk about that?"

"Sorry." I dribble and dodge by him, scoring.

We're warming up, waiting for the rest of our team. Dom isn't here yet, which is odd. He's usually the one waiting for us.

"Sorry? I waited at the bar for an hour, man."

"I told you. I got caught up at the office." I check the ball and bounce it back to him.

He shakes his head. "Who is she?"

Carm dribbles by me, and I have no energy to fight him. I was up half the night, trying to figure out why I hadn't landed the best account to come my way. A deal that should have earned me a seat at the table. Making partner at thirty-one? It's unheard of, but I deserve it. Or I did until yesterday.

"She? What the hell are you talking about?" I ask.

"You've never ditched me, except for that time that girl surprised you. Remember, the lingerie, the soft music, the dinner..."

"You're such a chick. How do you remember that stuff? All I remember from that evening is her on her knees, right about to deep throat me, then asking me to meet her parents the next morning for brunch. She was either brilliant or an idiot. It was a good tactic, but she didn't get one by me." I dribble and take a three-pointer.

Carm grabs the ball, dribbling to the top of the line. "You're such an asshole. If Ma knew what you do, she'd smack you upside the head." He throws the ball back to me to check, and I bounce it his way.

"You're judging me? I don't see any permanent fixtures in your life."

He shrugs and smirks.

"What? You dating someone?"

"Hell no, but I like to think I'm not as screwed up in the head as you are. That one day I'll make Mama understand why I'm her favorite." He winks, ducks left, then goes right for a lay-up.

"For starters, I'm not screwed up in the head. I like my life. I'm not anti-anything, I just like not answering to anyone. I like being a bachelor."

"And you *like* a different woman every week." He laughs, tossing me the ball.

"Variety is the spice of life, brother."

He laughs.

"Seriously though, it's not even about the women. It's the fact that no one's telling me I have to go shopping on

Saturday and dragging me around a million candle shops or taking me on a wild goose chase to find a certain color rug." I toss the ball to him for a check.

He rolls his eyes. "God forbid."

"Oh please, you can stop the whole holier-than-thou act. You're not exactly a put-a-ring-on-it kind of guy either."

He laughs. "True, but it's more fun making fun of you. For me, it's my schedule. I don't have the time."

"Speaking of, how's the new ad campaign going?" I step to the side and swish one in for another three-pointer.

"The cocky asshole image works." He shrugs.

A grin tilts up the corner of my lips. See, this is where I excel. Give me a sports car, a cologne, a deodorant, any product geared to the male persuasion, and I'll nail the campaign with one suggestion. But this whole diaper, baby, family crap is impossible to understand. I spent most of last night replaying the meeting with Coddle. Including the way Annie slid in and stripped their attention from me and saved the day.

"Hello?" Carm waves his hand in front of my face.

I blink, shaking my head before I spend all day today trying to figure out the missing puzzle piece.

"What's going on?" he presses when I dribble, and he blocks the shot without much effort.

"Nothing. Just work."

He glances at the clock. "Where the hell is Dom? Do you want to talk?"

I stare off to the side and wonder if I do. I'm not a touchy-feely guy, but this is work, and if anyone understands being at the top of your game, it's my brother. I nod, so we walk over to the bleachers and sit. We both sip our waters. Playing at my old school gym brings back memories of when I was a pretty big deal.

"This new account," I say. "It's for diapers, and as much as I hate to admit it, I'm struggling to come up with a great campaign."

He laughs, clutching his stomach. "Why the hell would they give you a diaper campaign?"

"Because it's the big fish and I've got the biggest hook."

He chuckles, crushing his empty water bottle. "Your ego amazes me."

"You share the same one, so I'm not sure why you're surprised."

The doors open and Dom busts in with his arms open wide. "The party has arrived!"

"Only one of us has a bigger ego in this family." Carm rolls his eyes. "Finally."

Dom drops his bag on the bleachers. "Sorry, guys. Had a hard time getting out of bed this morning." He hits the basketball from under my arm and dribbles it through his legs and spins it on his finger as though he's the next Globe-trotter.

"Do I even want to know?" I ask.

"We don't." Carm smacks the ball out of Dom's hand and dribbles to the hoop.

"She might be worth a second time." He clicks the roof of his mouth with his tongue. "And get this. After shower sex this morning, she's the one who handed me my clothes and said she had somewhere to be."

I stare dumbfounded at my older brother. "So hold up, you wanted to stay, and she told you to go? And that's a good thing?"

Dom steals the ball from Carm and throws it at me. "Yeah, it means she doesn't want strings. How fuckin' perfect is that? I've been searching for a consistent hook-up who isn't going to harp on and on about my time at the office, marriage, and babies."

"Way to have goals in life." I toss the ball to Carm, who dribbles past Dom and scores.

"It's the perfect plan. I don't have to leave work early just to butter up some girl at a club."

"Perfect. You can sit at your desk, have Uber Eats deliver your food, and now order sex on speed dial." Carm's sarcastic tone doesn't register to Dom.

"I know, right?"

I shake my head. "Let's just play."

I need to get my head away from my problems—one Annie Stewart and one diaper company—for at least the next hour.

ALL THREE OF us are sweaty messes when we arrive at my parents' house.

Walking in, the smell of garlic accosts us. I bet my brothers' stomachs rumble from the smell too. All three of us walk right through the living room into the kitchen, take forks from the drawer, and stab the simmering meatballs. We give my mom a wave because she has the phone pressed to her ear.

"Oh, Maria, I'm so happy for you. Yes, we need to get planning. Let us know when a date is set. Ciao."

My brothers and I stop and stare at one another, knowing we're walking into another rendition of "why can't you be more like your cousins."

Ma puts down her phone and smiles at us. Not one word about us digging into the meal she's yet to finish preparing. She doesn't tell us what furniture she wants moved to the basement so she can make a sewing room out of a bedroom. She just turns her back and stirs the gravy.

Our faces fall. Somehow, this is worse than the lecture.

We point at one another, trying to silently force one of us to make the first move. With that not accomplishing anything, we set our forks on the tray and run a game of rock, paper, scissors.

Our fists slam into our palms three times.

Dom chooses paper.

Carm chooses paper.

I choose rock.

Damn it.

My asshole brothers laugh and pick up their forks, smiles plastered to their faces.

"Ma?" I ask. "How's Zia?"

"Luca proposed. Wait until your dad hears when he gets home from work. He won't believe it. I'll let you boys know when we hear about a wedding date."

I close my eyes. The worst part about having three bachelors as sons is apparently having a sister who has three sons who all recently fell in love. This is the second proposal in the Bianco family, and I'm sure the third isn't far behind.

I place my hands on her shoulders and kiss her cheek. "I love you."

She pats my hand on her shoulder. "Love you."

We're in uncharted territory here. Ma usually raises her wooden spoon and tells us exactly what we need to do to fix her mood. She's not a hold-it-all-inside kind of woman.

I stare at my brothers, unsure of what to do. They shrug, still chewing their meatballs. When my eyes widen, they head over to Ma and gush over how great the food is and how much they love her.

"Grab some plates." She reaches into the cabinet and shoves them into my stomach. "Eat."

We do as she says, filling our plates with pasta and meatballs while Ma busies herself in the kitchen. Everyone is silent until we hit the dining room.

"What the hell?" I whisper-shout.

"Fucking Biancos." Dom shakes his head. "They've screwed us over."

I shrug. "Not really their fault."

"I only see one solution," Carm says.

"What?" Dom asks, taking a seat.

"One of us has to get married." He places his fork on the plate and prepares his hands for rock, paper, scissors.

I shake my head. "No."

Dom follows suit with Carm.

"You're both demented. I'm not gonna find some woman to marry because I lost a game of rock, paper, scissors."

"Because you always lose," Dom says as though it's fact.

"I've won plenty."

"Not really," Carm chimes in.

"I won last week. Let's remember who was first to jump out of the airplane."

Dom and Carm share a look as though they set that up for me to win. *Whatever. Jackasses.*

"Let's make Blanca do it," Dom suggests.

"Sure, we'll just hire out a groom for our baby sister?"

My little sister is only twenty-five and way too young to settle down.

"I bet between the three of us we know a lot of good guys," Carm suggests.

"I say oldest goes first." I smile at Dom, spiraling my spaghetti onto my fork.

Dom wipes his mouth. “Why the oldest?”

“You’re supposed to forge the path for us. You know, set an example.” Carm slaps him on the back.

“You’re the emotional one.” Dom nods at Carm.

“What the hell does that mean?” He looks at me to see if I’m in agreement.

I nod. “If any of us is going to settle down, it’s you.”

“Why?”

I almost laugh out loud at the offended look on Carm’s face. You’d think I’d said he’s a misogynist or racist or something.

“You were always hanging off Ma, telling on us when we were little. You used to sleep with her and Dad until you were, like, sixteen,” Dom says before piling a forkful of spaghetti in his mouth.

Carm sets down his fork. “I was eight and I suffered from night terrors, okay? You assholes were always watching those scary movies.”

Dom and I share a laugh.

“So it’s settled. You got the short straw.” I point at Carm with my fork.

“No.”

“Come on, Carm. Take one for the team,” Dom adds.

“Assholes,” he whispers.

“We gotta figure out something to make Mama happy,” I whisper.

“I say we throw this one to Blanca,” Carm says.

I think about it. Although it sounded horrible before, she’s the most logical choice. And it’s not like we’d ever let her be with some douche.

“Yeah, and then Ma gets to go dress shopping and plan everything. It’s perfect really,” Dom says.

I shrug. Better her than me. “Sure.”

"Then we're in agreement. Now, who tells Blanca the plan?" Dom asks.

We set our forks on our plates, knocking our fists on our palms three times.

Dom shoots scissors.

Carm shoots scissors.

I shoot paper.

They laugh and pick up their forks.

Assholes.

CHAPTER FIVE

Annie

Monday morning, I stuff my purse into the bottom drawer of my desk and boot up my computer while checking the messages for Mr. Beardsman.

After listening to his messages, I check my own. The first one is from Mr. Beardsman.

"Hi, Annie. I heard the great news about the Coddle account. You're in luck, because I must have caught something, and I'll be out today. I know you're going to have to go back and forth, so unless it's urgent, don't worry about me. Hopefully, I kick this today. Have a great day and congratulations again. You deserve this opportunity."

I hang up and turn off his light before shutting his office door. The news already traveled that fast?

My desk phone rings, and I pick it up. "Hello?"

"Miss Stewart, I'm waiting," Mr. Mancini says. *Click.*

What a jerk.

I stand, grabbing a pad of paper and a pen, then walk through the maze of cubicles to his office. Jake's eyebrows raise as I pass him and knock on the glass door labeled, Lorenzo Mancini: Senior Advertising Executive.

The first thing I notice is that Mr. Mancini's assistant's desk is still vacant. It's not like I thought they could fill the job so quickly, but I thought they'd at least call in a temp.

"Come in."

I walk in and notice his suit jacket hanging on a hanger inside a closet outside his bathroom. His sleeves are rolled up and he looks more as if it's five o'clock, not nine in the morning. What time does he come in?

"So you're aware, I'm an early riser, so you'll need to get here by eight. If I don't have clients, I take lunch in my office at twelve-thirty. You can check my schedule on your desktop. The old assistant had a list of my likes and dislikes there too."

My pen stops scrawling midway through when I realize I'm taking notes on things that don't pertain to me. "I'm sorry, why are you telling me this?"

He looks up from his computer. "You're my new assistant."

"What?" Jacobson and Earl aren't known for great communication, but I think if I'd been reassigned, someone would have mentioned it.

"Jesus. No one told you?" He scowls and picks up his phone. "Shelby. My office. Now." He hangs up on her.

The more I get to know him, the uglier he gets.

Okay, that's not true, but I wish it were.

Shelby knocks a minute later.

"Come in."

She's wearing another mid-calf skirt and blouse with a cardigan her cats must have used for a blanket. "I just got in.

You're way ahead of the game, Mr. Mancini. Miss Stewart was my first line of business."

I lean back in my seat, waiting.

"Please tell her the wonderful news." Mr. Mancini holds out his arm and leans back in his executive high back chair.

Shelby takes the chair next to me but sits on the edge as if she doesn't plan on staying long. "After Friday with Coddle, Mr. Jacobson thinks it's better for you to work directly with Mr. Mancini. Until we can hire a replacement for Mr. Beardsman, you'll have to cover both jobs, but I know Mr. Beardsman isn't a high demander of your time." She smiles.

"So you want me to do two jobs for one pay?" I clarify.

"Gutsy," Mr. Mancini says through a fake cough into his hand.

I refrain from rolling my eyes.

"Well, your time with Mr. Mancini will be more about working on the Coddle pitch. Mr. Jacobson really wants you to have a foot in this campaign. Working for Mr. Mancini will enable you to gain the experience you need to move ahead."

I absorb what she's saying. The question is will Enzo Mancini let me in or keep me out in the cold, stealing my ideas as though they're his own? "Mr. Beardsman is out today. He's sick."

Shelby smiles. "Perfect. That gives you time to get settled here."

"Am I supposed to move all my stuff from my desk?"

Shelby looks to the dictator sitting at his desk. He nods.

"Yes," she answers.

Since when does he make these decisions? Shelby is who I report to.

"My assumption is you'll be spending the majority of your time here." She looks at Mr. Mancini once more and he nods.

"Okay," I say, sounding about as thrilled as if the dentist told me I need a root canal.

"That's what's so great about you, Annie, you're so easy." She stands, straightening her cardigan and blouse. "If you two need anything else, please let me know. I think you two will work great together." She does that thing with her fingers—bringing them together—and leaves.

The door shuts, and I stare at Mr. Mancini typing on his computer. After a minute, he stops and swivels his chair forward. "Now that that's handled... I'm having a meeting with Billy this afternoon. You can sit in on it since it has to do with Coddle."

"Okay."

His gaze stays on me. Since he has nothing else to add, I stand. "I'll move my things."

"Perfect. Thank you for being so accommodating. I think you'll find you might learn more from me than you did with Teddy."

I give him a saccharine smile.

I'm not at my desk near Mr. Beardsman's office for more than two minutes before Jake comes up behind me. "What's going on?"

"I've been moved? I think. I have to move to the desk by Mr. Mancini's office. They're going to try to find someone to take over my duties for Mr. Beardsman because they want me to work the Coddle account with Mr. Mancini."

Jake's jaw drops.

Am I just having a hard time seeing the positive in all this because I'll have to grab lunch and answer phone calls for the biggest dick in the office?

I wonder if he *has* the biggest dick in the office?

I give my head a shake. *Really professional, Annie.*

Jake crosses his arms and smiles. "That's awesome."

"I guess so, but I'm still his assistant."

"You won't be for long. They're gonna see your talent and move you up to your own accounts."

He helps me by gathering my personal items as I grab my purse and coat. I stare at Mr. Beardsman's dark office and my stomach sinks. This change doesn't feel promising. It doesn't feel like the next step in my career. It feels more like the last step before I reach the edge of the cliff. Mr. Mancini doesn't keep his assistants long. What will happen when he's ready for me to leave?

BY THE TWO o'clock appointment with Billy, I'm cautiously optimistic. Other than a few phone calls to him and having his lunch delivered, Enzo Mancini hasn't been that bad at all. I've even been able to get some things done for Mr. Beardsman, so he doesn't return to a desk full of work. Maybe I underestimated Mr. Mancini's jerk level.

Billy walks by my new desk and backsteps to look me over. "Something's different here."

If I was looking for the exact opposite of Enzo, Billy's my man. He's easygoing and funny. Never takes anything too seriously. But that's like most of the guys in the art department, I guess.

"Well." I stand and grab a pad of paper and a pen. "I guess I've been promoted. Maybe?" I'm still confused myself.

"The fact you get to sit in on the campaign for Coddle is pretty awesome."

"True." I shrug.

He walks straight into Mr. Mancini's office, holding the door open for me. I think nothing of it until we step in and Mr. Mancini's scathing eyes are pointed right at me. He's standing off to the side near his bathroom so we couldn't see him through his glass door, but now that we're inside, I can see *everything*.

His shirt is open and it's like a magnet—my gaze dips to his hard, muscular chest on full display.

Jesus, how is it possible to look that good?

"Is knocking no longer customary?" he asks, his fingers buttoning up his shirt.

Then I see that his slacks are unbuckled and hanging open.

"If I was less of a man, I'd feel self-conscious around you." Billy grabs a soda out of the fridge and sits on the couch in the far corner of his office.

"Um... I'm sorry. I'll be right back." I swivel on my heels, my face heated to what I think might be the surface level temperature on Mercury. I'm getting a good idea of why the employee handbook has a strict no-fraternization rule.

"Not necessary, but next time maybe buzz me before just strolling in."

I still don't turn around, because there's no way I can see him like that and not have the image playing on repeat tonight as I'm alone in my bed.

"He's dressed now," Billy says a moment later.

I turn around to find Enzo buckling his belt. How on Earth am I supposed to work in this environment?

"I dripped some coffee on my other shirt."

I wave off his comment, wanting to move on, and sit on the couch across from the one Billy is seated on. Mr.

Mancini sits on the far end of the couch and places a white shirt between us, closer to me than him. I glance at it.

"I use the downstairs cleaner for convenience."

"That's nice." I poise my pen over my paper.

"No rush, since I have plenty." He nudges it a little closer, and I wiggle over until I can't go any farther.

"Are you asking me to take in your dry cleaning for you?"

"Oh, this is fun," Billy chimes in, putting his feet up on the table and resting his arms on his belly.

"You are my assistant, are you not?" Mr. Mancini opens a folder on the table, not bothering to make eye contact with me.

"Just so you know, most assistants do not pick up dry cleaning," I snipe.

"Since when?" He finally makes eye contact, but it's fleeting.

"Since the nineteen-seventies."

He looks at Billy, and he nods.

"Huh. No one's ever told me that."

I roll my eyes. "Not surprising."

"What does that mean?" He leans back on the leather couch, his arm outstretched along the back, positioning himself as though we're all buddies, sitting around and shooting the shit.

Billy chuckles, and my gaze shoots to him. I see we're on the same page.

"You're a good-looking guy. People tend to do things outside of the norm for you. To please you."

A mischievous smile forms on his lips. "You think I'm good-looking?"

"That's what you got from what I just said?" I deadpan.

He shrugs. "I think you're wrong. I think my previous

assistants knew how hard I worked, and they were okay dropping off and picking up some dry cleaning since it's right downstairs."

"And in the end, they all got fired." I tilt my head and smile.

Billy laughs again.

"One thing has nothing to do with the other."

"Really? Billy, go give your dry cleaning slip to Emma," I say.

His eyes shoot up. "First of all, I'm comfortable in my body, so I don't take offense to your comment. Second of all, I like my balls. My wife likes my balls, and she wants another kid, so I think I'll do that myself."

I laugh. "Okay."

Mr. Mancini ignores Billy, talking to me. "What about you? You're attractive. You're telling me you don't get perks for being good-looking?"

It takes me a minute to respond because I'm stuck on the fact that he said I'm attractive. "Um... no. We're on different playing fields."

His gaze drags over my body and back up. "No, we're not."

Does he not look in the mirror every day?

"Let's make a bet," he says with a smug smile.

"I'm not betting."

"Yeah, let's bet," Billy chimes in, and both of us look at him.

"You go out there to that guy you're always talking to—is he your boyfriend?" Enzo asks.

There's only one guy out there. "Jake? No," I scoff.

"Take this dry cleaning bag and tell him you're swamped and ask him to take it down for you." Enzo's face says he's dead serious. Demented and serious.

"No." I smack my pen down on my notepad.

"Why? I think he'll do it because he likes you."

"He does not like me. We're friends. Friends do friends favors. It wouldn't prove your point." I cross my legs.

"Nah. Let's do it." He holds the bag out for me.

"This is so childish." I stand and snag the bag from him.

"That's what's so great about it," Billy says. "I bet Jake refuses."

"He'll totally do it," Mr. Mancini says, crossing his arms and staring at Jake at his computer.

I huff. Why do I feel the need to prove this adolescent point?

I walk out of the office and approach Jake's desk. "Hey, Jake. Could you do me a favor? Um..."

He looks up at me.

"Could you take this to the dry cleaner for me? I'd do it, but I don't have a ton of time, what with covering both desks." I slide the bag onto the edge of his desk.

"Sure." He holds out his hands.

"Why?" I widen my eyes.

He tilts his head. "Why what?"

"Why did you say yes?"

His forehead scrunches. "Because you said you were busy."

My cell phone ringing from where it sits on my desk distracts us, and I rush over to silence it.

"It's my dad," I say to Jake. "Hey, Dad, I'm sorry, I can't talk. Can I call you back later?"

"Beth's having the baby. She's at Memorial."

I jolt, and Jake looks on in concern. "Oh. Okay. Um... I'll be right there." I hang up. "Beth's having the baby."

Jake jumps up and snags the bag from me. "Then I'm definitely taking this for you."

"No." I grab it back. "I'll tell you about this later."

I walk back into Mr. Mancini's office. His cocky smirk says he thinks he's claimed victory, but I still think our friendship is why Jake said yes.

"Sorry, I have to go. My sister just went into labor." I drop the bag on the couch.

"Go," Mr. Mancini says, motioning out the door.

"Really?" I ask. He's being way too understanding.

"Family always comes first."

I think he's serious. "Okay. Well..."

"This is perfect. You go with her." Billy claps his hands in front of him and nods between us.

"Why?" Mr. Mancini asks.

"Yeah, why?"

"So he can see the chaos before a birth and what it's like after. Just as you described in that meeting."

I shoot Billy a look that says he better watch his back tomorrow.

Mr. Mancini's eyes light up. "You're right. That's perfect, I'll grab my jacket."

"Um..."

Whatever. I can argue with him on the way over. Right now, I just need to get to the hospital because I'm going to be an aunt!

CHAPTER SIX

Enzo

We get out of the taxi at Memorial. Billy really is brilliant. To see a birth right before the Coddle pitch is perfect.

On the elevator up to the Labor and Delivery department, Annie glances at me. "I'm not sure my sister is going to be game with you witnessing her giving birth."

"Why?"

"Are you serious? She's not going to want you to see her hoo-ha."

"Hoo-ha? What are we, five?" I stuff my hands into my pockets. "Say the word with me, Annie. Va-gi-na. Vagina." I chuckle.

Her mouth hangs open. "You aren't serious, right?"

"No. I'll stay up by her head. You think I want to see that? Talk about scaring me off for the rest of my life. I'll never get it up to get laid again."

Annie laughs, and it dawns on me that it's the first time I've made her laugh like that.

The elevator dings open. Annie's steps come to a sudden halt before she's even cleared the elevator doors. She stares at the nurses' desk where a brunette stands with her back to us.

"What's wrong?" I ask.

A seething look crosses her face. "It's my mom."

"And?" I step out, holding the elevator open for her. I smile at the people waiting to enter.

"And I haven't seen her in five years," she continues on, and I follow.

Just as I'm about to ask a question, the brunette turns around. "Annie," she coos, holding out her arms.

"Nice of you to make it." Annie walks past her. Obviously, the texting in the taxi gave her her sister's room number.

The brunette looks at me. "Are you her boyfriend?"

"He's my boss, Mom, so hands off."

"That's unfair." The brunette walks faster in her heels, trying to catch up to Annie.

"How did you even know? Does Beth know you're here?"

"Your father called me. This is a big moment, and he understands that whatever is between us has nothing to do with me meeting my grandbaby."

I follow the two women. Annie's leading the pack while her mother keeps looking between her daughter and me.

"I'm Joyce."

"Hi, I'm Enzo."

We briefly shake before Annie disappears into a room to our left. Joyce doesn't fail to follow, but now I'm thinking that Billy is the stupidest person I've ever met. Annie usually has a smile in the office, and I've never seen her treat anyone with animosity.

Except me, I suppose.

I wait in the hall to give Annie a chance to speak to her sister about my being here. I hope she agrees. I think this could give me some great insight into what the client is looking for.

After a few minutes, an old man steps out of the room and approaches me. "Lorenzo Mancini?"

"Yes, sir."

"Franklin Stewart." We shake hands.

"Good to meet you."

"Where is he?" a woman from inside the room says.

I peek around the corner.

"Whoa!" The woman in bed falls back into the pillows shoved up behind her. "Mae wasn't lying about him."

Annie's cheeks are red, but she still has a sullen expression.

"So you don't mind if I stay and observe?" I smile, and her eyes gloss over. Then I spot the man holding her hand, his jaw clenched, and his eyes squeezed shut.

Annie's sister falls back on the pillows. "Oh good, not so bad."

The guy opens his hand and squeezes it shut. "Yeah, not bad."

"I'm Enzo," I say since Annie has taken on the role of pissed-off teenager in the corner.

"Beth. This is my husband, Sam." She motions to the man at the side of the bed. "We're fine with you sitting in but stay up near my head at all times." She looks over at Annie, a tentative smile on her lips.

"That's very agreeable of you. Thank you."

"I'd do anything for my little sis."

Before I can respond, Joyce pushes me away from the side of the bed and sits in the chair there. "Oh, sweetie, you look wonderful, but do you want me to put some makeup on you for the pictures afterward?"

"Yeah, you never know who might see you. Better look drop-dead gorgeous after you've squeezed a walnut out of a peanut shell." Annie picks at her fingernails, not looking up.

Beth shoots Annie another sympathetic look. "No, Mom, I'm good." She grips the woman's hand. "Thank you for coming."

My gaze remains on Annie. She rolls her eyes. Her dad goes to her side, touches her knee, and whispers something.

"Oh, God." Beth shoots up in bed and Sam grabs her hand, but she also still has her mom's hand. Her eyes squeeze shut.

"Beth, you're breaking my bones," Joyce whines, but Beth doesn't let go and a small smile creases Annie's lips.

Beth falls back on the bed. "They're getting more intense."

A nurse comes in to check on Beth. Joyce takes the opportunity to stand and shake out her hand, then she takes a seat on the opposite side of the room.

The nurse looks at the screen of a piece of medical equipment. "You're getting closer. I'm going to have the doctor come in and see where you're at."

As the nurse leaves, Annie takes Joyce's spot in the bedside chair. "You're doing great." Annie wipes away the hairs stuck to her sister's forehead.

"Never do this," Beth says to her sister. "This is torture."

"Okay." Annie laughs and looks at Sam. "Looks like you're a family of three."

Sam rolls his eyes.

"You think I'm being dramatic, Sam Reynolds? Do you want to change places with me?"

The room is silent.

"Of course not," Sam finally says.

"One kid is more than enough because you've never gone—OOOHHHH!" She grips Sam's and Annie's hands.

The longer the contraction goes on, the wider Annie's eyes get. Her mouth opens, and I watch her hold in the pain for her sister.

"Holy shit," Beth says when she can take a breath. "How did women end up on the shitty side of this situation?" She looks at Sam and my gut clenches. I can tell he's going to be her punching bag.

"Just the way God wanted it, I guess." He shrugs.

Even I know that's the wrong answer.

"I think what he means is, he'd change places with you if he could," I lean forward and add.

She falls back to the mattress as Annie rubs her arm. "You're dangerous." She smacks Annie in the shoulder. "Stay far, far away from him." Beth points at me. "Dangerous. Like Tom Cruise in *Top Gun* dangerous."

Annie giggles, although I can't see her face straight-on to know what she's thinking.

"You girls and that movie." Franklin shakes his head. "They must've watched that volleyball clip a million times that one summer."

"Summer of 2005," the sisters say in unison, and Annie's head falls on her sister's shoulder.

"Am I missing something?" Joyce asks.

"Just our entire childhood," Annie murmurs.

Beth's eyes find mine and she doesn't say anything as she runs her hand down her sister's hair, soothing her. These two are amazing to watch. I thought my brothers and

I were close. We are, but this is different. They obviously know each other's weaknesses, have shared many nights talking about their feelings and fears.

The doctor steps into the room. "Okay, Beth, let's see how you're progressing." She pauses and takes all of us in. "Full house. Are we allowing everyone in?"

"Um..." Beth says. "How many am I allowed?"

"We'll be back." Annie stands and heads out of the room.

I follow her because the stirrups are coming out, and yeah, I don't need to be here for that. Her parents follow me.

Joyce stands in front of Annie. "I really wish you could put your personal feelings aside. At least for today. It's supposed to be a joyous day."

"Sure," she says, but I can tell she has no intention of doing so.

"You're like you were at thirteen. So stubborn it's ridiculous." Joyce shakes her head.

Annie's hands ball into fists, and she glances at her dad.

"Joyce, you can't expect the girls to just understand."

I look between them.

"She's grown, let her speak for herself rather than you always putting words in her mouth."

"Words in her mouth? You left them. You're the one who—" He stops himself, pushing a hand through his gray-and-black hair, then inhales a deep breath. "Just... give her a break."

"Must be nice to still be Daddy's angel," Joyce sneers.

Annie's jaw tics. "I'm going to the vending machine." She walks off down the hall.

I stand there for a moment, not sure where my place is.

I'm going to kill Billy.

Eventually I follow her and find her in a small room off the waiting area, digging for money in her purse.

I pull a couple bills from my money clip and insert two dollars. "Anything you want."

"Oh, how nice of you." She hits the button to dispense change and two dollars' worth of quarters fall into the change area. "I'm not going to owe you anything."

She puts in her own two dollars and presses the button for mint Lifesavers. Bending over, she digs out the change and tries to hand it to me.

"I don't carry change in my pockets."

She guffaws. "Of course you don't."

She walks out of the small room, and I follow. When she sees a kid coming down the hall, she holds out her hand to him.

"Courtesy of Moneybags over here." She thumbs my way.

The kid's eyes light up, and he scrambles down the hall to the vending machine.

"Man, your family brings out the evil side of you."

She whips around to face me. "Clarification. My mother does."

I hold up my hands. "Okay. Your mom does. What's the story?"

Maybe if she talks about it, she'll feel better—or at least be civil to me.

"Yeah, I'm not going there today. It's a joyous day," she imitates her mom.

By the time we reach the room again, two nurses are rushing in behind us.

"Beth!" Annie hurries to her sister's side.

I stand in the doorway because all of a sudden, I realize

it isn't my place to be here. I'm intruding, even if this nice couple doesn't seem to mind.

Annie looks at me over her shoulder and waves me forward. "Come on, it's time."

I shake my head. "Nah, it's your family. I should probably head out."

Annie sighs and walks toward me. She takes my hand when she passes and drags me out of the room. "Beth's fine with it. This is where you'll see what I'm talking about and get a better idea of what we need to capture in our pitch. Come on."

She nods toward the room, and I find myself following her. I take my place up near the head of the bed and off to the side so I'm not in the way, and I watch it unfold.

"Come on, Beth, push," the doctor says.

She grunts and sighs, her face as red as a tomato.

"There you go, just one more."

"I can't believe I let you do this to me," Beth says to Sam through gritted teeth. "Never again. Never touch me again! Got it?" She falls back to the mattress, gasping for air. "This is worse than spin class. I was no good at that and I'm no good at this." Tears stream down her face.

"Come on, Beth. You got this," Sam says. "You're the strongest woman in the entire world."

Annie smiles at Sam.

Beth touches her husband's cheek. "Oh, sweet... JESUS!" She wails again, and her face scrunches. "Don't do it, Annie, don't." She shakes her head back and forth.

"A few more big pushes. I see the head," the doctor says.

"Is that really the head?" Joyce asks from her position at the foot of the bed. "Is that red hair? None of us have red hair."

Franklin narrows his eyes. "Shut up, Joyce."

"Sam, do you have red hair in your family?" Joyce looks quizzically between her daughter's legs.

"No."

"It's very common for blond hair to be red at birth," the doctor says.

We all look at Sam's mop of blond hair.

"Except isn't brown the dominant gene?" Joyce asks.

Annie's jaw tics again and she stares at her dad, silently willing him to step in.

"Enough, Joyce!" Franklin snaps.

"I'm just saying, it's unusual."

"Shut up!" Annie says. "Just shut up and be happy you were invited."

"Great, Beth. One more and you'll be done," the doctor says, ignoring the chaos around her.

"I can't. I can't." Beth's head moves from side to side.

"You can. Remember the last five minutes of a workout? Always the hardest. Soon you'll get to hold your baby as an award for all your hard work." Annie kisses her sister's forehead and wipes her sweaty hair off her face.

"Come on, babe, one more for our little boy or girl. Red hair and all." Sam laughs, which makes Beth laugh.

With the help of her sister and husband, she sits up and bears down.

"You did it!" the doctor says.

A second later, a cry echoes in the room, and the doctor holds up the baby.

I think I'm going to throw up. It's covered in blood and some other crap. Sure enough, there's a patch of red hair on its head.

"It's a baby girl," the doctor announces.

"She's adorable," Annie says.

After Sam comes around to cut the umbilical cord, Beth

relaxes. I watch intently how the nurse brings the baby to Beth and everyone fights to get a closer look. They count the baby's toes and fingers, pointing out the different features she inherited from her parents.

"She has our nose," Joyce says, wrapping her arm around Annie.

Annie doesn't pull away, and Beth smiles at them. "Three generations."

Sam snaps a picture.

"We're grandparents," Franklin says, hugging Joyce.

"We're parents," Sam says to Beth and kisses her temple.

Annie was right. A new baby trumps family drama.

CHAPTER SEVEN

Annie

I head up the elevator to work the next morning. I still can't believe Enzo witnessed me telling off my mom. No wonder he shot out of the hospital as soon as the opportunity allowed.

Wait… when did I start thinking of him as Enzo and not Mr. Mancini?

Probably about the same time he bore witness to my family drama and my niece's birth.

The delivery of flowers to my sister's hospital room an hour later was unexpected. I may have read the card more than once. It's not my fault—the man has a way with words.

Thank you for allowing me to be part of your special day. Wishing you many years of happiness with your new bundle of joy. Your beautiful little girl is the luckiest baby in the

world because she has the two of you to call Mommy and Daddy. Cherish one another.
~ Lorenzo Mancini

THE MINUTE I step into the office, Jake grabs my elbow and guides me into the copier room. From his urgency, there's clearly gossip to spill.

"Okay, what did I miss yesterday?" I ask.

"What was the dry cleaning thing?" he asks, his eyes frantic.

I wave him off. "Oh, some stupid bet Enzo initiated. I told him that his other assistants took his dry cleaning downstairs because he's good-looking. He said I'd get the same special treatment, and to prove it, I had to see if you'd take my dry cleaning down for me."

He steps back. "You were tricking me?"

"I told him it wasn't fair. That you'd agree because we're friends."

He nods, waiting for more information. I don't offer any because I forgot about the whole thing with all the excitement of yesterday. "Yeah, we're friends... but you know you're attractive, right?"

Jake and I have always been platonic, no underlying sexual tension between us. That's what I love about our relationship. But we're not friends who talk about our insecurities. Mae is the one who hears my rambling about the size of my thighs and my ass or how my hair will never do exactly what I want it to.

"We're not talking about this." I push past him.

He wheels me around again by my elbow. "Yes, we are,

because if you're going to work with Lorenzo Mancini, you need to know that you're at his level."

"Whoa, calm down on the pep talk." I laugh.

He doesn't. He's serious. "Don't play his games."

I tilt my head. "I'm not." The doorknob jiggles. "Great."

I storm over and unlock the door, and a pair of dreamy brown eyes meet mine.

"Miss Stewart?"

"Sorry, I'm coming now. Jake had an emergency paper jam and needed my expertise." I slide by Enzo, careful not to allow our bodies to touch.

"Please keep your private affairs off the office equipment," he says behind me.

"It's not like that." I toss my purse on my desk.

He holds open his door for me. "I need to see you."

"Can I take off my coat first?"

He huffs, continuing to hold the door open. "I suppose." He glances at his watch and taps his foot.

I roll my eyes, throw my purse in the bottom drawer, and grab paper and a pen. "How sweet of you to be so patient."

I walk into his office, and he shuts the door. I take a seat in front of his desk while he rounds it and sits in his chair, the skyline behind him. He's like King of New York right now.

"Listen, I don't care what you and your boyfriend do, but keep it off the clock, okay?"

My jaw hangs open. "You know he's not my boyfriend."

"Then why am I always finding you in the copier room with him?"

"Why are you going to the copier room? I know it's not to make your own copies."

He leans back in his plush chair, the pen in his hand

teeter-tottering back and forth. "I saw you come in and I followed. I gave you ample time to answer a professional question, then I sought you out."

"Ample time? You followed me?" I hold out my wrist. "Why don't you put a tracking device on me to save yourself time?"

He hems and haws. "I kind of like that idea." His smirk appears. The one that indents the one dimple on his left cheek.

I retract my wrist. "Not going to happen."

"Anyway, I wanted to speak with you to let you know that I sent you flowers." He changes topics faster than a round of *Jeopardy*.

"You did?" My heartbeat picks up. As sad as it is, I've never received flowers from a guy, except for my prom and homecoming dates.

"The florist couldn't deliver them because she had the wrong address." His perfectly shaped eyebrows rise as though I purposely gave him the wrong address. More like he went through personnel files or he bribed poor Mildreth down in Human Resources.

"I just moved." My voice is softer now, my attitude improving thanks to the fact that he sent me flowers. That thought shouldn't make me as happy as it does.

"Well, they'll be delivered to work now, and because I didn't want anyone getting the wrong idea, I had them scrap the card." He slides a small envelope across the desk. "This is for you."

I hold the white envelope and lift the flap.

"You don't need to read it here. It's just a thank you for letting me join in yesterday," he says.

Lorenzo Mancini civil? Thankful even? This is a revelation.

He straightens in his chair. "Make sure you change your address with Human Resources. And I rescheduled the meeting with Billy for this afternoon. And..." His gaze trails to the dry cleaning bag on the chair next to me.

I wait for him to say it. The bag is like a bomb about to go off.

"That's all."

I nod, biting my lip to stop myself from smiling. "Okay. Well, let me know if there's anything else."

"I will." He turns to his computer and, with his hand on his mouse, disregards me.

Once I'm at my desk, I discreetly open the small card. It's his chicken-scratch handwriting.

Thank you for allowing me to pry into your family for my own gain. You've gone above and beyond, and it hasn't gone unnoticed.

~ Lorenzo Mancini

I SIGH and close my eyes, stuffing the card back inside the envelope then into the bottom of my purse.

A half hour later, the mailroom comes up and leaves a dozen Juliet Garden roses in a soft apricot color on my desk.

When Mae comes to my desk to grab me for lunch, she leans down to smell the flowers. "These are beautiful. Who are they from?"

How did I not think of an excuse earlier? No one has asked because Jake has been in meetings all morning and has yet to see them.

"My dad," I lie, crossing my fingers under my desk.

"Your dad sent you roses?" Mae's forehead scrunches. "That's sweet and... weird."

"Mae!" I feign offense.

Enzo's office door is open, and I glance inside to find him at his desk, watching the scene unfold with a smirk, as if all he needs is a bowl of popcorn to fully enjoy my squirming.

Mae turns around and follows my vision. Enzo straightens, burying his head in his phone before Mae notices anything is amiss.

"I'm just saying, roses insinuate romance. I've never seen ones like these before." She inhales their scent again.

"I know, I had to google them. They're called Juliet Garden roses. They look like peonies, right?"

We admire the bouquet in the clear vase, smelling them and feeling how soft the petals are.

"You sure your dad didn't mix this up at the florist?"

My gaze shoots to Enzo. Once again, he's watching. A tingle skitters up my spine.

"Can we forget the flowers for now? My mom was in the delivery room," I say.

Mae's lips tip down.

Mission accomplished.

"She didn't..."

"She did." I grab my purse and pick up my phone, pressing Enzo's extension.

"That was entertaining," he answers.

I ignore his comment. "I'm going to lunch. I'll be back in an hour."

"What did you tell her? Who are those beautiful flowers from? An admirer? Your boyfriend?"

"My dad," I answer.

Mae peers down at the screen of the phone to see who I'm talking to, then she rolls her eyes.

"Interesting."

"What?" I shouldn't care what he thinks is interesting.

"That you went with your dad instead of someone you're romantically linked to."

My eyes flick to him through his glass door. He's smiling as if he's the big cat and I'm the small mouse trapped in a corner.

"Well, I didn't have a choice."

"Why is that?"

"I'm going to lunch. I'll pick up yours on the way back."

He chuckles. "Are you uncomfortable talking about relationships?"

The longer this conversation with Enzo continues, the more Mae is shaking her head with furrowed brows.

"Can we discuss this when I return?"

He laughs again. "Sure. Don't forget our meeting this afternoon with Billy." *Click.*

I inhale a deep breath. "Let's go."

I secure my purse crossways over my body, and I don't bother looking into his office to see if he's watching because I shouldn't care if he is. How did I go in a matter of days from never talking to Enzo Mancini to him sending me flowers and asking me about romantic relationships?

I don't have an answer, but one thing is for certain. Enzo Mancini is *not* what I expected.

CHAPTER EIGHT

Enzo

"Come on, Blanca." I hold the phone to my ear and swivel my chair around to look out at the Manhattan skyline. It's a gloomy spring day and I'm thankful my lunch will be delivered so I don't have to go out in the rain.

"What, did you lose at rock, paper, scissors?" my smartass sister asks.

"No. Why would you ask that?"

"Because this is the stupidest idea the three of you have come up with and my assumption is that you guys played rock, paper, scissors to see who had to tell me and you lost —again."

"Again? I don't lose any more than they do."

Rain pelts the glass, and unbidden, the vision of a drenched Annie Stewart comes to mind. I close my eyes to try to clear my vision, but all I can picture is a white see-through blouse when she returns.

"Yeah, you do, but that's not the point."

Blanca's voice pulls me from the daydreams about my assistant. I need to get a handle on this because I don't screw around at work. It's the one place I've always considered off-limits, but the flush that hit her cheeks when I told her I'd sent her flowers has been preoccupying my thoughts. I can't help but wonder what her personal situation is.

What kind of girl is she? Does she screw around or only with people she dates seriously? She finds me attractive, she told me that yesterday. She's hotter than hell, otherwise I wouldn't be envisioning her without her clothes on, but no way am I risking my job for a piece of ass.

"*Enzo*!" Blanca screams, and I swivel back around at my desk, alert and focused as though Mother Gertrude had just snapped her ruler on the table during history class. "Are you listening to me?"

"Of course."

"What did I say?" I can picture her now, copping attitude and jutting out one hip.

"That you won't do it."

"Dom's the oldest, he should be first. You're right about Mama hurting though. She thinks that you and Dom should've been married first since you guys are older than our cousins. Zia can't stop bragging about her soon-to-be daughters-in-law. Mama feels like she did something wrong."

"She has three successful sons. How can she feel that way?" I pick up my pen and tap it on the desk from end to end.

"None of you have ever brought a woman home. She

thinks she didn't teach you how to respect a woman, for one."

I huff. "What makes you an expert?"

"Hang on." There's muffled speaking through the line. I'm pretty sure I caught her lunch order.

"Where are you?" I ask.

"Out for lunch."

For the first time, I realize that there's clanking silverware and the other noises of a busy lunchtime restaurant in the background.

"It's raining."

"No shit, but I don't have an assistant to weather the storm for me, so I have to brave the elements myself."

"Make sure you don't get soaked. Don't want to get sick," I say.

"Is that your way of buttering me up so I'll get Ma off your back?"

"So it's a hard no?"

"You're incredible. Yes, it's a hard no."

"Fine." My shoulder sags and I lean farther back in my chair. It was a ridiculous idea anyway, but I always follow through on my bets. "How's the job going anyway?"

"It sucks. Not that you'd understand but being the low man on the pole sucks."

I chuckle. "First, I do know. You think I got to the top of the ivory building without scrapes and bruises? Second, it's better than working the pole."

"Har har, Enzo. The money would be better."

"Well, keep up the hard work and the rewards will come."

"Thanks for the pep talk. Report back to our dumbass brothers that a fake relationship is not what Ma needs. Find another way to make her happy. And seriously, stop playing rock, paper, scissors to solve everything. No one would think I was the youngest." There's some muffled noise and a thank you from Blanca.

"Enjoy your lunch, sis. Love you."

"Love you."

We hang up, and I sit at my desk, thinking about Ma wishing she has what Zia has. How can she possibly think it's her fault that none of her sons want to marry?

A knock sounds on my door, and I flick my gaze to Annie. I wave her in. She's dry as a bone. That shouldn't disappoint me, but it does.

"Here you go." She places my lunch on my desk.

"It's raining," I say, like a dumbass.

She stops mid-stride and glances over her shoulder. "Yeah."

"Thank you."

Her eyes scrunch up for a second. "You're welcome."

"I'm sorry about earlier. Your romantic relationships are none of my business and I shouldn't have pried."

She circles to fully face me. "Thank you for that."

I nod. "Meeting is at two, so bring your A game. Time to prove you deserve to be on this campaign."

The smile that was tipping the corners of her lips falter. "Okay."

And she's out of the office and behind her desk in a flash. With the remote, I click the blinds down over my glass door.

I really need to check myself. I'm talking nonsense. Apologizing for overstepping? Who the hell am I?

TWO O'CLOCK ARRIVES, and the buzz on my phone confirms how well Annie listens.

"Yes?"

"Billy and I are here for the two o'clock meeting. Are you dressed?" She laughs, and I hear Billy chuckling.

"Yes, you guys can come in."

Billy holds open the door and Annie walks in with a sketchpad and a notebook. She sits on the couch, crossing her legs and talking to Billy about when her niece was born and how pale I was.

"You couldn't have snapped a picture for me?" Billy asks.

"A little busy getting my hand crushed." She flexes her fingers. "I'm just getting the feeling back."

"My wife actually placed her hands around my throat and swore she'd never have another."

I eavesdrop while collecting my stuff to join them.

"My sister swore the same thing, but I already heard her tell my brother-in-law that they'll be having more."

Billy laughs. "Yeah, they're like tattoos, addicting."

"You have tattoos?" she asks.

My ears perk up. I wonder if Annie has one and where it might be.

"Just one. When I was in college. Peer pressure." He laughs. "You?"

I bury my head in papers as if I can't find what I'm looking for.

"Um... I have one." She's hesitant. Why is she hesitant?

"Where?" Billy's question is innocent; he's making conversation. I'm the perv wondering if she has one on her hip bone or right above her ass. Suddenly, the rabid urge to undress her and find it surges through my body.

"Let's just say only a few people have seen it."

I glance up to see her cheeks are flaming red.

Billy raises his hand. "Say no more. It's none of my business."

She shrugs. "I asked you first."

"Yeah, but mine is a Superman logo on my right shoulder blade. Yours sounds a little more private."

She giggles. "Thanks for understanding. You ready over there, slowpoke?"

"Yeah." I walk around my desk to the opposite side of the couch. "Who wants to go first?"

"Ladies first," Billy says, propping his feet up on my coffee table and resting his hands on his stomach.

Annie clears her throat, her gaze flicking between us. "I might've gone too much on the heartfelt side."

I offer her the advice I was given when I started out. "Don't come at us with a warning label. Just pitch your idea and be confident with what you have."

"Okay… um… how about we have two or three couples? Different circumstances. Maybe a teen birth, a couple who isn't married, and a married couple. We somehow show that life isn't perfect. Then at the end of the commercial, each baby is delivered, and everyone is happy."

"I need a little more," Billy says. "Also, do we really want to put teen birth out there?"

"It's risky, yeah, so maybe just a younger couple—early twenties perhaps. Maybe they struggle for money and you see an argument…" Her words trail off. Billy has already changed her mind on her original idea.

"Annie?" I wait until she's locked gazes with me. "This is just a shoot-shit-at-the-wall meeting. Relax. Billy's not judging your idea. He's poking holes at it because this is what a client does."

She nods. "I have some sketches." She opens up her book.

Billy's feet fall to the floor, and he leans in and looks. I have no choice but to slide closer to her. Other than when she fell into my chest a few days ago, I haven't been this close to her. She smells like a flower with a hint of vanilla.

"Are you an artist?" Billy asks. Her sketches *are* well done.

"I took a few classes in college, but no."

"I love the scenes at the end. I think we just need to figure out a way to get there." I hold out my hand to look at the sketches more closely. She allows me to have them, and I know it took a lot of trust for her to pass them over.

"How about we do an argument between a wife and husband, either before a holiday or maybe he didn't do something around the house? I can vouch for pregnant women being demanding." Billy chuckles.

Annie's eyes narrow on Billy. "Would you like to carry a human being around inside you for nine months?"

I smile, watching it unfold.

Billy grabs his stomach. "What do you think this is?"

"That's by choice."

Billy meets her gaze. "I stand by my overreacting pregnant woman idea." But his smile says he's joking, and Annie shakes her head, letting it roll off her back.

"We don't have a lot of time to portray this. Are we better pitching ideas for three different commercials that will run in rotation? We could have three drastically different couples." I place the sketchpad on the table.

"I think if we did them separately, we'd lose the feel that Annie's suggesting, but yeah, the time constraint is gonna be an issue," Billy says.

I walk over to the window to think for a moment.

"Maybe we concentrate on one family." I turn around. "Like your family," I say to Annie.

"Um..."

"I'm not saying your family specifically." The fear in her eyes that I'd exploit her family for an ad campaign stings, but I brush it off. "We show how everything isn't perfect between all members within the entire family."

Her cheeks flush, matching the shade of apricot in the roses I sent her.

For the next two hours, we shoot ideas around and Annie sketches a few more ideas. Billy adds to them.

When we part ways, I'm surprised by how far we got. Who would've thought we'd be such a great team? I've always worked exclusively with Billy, but I don't think either of us can deny how much Annie contributed to this pitch. I definitely underestimated her. I can't wait to see what other surprises she has in store for me.

CHAPTER NINE

Annie

Two weeks later, we're back in the conference room, except this time I'm not skulking in the corner of the room, ready if anyone needs a drink refill. I'm sitting up front with Enzo and Billy.

Mr. Jacobson walks in before the clients arrive, while I'm straightening all the proposal booklets. Neither Enzo nor Billy have arrived yet, telling me to stall because something must have happened to the video we prepared for the presentation.

"Miss Stewart, I'm eager to hear the new pitch." He unbuttons his coat and puts his hands in his pockets.

"I'm excited for you to hear it," I say.

"How are you getting along with Lorenzo?" He leans against the windowsill.

His older, more distinguished look screams successful man. Rumor has it he wants to retire soon. He spent his entire life building this company so he could enjoy a younger retirement, but with no kids of his own and since Mr. Earl passed away a few years back, he's been waiting for someone to hand the day-to-day off to. Lorenzo Mancini seems to be the man he trusts.

"Good, thank you for asking." I pour water into the glasses set around the table.

"Is he welcoming your ideas?"

I take a moment to think over his question. If he'd asked me three weeks ago, I would've said no way would an egomaniac like Enzo Mancini listen to one idea in my head. But the truth is, he's been receptive. He's added to my ideas and morphed his own to work around mine. The three of us truly were a team on this campaign. I'm as surprised as the next person by that, because the Enzo Mancini I saw before is not the man I've gotten to know. He still hangs up on me and he's still abrupt, but he's allowed me to be much more a part of the advertising than Mr. Beardsman ever did.

"Yes. Very. I will say Mr. Beardsman has been left with temps coming and going which..." I let my sentence trail off because like Mae told me, I have to take what I want once in a while. I realize that I don't want to go back to working for Mr. Beardsman.

"I'm aware of the struggles we've found in replacing you. Let's see how today goes and we'll move forward from there." He smiles, but his words pretty much mean if the pitch sucks, I'll be back with Mr. Beardsman, so let's not get ahead of ourselves. It's a mental slap to remind me what's riding on today's success.

"Perfect." I nod.

Elise's voice comes through the speaker of the conference room phone. "Annie, Mr. Peterson and company are here."

I smile at Mr. Jacobson. "I'll be right back."

Walking out, I inhale deeply the entire way to the front desk, doing my best to rein in my nerves.

"Mr. Peterson, so nice to see you again." I hold out my hand.

He turns away from his daughter, Blair, and shakes my hand. "Miss Stewart, we're eager to see what you've added."

I shift my attention to Blair. "Miss Peterson."

"Blair," she says with a smile.

I return her smile and continue shaking hands with the other employees in attendance. We file into the conference room, and I blow out a relieved breath when I see Enzo talking with Mr. Jacobson. They part and say their hellos before everyone is seated. It takes me a second to realize that Billy is still missing. Not a good sign.

I sit down and open my proposal to find a Post-it note inside, written in Enzo's scrawl.

Don't freak out. Video is gone. We're going old school with your sketches.

MY EYES WIDEN, my heart rate skyrockets toward the sun, and I look at Enzo.

He shoots me a look to say *yeah, we're kind of screwed*, then stands and addresses the room. "Thank you for giving us this second opportunity to show you how we can help you achieve your goals. As you're aware, we've added Annie Stewart to our team, and I say with confidence that she's brought just what was needed to give you what we think is a winning campaign for your diaper line."

"I hope so," Mr. Peterson says, eyeing me.

Blair beams at me since she liked my first idea. I hope I don't disappoint her. I'm all too familiar with what that feels like, given my relationship with my mother.

"That being said, we had some last-minute technical difficulties. We hired actors and filmed the shots, but unfortunately, the file was corrupted somehow... well, I'm not going to act like I have any idea what the technical details are, but the result is the same. There isn't a mock commercial to show you on the screen." He smiles to mask his annoyance. "Thankfully, Miss Stewart is a pretty great artist and we're going to act through some storyboards she prepared to pitch our idea, so be kind. My acting skills aren't stellar."

Everyone in the room laughs, and I tilt my head, trying to understand what he's talking about. We're not acting out the sketches. They speak for themselves.

Right?

But Enzo meets my gaze and his expression says, "Did you not understand what I meant from my Post-it note?"

He's got to be kidding. I cannot stand in front of these people and act.

He props up on the easel a sketch of the first scene, and his eyes shoot to me, silently telling me to stand. I slide my chair out from the table, my legs wobbly and shaking, and make my way over to him. He's totally joking. This is some initiation thing that he and Billy cooked up. No way can he be serious.

But Enzo continues. "The first scene is a couple arguing about family coming to visit. The wife tells her husband how his mother hates her..."

I see the lines I'm supposed to say, but I'm a deer in headlights, staring at Enzo.

All right, it's time for him to laugh and say he's just joking. But all he's doing is widening his eyes, telling me to start.

I clear my throat and place my hands on my non-existent belly. "Here I am ready to pop, and your mom is going to run her finger along every shelf, judging the fact that I don't dust every day." My voice shakes, but I get the line out.

Enzo smiles then schools his features. "She loves you."

"She hates me, and you know it."

Enzo rolls his eyes just like the husband is supposed to. "What about your dad? He's always being passive-aggressive with comments like 'it's a forest out there' because I only mow the lawn once a week."

"He's joking. That's what he does." I rub my belly since the actress is supposed to be resting from cleaning.

Enzo puts up the next card.

God help me, how many are there again?

"Your parents are here. Your dad double parked —again."

"You know he hates coming to the city," I say.

"So instead of him finding a parking spot himself, I'm supposed to go out there and drive around for an hour?"

I place my hand on his shoulder as though we're staring out a window together. My fingertips explode with tingles. The scent of his cologne hits my nostrils, and I suppress a full body shiver. "They'll be gone in a few hours."

I glance at the script. I'm supposed to kiss his cheek. Surely, he doesn't expect me to do that. But Enzo waits, his eyes imploring me. I rise to my tiptoes, my hand on his shoulder, and press my lips to his cheek as quick as can be, then I fall back down to my heels, pretending I didn't want to leave my lips there longer.

He pretends to walk out the door.

I pick up the next card since I'm closer.

Everyone is seated around a table, so he arranges four chairs at the front of the room, and we sit.

Enzo lowers his voice. "When are you going to move to the suburbs? The city is nowhere to raise a baby."

Then he moves over as though he's the husband, and I swallow a laugh.

"We like the city, Sam," he says in a different voice.

I glance at the card and see it's my turn to be two different people. "I'm more concerned about the cleanliness of the house with the baby coming. Illness can kill a newborn."

I slide over and bend at the waist, pretending to use a fork as if I'm eating. "Honey, want to help me in the kitchen?" I stand, rolling my eyes at Enzo, and he flips the next card.

When is this going to be over?

Enzo slides out a chair and I sit in it, dread coating my stomach because of this next scene I'm going to have to act out.

"Push, honey," he says, and I pretend to be my sister from three weeks ago. "One more."

Then Enzo stands and pretends to be the dad and the wife's dad, even putting a high pitch to his voice to be the mom. I grunt, pretending to push, and Enzo hands me a water bottle wrapped in paper towels as if it's the baby. I side-eye him, and he shrugs.

He goes around and does all the nice voices, hugging air to make it seem as though everyone is embracing. Then he comes to me and kneels, his fingers weaving through my hair and the other cradling the water bottle.

"We're parents. She's beautiful." He kisses the baby then my forehead like a real new dad might.

Our gazes lock, and I'm caught up in the moment for a second. I touch his cheek, and our foreheads rest against one another's. He stands abruptly, leaving me in the chair with the water bottle baby.

Mr. Peterson laughs and looks at Blair.

"Are you sure you two weren't in theater?" She smiles. "Very unconventional but interesting to watch as well. Shows a real commitment to making this partnership between our companies work." She gives her dad a look I can't decipher.

The door opens and Billy walks in with a big smile, holding up a USB stick. His button-down shirt is untucked, and he's panting as though he just ran a marathon. "I've got it. I was able to retrieve the file."

My jaw tics and I look at Enzo for a second then roll my eyes.

"Would you like to see much more talented actors than us?" he asks the Petersons.

Blair shrugs. "I think I can speak for the two of us when I say we love it. It's what we were looking for—the perfect mixture of humor, relatability, and love."

"So?" Enzo asks, holding up his hands.

"Congratulations," Blair says.

Enzo's gaze shoots to mine, and my head falls back in relief.

"So no one wants to see the video?" Billy asks, disappointment clear in his voice.

"Oh, we'll watch it, but it's not a deciding factor." Mr. Peterson rises from his seat and shakes Enzo's hand then mine. "Well done, you two. Anyone who would put themselves through that to get our account is someone we want on our team."

I cringe before looking at Enzo. Is that why Enzo Mancini is the man Mr. Jacobson wants to replace him? Because he'll go above and beyond to get what he wants? As much as I shouldn't care, it's sexy to see a man refuse to take no for an answer.

CHAPTER TEN

Enzo

We're all seated at the table I asked Annie to reserve for dinner in the hopes that we'd seal this deal today. Billy decided not to join us, having some commitment with his kid tonight. Mrs. Peterson joined Mr. Peterson and Blair on the trip up from Houston, so she's here too.

You know who else should be here? Annie. We've ordered drinks and appetizers, but she's yet to arrive.

"I'll be right back," I excuse myself, thinking maybe she can't find us in the private room in the back of the restaurant.

Since I never got her cell phone number, I have no way of getting a hold of her. Surely, she has mine though. I think back to our previous contact and realize none of it was by cell phone. She's always called the office line if she was out and needed to know what I wanted.

I approach the hostess, who smiles. Her gaze floats down my body and back up to meet my eyes. Hers are screaming "take me home tonight," but I ignore it.

"I'm looking for a woman. Brunette, brown eyes, about this tall." I hold my hand up to my shoulder. "I think she was wearing a gray blouse and a black skirt?" Unfortunately, my mind was on the presentation and not how many buttons Annie had clasped on her blouse today. Which is the way it should always be, but sadly, is not.

The hostess's mood sours fast. "Sorry. I haven't seen her."

I scour the bar area. No way would Annie tell Mr. Jacobson she'd be here and not show. I glance out the revolving doors. There she is outside, talking on her cell phone, a grin from ear to ear.

"Thanks." I knock on the hostess stand then circle through the doors.

Her back is to me, and since she doesn't see me, I lean against the wall to eavesdrop.

"I can't believe it. They loved it! I'm about to walk in there and have dinner with the owner of Jacobson and Earl and Lorenzo Mancini. How did my life change so much in such a short amount of time?" She pauses and presses her finger to her ear. "I know, but... Beth..."

Curious, I lean forward with the hope of having suddenly developed supersonic hearing so I can hear Beth's advice over the Friday traffic in Manhattan.

"Okay. I will. See you tomorrow." She turns and her face falls. "Gotta go." She presses End on her cell phone and slides it into her purse while staring at me. "Do you always listen to other people's conversations?"

"No, but I was searching for you. You're late for dinner."

She narrows her eyes at me before moving through the revolving doors. Following her to the coat check, I watch as she passes off her spring jacket. I applaud my subconscious for remembering what she was wearing. A tight black pencil skirt shows off her amazing ass. Without saying a word to me, she weaves through tables right to the back room.

So much for thinking she didn't know where to find us.

"Sorry I'm late," she says, finding the only empty chair—which is coincidentally next to me. "A pedestrian was hit by a cab, so I was stuck in gridlock on the way over. You guys must've been lucky and just missed it."

"That's okay, they just brought the wine," Blair says.

I snatch the bottle off the table and pour Annie a glass.

"Thank you, Mr. Mancini," she says before sipping the wine.

"So tell us about yourself, Miss Stewart." Mr. Peterson takes a sip of his scotch on the rocks.

"Well." She straightens in the chair, fiddling with her napkin on her lap. "I graduated from NYU, and I was lucky enough to secure a job with Jacobson and Earl a year after graduation. Before that, I was working a lot of odd jobs while interviewing for positions in my field. I've been here ever since." She looks at Mr. Jacobson as if she's thanking him, but I can tell he had no idea who she was nor whether he was responsible for hiring her.

"Are you from New York originally?" Blair asks.

She nods, sipping her wine. "For most of my life. I moved here when I was ten, from Connecticut with my father and my sister. I'm not sure I could leave now."

"Blair just recently moved from the city to the suburbs and it's been an adjustment, right, honey?" Mrs. Peterson says.

Blair sighs. "I miss the late-night restaurants, delivery

from anywhere, and just the buzz of the city. But once my husband and I had our second last year, we finally threw in the towel. Between car seats and strollers and groceries, it was too difficult. But we do keep a condo in the city to sneak off to once a month. Dad and Mom like to watch the kids anyway, right?" She smiles at her parents, and they both beam.

Mr. Peterson pulls out his phone. "They're the cutest grandkids to ever exist."

I take the phone and see a baby boy and a girl I'd put at five or six, then I pass it over to Annie.

She looks at the picture more closely. "Now my dad might argue with you there." She hands back the phone.

"Oh, you have children?" Mr. Peterson asks.

"No. My sister had a baby a few weeks ago." She pulls out her phone, displaying a picture of her and her niece, and shows it to the Petersons.

"Oh, what a cutie. What's her name?" Blair asks.

"Cecilia. You want to hear a funny story?" Annie eyes me, obviously pretty comfortable now that half of her glass of wine has been consumed.

"Always." Blair sits up straighter and props her chin in her hand.

"To prepare for the pitch, Enzo attended the birth. It wasn't pretty. My sister was screaming at my poor brother-in-law the entire time, but"—she puts her hand on my shoulder—"he didn't pass out or throw up, so I say that's a win."

Blair laughs. "You did all that for our ad campaign?"

I nod, my words lodged in my throat. I'm a little surprised that she threw me under the bus, but the client loves it, so her judgment was on point.

"He did, and my family is not easy, believe me." She pats my shoulder again then removes her hand.

Even after her hand is back on the stem of her wine glass, I feel as though she's still touching me. Which is weird, right?

"Way to go above and beyond." Mr. Jacobson beams at me, and I nod in appreciation.

We continue talking about life and kids. Annie and I the only ones without much to add, but we contribute to the conversation where we can. When dinner has drawn to a close, the waitress hands me the bill and I discreetly hand her my company credit card.

"We better go. We have an early flight." Mr. Peterson stands.

We all head to the coat check to say our goodbyes. Hands are shaken, and Mr. Jacobson pulls me aside for a moment.

"I assume you took care of dinner?" he asks.

"Of course. Have a great night."

He nods then pushes his arms through the sleeves of his coat. "Thank you, and make sure Miss Stewart gets home safe."

I glance at her as her hands stop mid button on her coat. I push my hands into my pockets and smile. "Of course."

They say their goodbyes, and the waitress returns with my credit card slip. I leave the tip, sign my name, and pass it back to her, folding the receipt into my billfold to expense.

"Want to share a cab?" I ask Annie.

"Oh, you're not going my way."

My forehead creases. "How do you know?"

"Trust me on this one." She takes a few steps toward the revolving doors.

"You heard Mr. Jacobson. I need to see you home."

We say goodbye to the hostess, who either has a resting bitch face or thinks I've scorned her in some way because it appears that Annie is my date.

"You don't," Annie says when we get outside.

The cool spring air hits us in the face, and I inhale a deep breath. The sky is dark now, but the sidewalk is still bustling with people.

"What if something happens to you? I can't afford to be fired right before I make partner." I wink.

The valet flags down a cab for us, and I tip him before opening the door for Annie.

"It's out of your way," she says, her feet firmly planted as though she has no intention of getting in. When I don't break her gaze, she rolls her eyes and gets inside, sliding across the seat to the other side.

"Think of it as a thank you." I wait for her to tell the taxi driver her address.

Her shoulders fall. "Go to Inwood." She glances at me before spitting out her address.

The cab pulls away from the curb.

I chuckle. "Do you think I'm going to stalk you or something?"

"What? No." She shakes her head. "It's just... forget it."

"What?" I'm intrigued by why this is a problem for her. I shift in my seat so I'm better able to see her.

"You probably live around here, and I live in Inwood. I'm not ashamed, I'm proud of where I live. I worked hard to buy my condo, but to you it's Inwood."

I laugh. "You're kidding, right? You think I'd think less of you because you live in Inwood?"

"Well, I'm assuming you have a doorman on the Upper West Side."

I shake my head. "You assume wrong. Tribeca."

She appears genuinely surprised. "And here you are going out of your way to take me to Inwood."

"Please, I go to Brooklyn every weekend to see my parents. I'm not some snob who's never left Manhattan."

She looks out the window. I can tell it's still bothering her that I'm escorting her home, but she has nothing to worry about. I was there once. Moving out of my parents' before I was able to crack into the ad business sucked. She thinks Inwood is bad? I shared a two-bedroom with three buddies in Flushing. With one bathroom, I might add.

"That's where you grew up?" she asks after a minute.

I nod. "Born and raised. My parents are immigrants. My dad works for the city, and my mom does odd jobs at home. Caters out of our house but keep that on the down low."

She smiles at me. Maybe a little of my history will convince her that I'm not judging her.

"What about you? Where does Beth and your dad live?"

She turns to face me. "Beth and Sam are in Soho, and my dad lives in Midtown."

"Why did you guys move to the city from Connecticut?"

"My dad is an attorney and he would commute, but then my mom decided the last thing she wanted to be was a mother, so she left. My dad moved us to Midtown because otherwise he'd never see us."

"How did you like growing up in Midtown?"

She rolls her eyes. "It wasn't Connecticut. Ever have those memories where you think maybe you're making it more than it was? I think those years in Connecticut were happier for me than anyone else in the family. My dad much prefers living in the city. But

Manhattan is home now. I'm used to it. It'd be hard to go back."

"It's weird how you think you'll never get used to something at first, but then it becomes your new normal and you can't imagine how it could be any different."

She nods. "Oh, this is me." She leans forward to tell the taxi driver.

How on Earth did we get to Inwood in so quickly?

She digs into her purse. "Here."

I raise my hands. "I'm not taking your money."

"Please. Come on, Mr. Mancini."

Even I notice how weird that sounds coming from her mouth now that our working relationship has turned into more of a tenuous friendship. "Enzo."

"If I call you Enzo, can I pay my share?" She bats her eyes a few times.

I twist my lips, thinking about it. The taxi driver huffs, annoyed that we're holding him up. "Sure."

"Please, Enzo?" she says, stressing both words.

The sound of her voice saying my name like that spurs images of her naked on my bed, begging me to fuck her. Her back arched, her delectable tits prominently on display with her legs spread. I shift in my seat to hide my growing hard-on.

She drops the forty dollars onto my lap and opens the door, leaving before I come back to myself. I lift the forty off my half chub, concocting a plan to get this back to her without her knowing it.

Her voice rings in my head one more time. *Please, Enzo?*

I might as well admit defeat. Tonight my dreams will be filled with me, Annie Stewart, and the word please.

CHAPTER ELEVEN

Annie

Monday morning, I walk into work, not sure what to expect. Friday night, I had dinner with Mr. Jacobson and the huge client we landed, then Enzo Mancini shared a taxi home with me even though it was way out of his way.

I'm not seated at my desk for more than a minute before my phone rings.

"Good morning Mr. Mancini," I answer.

"Enzo."

"Okay."

"Let's practice. Repeat after me. Good morning, Enzo." He puts a lilt in his voice that makes me smile.

"Good morning, Lorenzo." I turn on my computer and turn my back to his office door, hoping to hide my smile.

He huffs. "Try that again."

"What's wrong with Lorenzo? It's your proper name, isn't it?"

"Yes, but it's generally only used when I do something bad. Did I do something bad, Miss Stewart?"

His voice is full of innuendo, and a rocket from nowhere shoots right between my thighs. The ache grows the more his words repeat in my head. *Bad. Miss Stewart. Bad.*

I snap back to reality when I see his dry cleaning slip on my desk. "Totally inappropriate."

"Noted. But it's Enzo, and we're going to get very little work done until you call me that."

"Noted," I mimic his answer. My other line rings. "Shelby's calling me."

"Go."

He hangs up, and I switch over. "Good morning, Shelby."

"Good morning. We need to meet in Mr. Mancini's office in ten minutes."

"Okay."

She hangs up, and Jake looks at me with wide eyes. I pick up my phone and dial his extension.

"We landed the Coddle account, so I think I'll hear today what's going to happen with my position in the company."

His mouth hangs ajar until I laugh. "That's awesome. Congratulations! You're going to let me follow you down the golden path, right?"

"Just hop on my colorful train."

It's good to have a coworker who cheers for you to win instead of fail. Jake started right after me, but close enough that we're in a gray area regarding which one of us will move up the ranks first.

"I heard there was a dinner?" He waggles his eyebrows.

Seriously, who does he get his info from?

"There was."

"And you were invited?" he asks.

"I was."

"Oh, Annie, you're big time now."

My hand falls to my stomach. "Don't scare me. I'm terrified."

He shakes his head. Is it odd that we're having this conversation on the phone but still face-to-face? "You got this. Just remember what I said. Don't let him railroad you."

"I heard you."

I want to tell him don't worry. That Enzo Mancini isn't the man we thought he was. That he's given me more say and more credit than Mr. Beardsman ever did. Jake is blessed to work with Mr. Zilroy, who lets him pretty much follow his every move. He's also about a hot minute away from retirement. I'm pretty sure Mr. Zilroy naps after lunch every day, but Jake, being the good assistant he is, makes excuses for him. One day it could be Jake and me in these offices.

Mr. Zilroy walks out of his office behind Jake.

"Turn around. Bye." I hang up and go through my emails.

I try to get through them all, but I keep checking the clock. It'll be nice when I can get rid of Mr. Beardsman's correspondence from my list of responsibilities, but a rock of guilt sits in my stomach for abandoning a man who treated me so nicely for two years. The temps they've brought in are struggling, and I see now why Enzo probably went through so many. Maybe *he* wasn't the problem. Then my eyes fall to the dry cleaning slip.

Nope, he was the problem.

"Ready?" Shelby knocks her knuckles on my desk. She's

wearing a full-fledged cat sweater. I mean that literally. Little floating cat heads with sequin eyes and mouths cover her green cable-knit cardigan.

"Yes." I slide my desk chair out and grab my pen and paper. It isn't until after I step away from my desk that I remember to grab the phone. "Hold on one second."

"Yes?" Enzo answers.

I look through the glass door to find him leaning back in his chair with a smirk plastered on his face. I grip the phone tighter. This isn't going to be good.

"Shelby and I are ready if you are, Mr. Mancini."

"What did we just talk about?"

I clear my throat. "Are you ready?" I smile at Shelby, who looks at me quizzically.

"Say it."

My jaw clenches and I lower my voice. "This is ridiculous."

"Let's practice again. Let it roll off your tongue. Ennnzzzooo."

I glare into his office, and he looks as though a laugh is about to break his composed stature. I huff, and Shelby wanders away to tell Jake about the game of hide-and-seek she played with her cats this weekend and how Spunky found her every time.

I shield my mouth and the receiver. "Shelby and I are here… Enzo."

He cradles the phone in his neck and applauds.

I roll my eyes, done with this game, and hang up. I try to mask my annoyance. "Ready, Shelby?"

She seems surprised, having been entranced in her reenactment of quality cat time this weekend. Jake widens his eyes and mouths "thank you" behind her back.

We step into his office, and Enzo's smile at the two of us

feels weird. Before I started working for him, I could probably count on one hand how many times I saw him smile.

"Please." He signals to the chairs in front of his desk.

Shelby sits and crosses her ankles before pulling some papers from a file folder. Enzo straightens in his chair.

"Congratulations to you both on the Coddle account. I heard there was a snafu but you two hung in there."

"Thank you, Shelby," I say.

Enzo nods.

"Mr. Jacobson sent me an email Saturday morning. You'll no longer be reporting to Mr. Beardsman, Annie. Your time needs to be on the Coddle campaign with Billy and Mr. Mancini. We'll find someone permanent to work for Mr. Beardsman, but I do ask that if the new assistant needs any help that you help her find her way. I'll try to step in as much as I can, but you'll be hard to replace."

My stomach flutters with excitement. "Of course."

"That being said, you're receiving a raise since Mr. Mancini is one of our busier ad execs." She beams at Enzo. "Due to the larger accounts he handles, and the confidentiality perspective, Mr. Jacobson would like to offer you this." She hands me a paper that details their offer.

Enzo leans back. I wonder if he's behind the scenes on this decision. Does he know how much they're offering?

"What exactly will be my new position?" I ask.

"You'll be Mr. Mancini's assistant exclusively."

I tilt my head and glance at Enzo, who's smiling as if he just got his Christmas wish granted. I can't help the way my shoulders sag in disappointment. "Oh."

Shelby pats my arm. "This is a good thing. I think it's the first of many moves for you."

I wonder if she believes the bullshit she's throwing at me. Am I really supposed to sit here and give away all my ideas, but still make sure Enzo gets his coffee and lunch daily?

She takes the paper from my hand and sets it in front of us on the desk. "I just need you to sign here and here. We're extending your confidentiality agreement and non-compete."

I place the tip of the pen to the paper. A non-compete means I can't leave if they take all my ideas and never give me credit for them.

I drop the pen. "I need to think about this. Can I have today?"

Shelby rears back as if I slapped her.

Enzo's bolts upright in his chair.

Both of them look at me as though I just flew in through the window in a Supergirl costume.

"I thought you'd be happy?" Shelby asks but quickly waves. "Of course. Take today and we'll discuss it tomorrow." She stands and exits the office.

Before I have a chance to sneak out with her, Enzo stands, rounds his desk, and sits on the edge right in front of me. "Forget the whole name thing. You want to call me Mr. Mancini, go for it."

I lean back in the chair and shake my head. "It's not that." I'd never admit it, but I like his playful side.

"What is it then?"

I look at him. "Would you be happy remaining an assistant if you were part of the reason your firm scored the whale?"

He crosses his arms, his shirt straining along his strong shoulders and biceps. "You want more money?"

I shake my head, standing. "No." I take a few steps toward the door.

"Help me understand."

I whip around, but he's still leaning against the desk, except his hands are gripping the edge now. And all I can think about right now is how hot he looks.

Hot. Powerful. Intense.

What the hell is wrong with me? I'm at the pivot point of a change to my career, and all I can think of is how I want to jump my boss.

I'm a disgrace to women everywhere.

"You know what, forget it. I'll sign it." I wave him off, but when my hand moves for the doorknob, it clicks locked. "What the—?" I turn around as Enzo's hand slides out from under his desk. "You mean people actually have that?"

He doesn't smile or act cocky or even answer. "Is it because you'll be working for me?"

I plant my hand on my waist and cock out my hip. "First of all, I'm not cool with you locking me in your office."

He reaches down and I hear the lock click again. God, I hope no one else heard that outside.

"It has nothing to do with you. I thought I'd maybe be promoted to junior ad exec or something. I didn't think it was going to be a 'when you have free time between catering to Lorenzo Mancini, think of some great ad concepts, will ya?'"

He crosses his arms and tilts his head as though he's rolling my words over in his head. "Everyone pays their dues. When I started, it took a long time before I made junior and a ridiculous amount of time to become a senior exec."

"You're thirty-one," I deadpan.

He shrugs. "True, but there were lots of late hours and no sleep. I didn't get to where I am without sacrificing."

"Really?" I cross my own arms, matching his stance. "Were you someone's assistant for two years only to get to pitch to the firm's biggest client, and then be told, 'oh guess what, you still get to be an assistant, but you can do a lot of the work of a junior ad exec too?'"

He rounds his desk, stares out the window for a second with his hands in his pockets, then turns back to me. "Okay. I get it. This is the opportunity you've been waiting on pins and needles for."

"You're right. It is. I just thought..." I let out an exasperated breath. "Women are constantly overlooked in this office."

He says nothing, but from his confused expression, he's either never thought about it or he's recounting how many women he's demeaned in his own career.

He picks up his phone. "Shelby, can you come to my office for a moment?"

"Don't." I step away from the door. "I don't want this made into a huge deal because I'll be seen as a problem and I'll be fired."

His forehead crinkles. "You're not going to get fired. I can guarantee that. I'd handle this myself, but technically Shelby's your boss. If I go above her head, it won't be good for either of us."

"Why would it be bad for you, golden boy?"

"I'm allergic to cats. One sweater smother from Shelby and I'm dead."

I laugh.

"I like you much better smiling," he says in a soft voice.

My laugh dies on my lips and we stand there with our gazes locked, in silence. My stomach flips. *Do not fall for the boss.*

Shelby's knock on the door breaks the spell, and Enzo waves her in. She takes a moment to appraise us and waits.

"I think we should go back to Mr. Jacobson and suggest

that upon agreement of two or more Coddle product ad approvals, Miss Stewart is promoted to junior ad exec."

Shelby's eyes widen. "You want *me* to do this?"

"The org chart says you're her boss. I'll gladly fight for her, but it's not really my place."

Shelby blows out a big breath. "This is why you don't want to sign?"

"I don't want to be a pain, but with this non-compete, I can't take my talent somewhere else, yet I'm still an assistant."

She nods. "I see. Okay, I'll go to bat for you. We'll see what happens." She points at Enzo. "You have to back me up on how much she deserves this."

Enzo holds up his hands. "Done."

"I'll let you two know what happens." She leaves, and I shift my weight from one foot to the other.

"Thank you," I say.

He rounds his desk and sits in his chair. "Don't thank me. I didn't do anything. You could've signed those papers with no complaints."

"I know but..."

He places his hand in the air, silencing me. "I'll be out for lunch this afternoon. Coddle sent an email saying we're receiving a package of their products tomorrow, so we'll be busy most of the day with Billy. Make sure you tie up any loose ends with Mr. Beardsman today."

The conversation is clearly over, based on his standoffish vibe. This man switches moods faster than my sister did when she was in labor. At least she had a reason.

CHAPTER TWELVE

Enzo

"If I tell you this, there's no telling Dom," I say to Carm.

He increases the speed on his treadmill. Dickwad. He's purposely making this a contest. Everything's a contest to him.

"Okaaay." He draws out the word.

"I'm conflicted."

"Conflicted?" Carm laughs, upping the incline on his machine.

I press the buttons on my treadmill to match his speed and incline. He snickers but doesn't change the setting. We can do this all day because I have more endurance than him and we both know it.

"I have a new assistant."

"And she quit already? What do you do to these poor women? It's really not that hard to treat people well." He flashes me his billboard smile. The same smile that's made him a shit-ton of money.

"Anyway, she's working on the Coddle campaign with me."

"Look at you, growing up! I'm proud of my big brother. He's learning how to share." His breath is labored while his feet pound on the treadmill.

"Will you just listen?"

My patience was thin to begin with, but it decreases when two girls come over, one on either side of us, and jog on the treadmills as if they're on the slow-mo reel in *Baywatch*.

Carm and I share a look that says, you want to or not?

I'm a no.

Carm's a yes.

I really need to talk to someone about this shit rolling around in my head. One minute I'm flirtatious with Annie, then mean, then polite, then indifferent. I thought I had my attraction to her under control, then I go and negotiate a new contract for her. What the hell?

The look on Mr. Jacobson's face when he called me into his office to discuss moving Annie up the corporate ladder was shock. I wanted to say yeah, I get it, I feel the same way. I think I've been abducted too.

At first it was the way her skirts clung to her curvy hips and ass. And the way one button would fall open on her blouse midday, giving me a glimpse of her bra. Sometimes it wasn't even a sexy lacy bra, just a basic nude-colored one, but my mouth always waters to find out what's hiding behind the fabric. Are her nipples a dusty rose or a light brown?

When did I become such a fucking pervert?

When Annie Stewart came to work for me, that's when.

But my draw to her appearance has been buried by my admiration of her mind. I know. Who the hell am I turning into? Being attracted to a woman's mind? What does that even mean?

By the time I get out of my own head, Carm's flirting with the woman next to him, his speed and incline increased so much it's like he's trying to sprint up Mount Everest.

I glance to my right. A smiley blonde turns her head to face me, and dread settles in my stomach at having to play wingman for Carm. I was seconds away from baring my soul, giving my baby brother reason to razz me for life, but instead I'm going to plaster on a fake smile and keep the girl beside me occupied so that he can get laid.

"I'm Trina." Her ponytail swings along her back. Her full face of makeup says she's not here just to workout. She's here hoping to pick up a guy.

"Enzo."

She presses the button on her treadmill to lower her speed. The running was an obvious ruse to grab my attention. "Do you come here a lot?"

"Usually in the morning, but I had a hard day at work." I move my attention from her to my machine.

Meanwhile, Carm has slowed his pace, laughing with the girl next to him.

This is ridiculous.

"It was nice meeting you." I press Stop on my machine then pat my brother on the back. "I'm out."

He looks over and nods, but my words register a half second later. "What? No!" He stops his machine, riding the belt to the end and hopping off.

Show-off.

He winks at the girl he was talking to. "I'll be right back."

I throw my towel in the hamper and head toward the locker room.

"Enzo!" he calls, but I don't turn around. I could recite what he's going to say. "What the hell?"

"I'm not in the mood," I mumble, pushing open the locker room door.

"Not in the mood? Since when?"

"I just wanted to work out." I open my locker.

He rests his back on the lockers next to mine. "You're acting like a chick."

I glance at him and grab my jacket from my locker. "I wanted to get rid of this tension piling down on me with this big campaign."

"I thought you wanted to talk about your conflicted feelings?" He smirks.

See, my brother's not stupid. He knew I needed to get something off my chest, but to him, pussy is the priority. Unless there's a real estate deal to be had.

"Forget it. Go back in there." I wave him off and shrug on my jacket.

"Don't you think blondie might be the best way to get over these 'conflicted feelings'?" He puts the words in air quotes.

I shake my head, sitting on the bench between the row of lockers. "This time I don't."

He straddles the bench, facing me. "Whoa. Okay, what's going on?"

I glance up from untying my runners. "I find myself being nice to her. Like going out of my way to be nice. Hell, I shared a taxi with her to Inwood the other night."

His eyes widen.

"Today I helped her get a new contract that will give her a hell of a promotion."

His eyes bug out like they did the first time he saw a nudie magazine when he was ten. We can all thank Dom for that.

"Yeah, I'm fucked." I pull off my shoes and toss them in my gym bag.

"My guess is she's attractive?"

I nod.

"Have you banged her?"

"No. I would never."

He tilts his head.

"You know my rule about that. But I still find myself flirting, and then when I catch myself, I shut down." I grab my other shoes from the bottom of the locker.

He nods a few times. "Maybe you're just being nice. Like you respect her. You said she helped you with the diaper campaign. Maybe it's a platonic thing? You've never had a woman coworker before, have you?"

I crinkle my forehead while I do up my laces.

He holds up his hands. "I mean, like, someone who challenges you and your ideas. You've had assistants, but Jacobson and Earl isn't exactly known for their women ad execs."

Now that he mentions it, he's right. There was Viv Beacon back when I first started, but she left and started her own company. Other than her, all the women in the office are assistants. Shelby's the highest-ranking woman, at least on my side of the building.

"Maybe you going to bat for her contract is just a nice thing because you like having her around the office and you value her input. And you're not blind. If she's attractive, your body is going to have a natural pull to her. Just don't act on it." He pats my back.

He's right. Why am I in a tailspin? If it was that Jake guy I was helping, I wouldn't think twice. It's appreciation for a coworker and wanting them to get the recognition they deserve, that's all.

"You might be right. Thanks. Who would've guessed my baby brother was so smart?" I pinch his cheek, and he smacks my hand away.

"Good. Now let's go get laid." He stands to head toward the entrance to the gym.

"Nah, I'm heading out."

He throws his hands in the air. "You're kidding me. I just did my best psych one-o-one and you're gonna leave me hanging?"

I stand and position the strap of my gym bag on my shoulder. "Take them both home and have some fun." I smirk.

He contemplates that for a moment. "Do you think they'll go for it?"

I shrug. "You don't know until you ask. You know better than anyone that selling anything is a numbers game."

"I better go before they find someone else. See ya." He waves, already halfway to the door.

"Good luck," I murmur, heading out the opposite way and feeling lighter.

How did I not know the difference between appreciation for a coworker and wanting to nail my assistant? In all honesty though, I'm in uncharted territory here.

CHAPTER THIRTEEN

Annie

"We've got some packages for you," the guy from the mailroom says.

I turn around from my desk and see two guys there, each with a dolly carrying two boxes.

"Seriously?" I peer over the edge of my desk and see Coddle's name on the return address label. "Give me one sec." I pick up my phone and call Enzo's extension.

"Yes?"

"Mind if I let the mailroom guys in?"

"Sure. And then order us lunch. Billy's kid is sick. It's just us today."

I sink down in my chair. Why didn't I know about Billy? Because I'm not on the need-to-know list.

"Is that a problem, Miss Stewart?"

I sit up straight in my chair. "No. I'll let them in."

He hangs up, and I stand. Now I have to be alone with

Enzo for an entire day? God help me. The faster we get through this, the faster I can become a junior ad exec and work with someone else.

"Follow me." I round the desk and open the door to Enzo's office.

"Mr. Mancini." They each nod to him in hello. "Where would you like these?"

"Over by the couches." He absentmindedly points, clearly distracted by whatever he's looking at on his computer.

They do as he says and say their goodbyes.

"Thanks, guys." He nods, sliding his chair from his desk.

He's wearing a brown suit today. He's almost always in black, blue, or grey, but the brown somehow pulls out his olive skin tone even further, and the blue tie adds a flash of color. I wonder if he has a personal shopper who puts his looks together? Probably. His suits are obviously tailored and cost way more than anything in my closet.

"Miss Stewart."

His voice is close, and I blink, finding him right in front of me. His hand touches my arm in an are-you-okay manner, not in an I-know-you-were-daydreaming-about-me way. Thank God.

I smile. "Yes?"

He sits down on the couch, opens the pocketknife in his hand, and cuts open the box. How long was I daydreaming that I never even saw him grab the Swiss Army multi-tool thingy?

"Are you joining me?" He looks up at me through his long eyelashes.

If we had babies, would ours be blessed with those gorgeous lashes? *Oh. My. God. What is wrong with me? This is ridiculous. I'm not even close to the kind of woman he'd go for.*

"Yes, of course." I walk over and bury my head in a box. "There's so much in here."

He flashes me a cocky smile. "Part of the perks."

"Too bad it's not beauty items."

He tosses me a colorful box, and I catch it at the last minute.

"I think you're the only one of us who will use these."

I forgot that Coddle has a whole line of health-related items. Cue the mortification as I look at the box of tampons in my hand. My cheeks heat, and I have no idea why. It's a natural thing, and what do I care what Enzo Mancini thinks? Women get their periods. Big deal.

"I think we'll choose those as our last item to do a campaign for."

I tap the box on my thigh, thinking of all those stupid tampon commercials. The ones where a girl is dressed in white pants and riding a bike like life couldn't get any better, not like it feels as if her uterus is trying to claw its way out of her body. Great, she won't leak. Doesn't mean she feels like taking on the world. "I don't know, I have some ideas."

He stops, holding a bottle of baby shampoo, and looks at me. "That might have to be all you."

We laugh, and I place the box on the other side of me before digging for more treasure.

Enzo finishes sorting through one box and is starting the other when he stops. "This one has your name on it, and there's a note inside." He slides the whole box my way.

"Oh, I love surprises." I open the flaps and take out the small note. "It's from Blair for my sister." I move all the paper around to see bottles upon bottles of everything she'd need for the baby. "She's going to love this."

Enzo smiles. He's stopped pulling items out and he's studying me.

"What?" I hide my face by turning away from him.

He clears his throat. "Nothing. You must *really* like surprises. Your face lit right up."

"Well, you just learned something about me. But it takes a lot to surprise me."

He rests his back in the corner of the couch, ignoring the boxes. "Really? Why is that?"

I shrug, pushing the box for my sister aside and bringing my attention to the next box, ignoring Enzo's eyes on me. "I anticipate people's actions."

He laughs. "No way can you anticipate everyone's actions."

I sit up straighter. "You know when you're dating someone—"

A cloud of confusion covers his face.

"You don't know what I mean?"

"I don't date."

I tilt my head. "You don't date? Like, ever?"

He does seem like the habitual one-night stand kind of guy. Or maybe he has a girl he keeps around strictly for sex. For the past two years, he's come stag to the Christmas party, but I've never seen him hitting on anyone either. There are no rumors about him being a player. Maybe that's because he goes through assistants so fast that no one has time to learn anything about his personal life.

"In high school and college, sort of." His face crinkles, and he shrugs as though that wasn't really dating. "Once I got out of college, I didn't have the time. I had goals and I knew a relationship would jeopardize me achieving them."

Huh. I have something in common with Lorenzo Mancini.

"What?"

I try to mask my revelation with a smile, but I'm too late. "It's just... I feel the same way."

"You don't date?"

"I have, but I decided I want to stand on my own. Make sure I owned a condo, had money in the bank, a secure future before I invite someone else to join me."

He seems to think about that for a moment. "And have you? You're on your way to junior ad exec, and you just bought your own condo."

I shrug. "I always had thirty in my mind, but I thought it would take me that long to accomplish it all. I might have to hold out for becoming a senior ad exec before I start dating." I laugh.

He doesn't.

He's staring at me, and I swear there's a crackle in the air. I suck in a breath and hold it, locked in his gaze.

"But when you did date, you were able to figure out when he was going to surprise you?" He changes the subject and sits up straighter, grabbing a bottle of lotion from the box.

The moment between us is gone so fast, I have to wonder if I imagined it.

"Well, yeah. They'd always miss a step somewhere, and whatever they were setting up, I'd find out. Nothing is worse than having to pretend to be surprised. Especially when the person asks if you were surprised and you have to lie."

He chuckles. "You lied?"

"I didn't want anyone to feel bad."

"Oh, how different we are from one another." He

shakes his head and grins.

I don't mention that I think he likes to think he's a tough ass, but what he's done for me since I started working with him is contrary to his reputation for being an asshole.

"What do we want to tackle first?" I stare at the abundance of products in front of us and pick up some lotion. "Baby bath time?"

He picks up his own bottle because they sent us three of everything. "What is that, lavender?"

"Yeah, this one is how Cecilia smells."

"How are they doing?" He arranges the bottles in a straight line, putting the alike products together.

"They're good. I go over there on Saturdays to help out. I mostly clean and let Beth take a nap."

"Babies are scary."

I laugh. "Should that be our pitch?"

A deep rumble of laughter falls out of him, and it surprises me. I've heard him chuckle or laugh with clients, but never have I heard him full-on belly laugh. It's hearty and sexy and—oh my God, I need to stop dissecting everything about him. A promotion is on the line here, and I don't want to be fired for fraternization. Not that he would cross that line either.

"I say we tackle the bath products—babies to adults. It could be a three-in-one campaign," I say.

"Done. Good choice." He separates them out from the others.

"And the tampons."

"No way." He shakes his head and puts up his hands as though I might toss him one of the three boxes.

"Ideas are already spilling out of my head."

"I know nothing about those things. I mean, I know where they go and their use, but..."

I'm sure he's more than familiar with the hole they go in, I think but don't say.

"Well then, isn't it better that I'm here to help? What if I quit when they don't give me the junior position and you're left all by yourself to do a tampon campaign?" I smile, hoping my twinkling eyes will work some sort of magic and he'll agree with me.

"First of all, you're going to get the junior position. Can't we leave the tampons for last?"

"I'm sure that's what they expect. I bet if it were condoms, you'd be all over them."

"Speaking of." He digs into the bottom of one of the boxes and tosses me a pack.

And here we are, already prepared if the need arises.

Lord, save me from myself. There is definitely something wrong with me. I take a breath to recompose myself. "Let me guess, you want to do the condoms?"

"Well, I am a professional on that one." He shrugs.

I narrow my eyes. "It's not like I don't use condoms."

"You *feel* the condom, but you don't *use* the condom."

"True." I hold up the boxes of tampons and condoms, one in each hand. "Which will we choose?"

His eyes focus on the condoms and his eyelids grow heavy. His smoldering gaze shifts to me, and I can't help but wonder if he's also thinking of testing them out.

I drop the boxes. "Let's concentrate on bath time first."

He swallows audibly. "Good idea."

I stand. "So, um, I'll go order us some lunch before we get started."

"Perfect."

I practically run out of his office and shut the door, gasping for a breath of fresh air that isn't mingled with the scent of Enzo.

CHAPTER FOURTEEN

Enzo

I weave by the patrons waiting to be seated, finding Dom at his usual table at the Trading Post. He's already scarfing down his lobster mac and cheese. Most people would say Dom is intimidating as hell, but I don't think they'd have the same opinion if they saw him eating mac and cheese for lunch. Come to Trading Post any Thursday and you'll find Dominic Mancini in the flesh.

Before sitting, I shrug off my jacket. Seriously, when is summer going to arrive? "How nice of you to wait for us."

Dom barely looks up, chewing his mouthful of pasta.

Our waitress arrives almost instantly. "Hey, Enzo."

"Kate, how's it going?"

She grabs the pen from behind her ear and positions her notepad even though I'm sure she knows our orders by heart. "Doing all right. You?"

"Good. I'll have the goat cheese pizza and a water for right now."

She nods, doesn't bother writing it down, and peers across the restaurant toward the doors. "Carmelo coming too?"

"Yeah."

"I'll grab his Stella."

"You're the best." I smile at her before she leaves.

Dom wipes his mouth with his napkin. "Since you failed at your mission, we have something new to discuss."

"Which is?" I unroll my silverware from my napkin and place the napkin on my lap.

"I don't want to waste time telling just you. We'll wait for Carm."

I nod. "So what, I'll watch you eat?"

"I have shit I need to take care of. Do you have any idea what happened today?" He grabs his fork again.

"Do you carry antacids around with you, big brother?"

He narrows his eyes, piling another mouthful of food onto his fork.

"Sorry I'm a few minutes late." Carm walks in, sans coat, and sits down, eyeing Dom already halfway through his meal before shifting his vision to me, silently asking 'what the fuck?'

"He's in a hurry," I say.

"Hurry? Do you know how long it took me to get all the way down here? How many times have I said we shouldn't meet at lunch?"

"Yet here you are," Dom says.

Carm rolls his eyes, then smiles and looks at me. "Hey, thanks for the other night. Turns out Trina and Kitty were into having fun as a group."

"You know those are fake names, right?"

"No. Why would they use fake names?" Carm seems alarmed by the thought. "Should I have used a fake name?"

"Since your half-naked body is plastered on Times Square, I'd say don't bother," Dom deadpans.

"Here you go." Kate comes by and puts down our drinks.

"Kate!" Carm's boisterous personality alerts everyone in a five-foot radius that he knows our waitress.

"Hey, Carm. What can I get you?"

"Ah." He looks at the menu and ponders for a minute as if we're not here every week. Even Kate, who I think might have a thing for him, looks as if she wants to scream. Carm can be blind to the obvious sometimes, so he probably doesn't even notice the lunch rush. "Salad. Chef. Just balsamic."

"Got it." She lightly touches his shoulder, moving on to the next table.

"It took you five minutes to order the same thing you do every week?" I grab my water.

He flashes me his toothy smile. "I almost changed it up. The mac and cheese looks awesome, given the shit day I'm having."

"What's going on?" I take a sip of my water and set it back on the table.

"That stupid chick who keeps advertising how to sell your house yourself rather than use a realtor? She's won some big clients lately and it's pissing me off."

"*Oh.*" Dom points with his fork. "She's hot as hell. I saw her billboard the other day."

"If you can see past her evil self." Carm rolls his eyes.

Dom pushes away his bowl and sets down his cutlery. "So Enzo fucked up the Blanca thing."

"What?" Carm's head swivels in my direction.

"She's not buying it." Dom leans back in his chair and crosses his arms.

"Did you honestly think she would?" Sometimes I think I'm the only Mancini brother with a functioning brain.

"I have a new idea anyway. I went over to our parents' last night because I had to grab something from the basement."

"What?" Carm asks.

Dom's forehead creases. "What?"

"What did you need?"

Dom shakes his head. "It doesn't matter."

"I know, but I wanna know." Carm's like a dog with a tug toy.

"Anyway"—Dom ignores Carm's questions—"I overhead Ma talking to Dad. She kept saying she didn't raise us properly. Going on and on about how she'll never see grandkids. You know how she can get carried away."

Carm and I nod. Whether it's good or bad, Mama takes everything to the extreme.

"You'd think we were fifty or something," Carm says.

"In Italian terms, we kind of are. And I think we're all in agreement none of us are ready to settle down any time soon?" Dom looks around the table, making eye contact with each of us.

We nod like good younger brothers.

Dom claps his hands together and rubs his palms. "Lucky for us, Ma and Pa had the oops baby, Blanca."

"Was she an oops?" Carm asks.

Dom shoots him a look that says *shut the fuck up and listen.* "We just need to find her a guy she can be serious with."

"This sounds like a bad plan. Like something from a

movie," I say. Blanca is way smarter than he's giving her credit for.

"It's brilliant. If there's not a movie, someone should make it into one. Blanca's always watching all that romance shit. I mean, how many renditions of *Romeo and Juliet* have we seen because of her? Hell, she convinced Ma that we should go to the play as a family."

"Technically, I'm not sure *Romeo and Juliet* is a romance," Carm chimes in, and we both stare at him as if he's sprouted another head. "What? It's true. I think romance has to have a happy ending. Name another movie where a main character dies?"

"*The Matrix*," I say.

"*Braveheart*," Dom says.

We high-five each other.

"Those aren't romance movies," Carm says.

Dom stares blankly at Carm. "Anyway… one of us needs to find her a guy she can't refuse. Then hopefully sparks will fly, and a whirlwind romance begins. Truthfully, all we really need is Blanca to bring the guy home to dinner. Mom's spirits will be lifted, and we won't be compared to our cousins, the wonderful Bianco brothers, anymore."

"I talked to Luca the other day," Carm says.

Kate slides our dishes onto the table. We each say our thanks while Carm waits for one of us to ask him about his conversation with our cousin Luca.

"Good for you." Dom puts his hands over our dishes before we have a chance to eat. "Let's see who has to be the one to find someone for her first." He rests his hand on his open palm.

"I'm not doing rock, paper, scissors," I say.

Dom and Carm look at one another, snickering.

"Because you know you'll lose." The grin on Carm's face makes me want to smack him.

"I don't lose every fucking time." I tear apart my pizza, not giving one shit what Dom says.

"Then why won't you do it?" Dom asks.

"Because this whole thing is childish. Finding our sister a date? I'm trying to make partner at work. I don't have time for this."

"I'm responsible for millions of people's money."

"Slight exaggeration." I take a bite of my pizza. God, that's good.

"What about me? This for-sale-by-owner woman is stressing me out. I have to stay one step ahead of her at all times."

"See? We're all busy, so it's only fair. We rock, paper, scissors and loser finds the date." Dom puts his fist on his palm again.

I shake my head.

"Stop being a baby," he goads.

"I'm not being a baby. If you're so worried about it, you find her the date." I have another bite of pizza, downing it with my water.

Kate breezes by. "I'll grab your bill, Dom?"

"Perfect. Thanks." Dom waves and sets his attention back on us.

"Let's just get this over with." Carm mimics Dom.

"Don't you think we're too old for these games?" I ask.

"No," they answer at the same time.

"And you're not going to let this go?" I ask, wiping my hands on my napkin, preparing to play their stupid game.

"Unless you want to bring a girl to Sunday dinner, this is our only way to get Ma off our back for a while." Dom smiles and winks.

I position my fist on my palm. "Fine. Two out of three."

"Nope." Dom's forearm muscles tense.

"It's one round unless there're two losers." Carm rehashes the rules we made when we were young and stupid.

"One." Dom pounds his fist. "Two." He pounds it again. "Three."

Dom shoots rock.

Carm shoots scissors.

I shoot scissors.

Dom leans back, grabs his money clip out of his pocket. "It's between you two losers now."

He leans over, handing Kate money before she can give him the bill. That's what happens when you come to the same restaurant and order the same thing every Thursday.

Carm faces me. His salad is still untouched.

"One," I say, my voice void of any enthusiasm. "Two." I pound my fist. "Three."

I shoot scissors.

Carm shoots rock.

What the fuck? It's a conspiracy. I know I win at this game sometimes.

"Woo hoo!" Carm stands, high-fiving Dom as he slides out of his chair. "Loser." He points at me with both of his forefingers and swivels his hips into some lame-ass dance.

Dom's big hand clasps my shoulder. "Good luck. Better you than me. All I know are traders and they're selfish pricks."

He leaves the restaurant without so much as a goodbye, and Carm slides back into his seat.

"Man, you really suck at this game."

I ignore him, continuing to eat my pizza.

"Oh, don't sulk." He chuckles.

I'm not sulking though. I'm running through the list of guys I know, but none of them are good enough for my baby sister.

We eat our lunch while Carm regales me with a detailed account of his time with Trina and Kitty from the gym. Carm's lucky I haven't thrown up from his very detailed description. I've told him to stop talking about five times now.

My phone vibrates in my pocket as I finish my last slice. I slide it out of my pocket and see the time.

"Shit. I gotta go." I wipe my mouth. "See you later."

"Don't work so hard," he jokes because the three of us could start our own support group for workaholics.

I'm in the cab, headed back to the office when a text message comes through.

Carm: *Jackass. You left me with the bill.*

I laugh, knowing full well what I did.

Me: *Sorry. I'll get you back.*

Never. He and Dom have no problem with their rock, paper, scissors shit. If I have to go search out guys for our sister, Carm's buying my lunch. Where do I find an available guy deserving of my baby sister? There's only one woman I can think to ask.

CHAPTER FIFTEEN

Annie

Enzo and I sit on the one side of the double-sided mirror, looking into the room with the test group. We're alone at the moment because Billy is on some emergency campaign problem with Mr. Zilroy and Jake.

In the room are parents with their babies, most playing with toys. Others rock their newborns. A changing table has been set up to see which products they choose when caring for their baby.

My notes are minimal and I'm already doubting this process will help us come up with a campaign, but I'm the newbie here, so I keep my mouth shut.

"You're single, right?"

Enzo's question throws me. I turn toward him. His eyes are still on the parents and their kids. "Um..."

"Yeah, I know it's probably against the code of conduct that I ask, but are you?"

I tap my pen on the table. "I am. I thought we went over this the other day?"

Is he going to ask me out? Does he want to know because this slow-burning sizzle between us hasn't gone away yet? What will I say? As much as I want to explore this thing between us, I won't put this junior executive position at risk.

"Where do you find guys?" he asks.

I glance at him. Once again, he's not looking at me. Maybe he's embarrassed? "The usual places. Bars, Tinder... it all depends on the mood I'm in."

"Mood?" His gaze finally meets mine.

I purposely look away because I'm not sure I can keep a straight face. "Whether I want to just hit it and quit it or if I want to snuggle afterward, you know?"

He turns his chair to face me now, his legs splaying open. He seems relaxed. His suit jacket has been discarded on the couch. His shirt sleeves are rolled up, revealing corded muscles in his forearms. He taps his pen on the table, the only hint that there's any tension brewing inside him.

"Hit it and quit it?" He raises an eyebrow.

"Don't act like you don't do Tinder when you're horny." I bite my lip to keep from laughing.

"I've never used Tinder." From the steady rhythm of his words, I'd say he's telling the truth.

"You're missing out." I sip from my water bottle before I lose it.

"Shut up. You're on Tinder?"

"Uh-huh."

He grabs his phone from the table.

A baby cries in the room, and I turn my attention to the mirror to make sure everything is okay. A mom changes her baby on the changing table and he obviously hates the experience, kicking his feet and swatting his hands at her. Her face is flushed with embarrassment as she peers around to make sure her baby isn't bothering anyone else. I jot a few notes about moms worrying about what others think. Babies who don't like their diapers being changed.

My phone dings next to me. I pick it up absentmindedly, my mind solely on whether we can do something with what I just witnessed. The Tinder app I let Mae convince me to put on my phone has a notification.

I side-eye Enzo, knowing he has something to do with this.

I click on the app. There's Enzo's picture with a big blue box that says, "Super Liked." I shake my head, placing my phone face down on the table.

"That's disheartening," he says.

I swivel my chair toward him, and my legs knock his. "I thought you didn't use Tinder."

"I don't, but I'll admit to downloading the app. You never know." He shrugs those strong shoulders of his.

"Hmm... I don't believe you."

He tosses his phone in front of me on the table. "Have at my history."

I push it aside. "No thanks."

"Are you going to like me back?"

"Why do you care?" I circle my chair to face forward.

"It's insulting to have a super like out there and not get one in return. I don't pay, so I only get one of those a day."

I chuckle. "For someone who doesn't do Tinder, you sure know a lot about it."

"My brother Carm loves it. Told me it would change my life."

"Sounds like a great guy."

"I wouldn't suggest you swipe right for him. No."

I zero in on the study group because this whole getting-to-know-each-other thing feels weird and awkward, but I'll admit that it's enlightening. The man I thought was a grade-A asshole is turning into a grade-A piece of goodness. "What's with all the questions anyway?"

His pen seesaws on the table. *Click. Click. Click. Click.*

"Babies are boring," I change the subject since he doesn't seem to want to answer.

"I lost a bet to my brothers."

This should be good.

"How many brothers do you have?" I glance at him.

"Two. One older, one younger. And a baby sister." He focuses on the group.

"Was the bet about Tinder? Or where to pick up guys?"

He laughs. "No. My three cousins just found love and my mom's depressed because her three boys are all still bachelors."

I nod in understanding. "Getting some pressure from your mom about settling down?" I jot down another note about two moms interacting and how one walked away rolling her eyes after the other tried to instruct her how to position the bottle.

"All my life. I'm Italian."

"Really? I never would have known," I deadpan.

"Now that my cousins are in love and two have already fallen on bended knee, my mom seems like she's in a depression or something. Especially since none of us even have a girlfriend."

I flash him a smile. "I don't know what that's like. My dad doesn't say much about me being single."

Correction: My dad doesn't say anything. He doesn't ask about my love life, and I don't think he cares if I end up a spinster with fifty cats or if I marry next year. He's always been about Beth and I being happy.

"You're lucky."

We sit in silence, both of us jotting down notes. Truthfully, I don't see how we're getting anything from this. Just when I think the conversation is over, he starts it up again.

"My brothers came up with a plan."

"I can only imagine."

"It's a good plan. Sort of. It's more my brothers' plan, but I see the possibility of success."

"You're being vague."

He laughs, his pen playing a game of teeter-totter again. "I have to find a guy for my sister." The pen stops moving.

A laugh bursts from my mouth so loudly, I fear the other side will hear me.

"Why is that funny?" He looks offended.

I stand up to grab another water bottle from the mini fridge. "Most brothers try to keep guys *away* from their sister. You know, the whole 'no one is good enough' cliché?"

He remains silent.

"Why are you the one in charge of this? There're three of you."

His shoulders sag a bit.

Okay, I've always found Enzo attractive. A successful man gets a checkmark right off the top, and to a certain extent, as bad as it is to say, his assholish demeanor ramped up his sexiness. Only because I'd wonder why he was an asshole. Did some girl hurt him so badly it ruined him for the rest of us?

But these weeks that I've been able to see a more vulnerable side to his personality have made me even more attracted to him. He has a depth I didn't expect.

"I lost."

"You lost? What does that mean?" I slide back into my chair, unscrewing the cap on the bottle. The cold fluid is a relief from where my mind keeps wandering.

"We hashed it out and I got... picked to find the guy."

"You're giving me bits and pieces and I'm still not sure what you're saying."

He throws his hands up, swivels his chair, and heads to the mini fridge. "We play rock, paper, scissors and they say I always lose. I don't. But I did this time."

"You guys play rock, paper, scissors?"

"It's the easiest way for us to come to a decision when none of us wants to do something."

I tap my pen against my lips and his eyes focus on the motion, so I put the pen on the table. "I'm just curious, you guys do rock, paper, scissors to decide which of you will find a date for your sister that'll hopefully turn into something serious, but you don't do the same to choose which of you should find a woman to maybe marry?"

He tilts his head as if this is the first time he's thought of it. Then he shakes his head. "Blanca wants to get married."

Blanca? What a beautiful name. I get Annie and she gets Blanca. Life is so unfair.

"Are you sure?"

He sits back down, opens up his bottle, and downs half the contents. "She's a girl. Don't all girls dream of their wedding day?"

I stare blankly at him. He's joking. Any minute he's going to laugh.

He doesn't laugh.

"No. They don't."

"Really?" A crease forms between his eyebrows.

"Do you think every woman you sleep with is waiting for a ring the next morning?"

He shrugs, sipping more water.

"*You do*!" I point. "So if we slept together, you'd be thinking I want to be your wife?"

He tilts his head and locks eyes with me. "Why are you putting yourself in this scenario?"

I look away and my eyes fall to the opening of his legs. Damn it. I tear my eyes away, but the smirk on his face says he saw me.

"It's hypothetical. Forget it. You're delusional, and it sounds like your brothers are too. I feel sorry for your sister."

He coughs and chokes on his water.

Good.

"We've been great brothers," he argues.

"Great. Sure. You're going to try to marry her off to the first guy *you* think she'd like instead of being adults and having a conversation with your mom. Why are you so hell-bent on being a bachelor for life anyway?"

"We've been over this."

"Have we? You said it was so you could achieve your goals. Newsflash, you're about to become partner, you probably live in a high-rise penthouse, and I'm sure you have plenty of money in your bank account, so I'm not sure your original reason holds any weight." I sound angry for some reason. What do I care? It's none of my business how he lives his life.

Before he has a chance to respond, I place my hand in the air. "I'm sorry. It's none of my business. I think I was getting protective of your sister, who I don't even know. So forget it. Don't answer that question. I'm going to the restroom."

I leave before he has a chance to say anything. Once I'm securely in the bathroom, I stare at myself in the mirror. What is wrong with me? I'm such an idiot.

I pull out my phone and pull up my group chat with Beth and Mae.

Me: *I need help.*
Beth: *Come over tonight and we'll make cookies.*
Mae: *Yay! Cookie night. I'll bring the milk, mama.*
Me: *Thanks girls.*

Just like that. No questions asked and my sister and bestie are ready to guide me out of the jungle of emotions I find myself lost in. They might have to send a chopper because I'm in deep.

CHAPTER SIXTEEN

Enzo

Annie walks back into the room, her cheeks still flushed. When she was going off on me, all I thought about was kissing her. I need to get her out of my system because she's right. Those reasons were legit way back when. But they don't feel so valid anymore. I get the feeling that Annie is becoming a game-changer, and I don't like it.

I gave her a Super Like on Tinder. The one and only time I've ever used the app. The only reason I even know what a Super Like is, is because of my pervy brother Carm.

"This was a complete waste of time," she says and takes her seat.

"I know, my notes are minimal."

I guess we're ignoring her outburst. Works for me.

"We need hands-on experience. Should I ask my sister? We could watch her with Cecilia all day or something."

That sounds like as much fun as spending the day at

Chuck E. Cheese.

"Why don't we make up a list of questions? We can ask parents about their nighttime routines. Make up a questionnaire and have them answer." Her face contorts, and it's clear she thinks that's the worst idea ever. "Or not."

"Sorry. I don't even know how it was with my family. Did my parents have a routine? I have no idea."

"I could ask Ma." It's out of my mouth before I can snatch it back. If I ask my mom, it will open up Pandora's box. She'll be missing when we were babies, thinking of how she's never going to have her own grandbabies.

"Okay, but I really think watching Beth and Sam might be our best bet."

"Perfect. Let's go with that." Thank goodness. I'd rather spend my night with a newborn than asking my mom about babies.

"I'm going over there tonight, so I'll find out a day that's good for her."

"Sounds good."

We both stand, and I open the door for her. She's in a pantsuit today, which disappointed me this morning, since I love her legs. Even though I shouldn't. I have to keep reminding myself of that.

After we thank the focus group for coming, we head down the elevator to the lobby of the building.

"Are you taking the products to your sister's place?" I ask.

We step out onto the street, and for the first time in weeks, sunlight shines down on us.

"Oh my God. Feel that on your face. I thought the clouds and rain were going to last forever." She tips her head up to the sky, granting me time to admire her long neck.

If she was mine, my first line of business would be licking up her soft skin until I captured her lips with mine.

"This makes the day so much better." She inhales a deep breath, and her smile says she doesn't smell the garbage set out at the curb, but something else. "The flowers, the grass. It's like everything is coming to life again."

I glance at my watch. It's three o'clock. We can get back to the office and get a few more hours of work in before the day is over. Her head falls down, and she digs out a pair of sunglasses from her bag and positions them on her face.

"Should we head back?" I ask.

She nods, but it's clear she's reluctant.

I flag down a taxi and open the door for her, but she doesn't step forward. I can't read her eyes because of her sunglasses, but I think she's staring at Central Park across from us.

Pushing her sunglasses up on her head, she steps forward but places her hand on my forearm. "Do you mind if I meet you back at the office?"

I crease my forehead. "Sure."

"Thanks. I won't be long."

Before I can say anything else, she walks across the street and into Central Park.

I peek my head in the taxi. "Sorry." I shut the door.

He flips me off and speeds off around the corner, almost hitting another pedestrian. I dodge traffic, playing a mild game of *Frogger* until I'm safely on the other side of the street.

"Annie!" I call.

She stops and turns. Her lips tip down. Shit, I didn't realize I was intruding on her. Maybe there's a reason why she wants to walk through Central Park.

"Did I forget something?" she asks.

"Mind if I join you?"

A smile rushes to her face and reaches her eyes. My heart does this weird sputtering thing.

"Not at all."

A rainy spring has nourished the plants and flowers. The park is green and colorful now, as if it all appeared out of thin air. People ride their bikes and walk the paths—a mix of parents pushing strollers and athletic types getting their exercise.

"I love spring because all the people come out of hibernation." She twirls in a circle and continues walking forward as though she's soaking in much more than the sun. "The city comes alive."

I could argue that the night is when this city comes alive, but I'm mesmerized by her. I've never seen her so carefree and relaxed. After a few twirls with her head tipped up to the sun, she stops and looks at me.

"I can name all the statues in Central Park." She laughs. "I know. Stupid fact, but my dad's a history buff, and when we moved here, he'd take us out every weekend from May to October. We'd walk the path and he'd tell us all about the person the statue honored."

Any words I might say are trapped in my throat. What is it about this woman that continues to draw me in?

"You're probably like, 'Whatever, Annie. That's so stupid,' but days like today, I feel like I'm ten again and my dad's telling the story of Alexander Hamilton or King Jagiello and the Battle of Grunwald."

We continue down the path until we pass the *Alice in Wonderland* statue.

"Oh." She touches the bronze sculpture. "My dad made a whole day about *Alice in Wonderland* once. He rented the movie." She tips her head. "The 1951 version. I became obsessed, and we watched each remake to decide which is best."

"And the winner?" I ask.

"Don't tell anyone, but I love the 2010." She cringes as if she should be ashamed.

"I've never seen any of them."

Her eyes narrow. "Oh, you need to get out more."

"Wouldn't I need to stay in more?"

She thinks for a moment, her eyes shooting toward the blue sky. "Maybe." She bumps me with her shoulder. "Want to know another fact?"

"Sure."

A sensation like we're in a movie and should be skipping through Central Park runs through my mind. It's like the sun and warm weather has intoxicated her. Shit, she's intoxicating me.

"There're no statues of women. I mean, not real women. There's Alice and angels and animals that might be of the female sex, but not one of a real-life woman."

My head draws back. There's no way that's true.

She points at me. "You think I'm wrong, but it's true."

I hold up my hands.

"In 2020, there's supposed to be one of Elizabeth Cady Stanton and Susan B. Anthony displayed. Those will be the first."

Huh. I never think about these things. But I remember the way she was upset when they wanted her to continue being an assistant after she contributed to the Coddle campaign. I thought she'd be ecstatic, and after she almost declined the opportunity, I realized how differently Jacobson and Earl makes decisions between her and me. After the first campaign I had a hand in landing, I was promoted to junior ad exec right away. Actually, I never even assisted. They called my job an apprenticeship, but I was paid.

Now, in 2019, there's not one statue in this famous park of a woman who made a difference in the world?

"I think it's sad for little girls, you know? Don't get me wrong, Alice in Wonderland and Juliet are fine, but girls walk through this park and see statue after statue of men who, let's be honest, probably had a hand in keeping the women below them down. Kids are smart, they see the difference." She sits at a water fountain and pats the spot next to her then digs into her purse, grabs two pennies, and hands one to me. "I'm doing all the talking. Make a wish."

She's been rambling since we walked in, but I'm enjoying listening to her. I like that she's sharing who she is with me. She has such a great head on her shoulders. No wonder it feels impossible not to be taken by her, even if she does work for me.

She closes her eyes, kisses the penny—which I'm not sure is a good idea—and tosses it in. We watch the penny swirl until it hits the bottom of the fountain.

She smiles before turning back to me and knocking me with her shoulder. "Come on."

I make a wish in my head and toss my penny into the fountain.

"Don't tell me," she says.

"Okay." Although if it does come true, it will benefit us both. Winning all the Coddle products would make sure everyone in advertising knows who we are.

"One last stop and then we can go back to the office, okay?" She has her hands up in front of her in a prayer pose as though she's begging.

It's funny that she thinks she's easy to say no to.

I shove my hands into my pockets before I can give in to

the temptation to take her hand and allow her to lead me wherever she wants. "Sure."

A few minutes later, we arrive at the *Romeo and Juliet* statue.

"Funny, I was just talking to my brothers about Romeo and Juliet the other day," I say.

"Really?" Her dreamy eyes say she won't be in agreement with us.

"My brother Carm says it's not a love story."

She balks, her mouth hanging open. Then she must think on it because her expression changes. "I guess I can see why people might think that but… you know what I love about their story?" She stares at the statue. "I love that it was such a forbidden love. So many odds were stacked against them, but they had this pull to one another they couldn't resist. Their love was too powerful to be ignored."

"You do know it only happened over three days?"

She turns to me, tilting her head. "Do you not believe in love at first sight?"

"No."

Her lips dip down. "You don't think that one day you'll be walking through, let's say, Central Park and you might spot a woman. Your eyes connect, and bam, there's that spark of electricity and suddenly the former bachelor known as Lorenzo Mancini is off the market." She laughs.

"Not at all." I lean in closer. "Want to hear another confession?" I whisper into her ear. "I don't believe in soul mates either."

She shakes her head then smiles and walks down the path, so I follow. "I don't either. I mean, if there's one guy out there for me, I'm never going to find him. I live in a city with almost nine million people. You're telling me that one day Cupid is gonna come down with his arrow and shoot us both? Not likely. But love at first sight? I do believe in that. Well..." She giggles and damn if it's not the cutest sound in the world. "I guess maybe it's more intrigue than love, and the desire to find out what's between you."

"Hate to break it to you, but that's not love at first sight."

Her lips tip down, and I hate seeing that. "Yeah, I guess not. Who would have thought I'd agree with Lorenzo Mancini? Not me."

"I'm curious, what did you think of me before we started working together?"

Her face flushes and she sucks on her top lip.

I cringe. "That bad?"

"No." She waves me off. "I thought you were difficult to work for."

"And now?" I stop us before we exit the park. It shouldn't matter what she thinks, but I want to know so badly.

"I think you're pretty great," she says.

Our eyes lock for a moment and I step forward, my arm extending. Her tongue slides out of her mouth, licking her bottom lip, and I want so badly to bite that lip.

The air between us feels electric, and my heart rate picks up as I lean forward.

My phone vibrates in my pocket, and she blinks, shakes her head, and steps back.

"I'll let you get that." She walks a few steps ahead, turning away from me.

Thank God for my phone, because I almost did the stupidest thing I could ever do. Kill my chances at making partner.

CHAPTER SEVENTEEN

Annie

"I almost kissed him." I flail on the couch and throw my arm over my eyes.

"I hate to break this to you, but rumors are flying at work."

I bolt up, lasering my focus on Mae. She nods, answering my unasked question.

"Why? We've been nothing but professional."

She raises her palms as though weighing them back and forth. "Didn't you just say you almost kissed him?"

"This is amazing. I'll write a thank you note for you to send them." Beth keeps pulling out items Blair Peterson was nice enough to send to her.

"I'm so screwed. You have no idea how much sex appeal he has." I slump back into the couch.

"Oh, I know." Mae grabs a cookie from the table, sitting cross-legged on the chair and staring at me as though she's happy it's me and not her. "We've been drooling over him for the past two years. Well, me only a year, but let's not forget your first day at Jacobson and Earl."

"*Ugh*." My throat strangles the sound of my frustration. "How can I forget?"

"I think he knew *of* you." Mae smiles to make me feel better. She's a good friend.

"Seriously, we have enough to stuff to last a lifetime, Sam!" Beth yells.

"Awesome!" he yells back.

The baby screams a second later.

Mae and I laugh.

"I'll be back," Beth stands.

"I got it, babe," Sam calls, and Beth sits back down, digging through the box as if it's from Sephora. I don't get the appeal. It's a bunch of lotions and soaps and diapers.

"That's a good guy in there," I say.

"He is," Mae says.

"For sure," I add.

"Back to your first day. Remember?"

"Yes, Mae, I remember. I remember every embarrassing moment of it."

"Why don't I know this?" Beth looks up. I didn't even think she was listening.

"Because you were in Samland. Newlyweds don't really see what's going on outside of their love bubble." The bitterness in my tone surprises even me. Beth's forehead crinkles, and I feel guilty for her thinking I'm not happy for her. My shoulders sag. "I didn't mean it like that."

Her gaze falls down, and she buries her head back in the box.

"She was in the lobby, getting her security pass, and afterward she was running late, so she ran smack dab into him," Mae says, and I can tell she's enjoying sharing this with my sister.

"I didn't account for how long it would take at security. I had to show my license and sign something. I figured they'd have called down and already have my tag ready." I use the same excuse I do every time we travel down this particular memory lane.

"That's it? That's not so bad," Beth says, her head still in the box. I make a mental note to get her baby supplies the next time I piss her off.

"The two of them ran into one another at the elevators."

My heartbeat picks up just remembering that day. I toss a pillow at Mae but miss.

"It can't be that bad," Beth says, a bottle of lotion in each hand, one lavender and one regular. "I feel like it's my birthday. How sad is that?" She chuckles.

"It's not nearly as bad as she's making it out to be." Mae sips her wine and grabs another cookie. "They get off the elevator."

"You're missing a crucial part of the story," I remind her, grabbing another pillow from beside me and pulling it onto my face.

Mae tilts her head and looks at me. "What?"

I move the pillow away from my face for a second. "I saw him when I interviewed." I put it back over, as if covering my face makes the embarrassment somehow less.

"Lorenzo Mancini isn't a guy you forget, so yes, she saw him at the interview. Knew on the ride up that they'd get off on the same floor. She hangs back because she doesn't want him to stare at her ass while she walks in front of him out of the elevator."

"My modest little sister." Beth nudges my arm.

I scream into the pillow.

"So she follows him."

I take the pillow off my face again. "Keep that amused tone out of your voice."

Mae laughs. "Long story short, she followed him right into the men's room."

"Oh, that's nothing," Beth says. "Please."

I sit up straight. "I followed him into the bathroom. He didn't notice right away. Put his tie over his shoulder and unbuckled his pants until he must have sensed me. I was standing there, staring at him."

"For how long?" I can tell my sister is trying to hold back a laugh now.

"I don't know." I fall headfirst into the couch.

"He doesn't even remember," Mae says.

"Because I'm *that* unmemorable. I'm pretty sure I'd remember someone who followed me into a bathroom and acted like they were going to watch me pee."

"That was two years ago. Things have changed. I saw it." Beth tucks her legs under her on the couch, finally ignoring the box of goodies.

"You never saw us until the hospital."

She shrugs. "You guys have chemistry."

"No, we don't. We're opposite sexes who work together. The lines are blurring, but they'll straighten out."

Beth looks at Mae, then to the side when we hear footsteps in the hall.

"Sorry, babe, she's hungry." Sam comes out of the back hallway looking like death. He's in shorts and a T-shirt with three stains around his shoulders. "Ladies."

"Sam, man, you need a shower. What's that smell?" Mae cringes with me.

"It's called fatherhood, Mae."

Her cringe intensifies from his snarky attitude.

"Go get some rest. I got her." Beth opens her arms, and Sam places Cecilia into them. Beth pulls up her shirt and opens some flap on her bra, her huge breast falling out.

"Whoa, did you get implants?" Mae asks.

I really hope she's joking.

"Yes, I did, Mae. After I pushed an eight-pound baby out of my hoo-ha, I said, 'Hey, doc, how about some bigger knockers?'"

"Jeez, I was joking." Mae tips her head down into her wine glass.

"Sorry. I'm just moody." The baby latches to Beth.

"They look great," Mae says, grabbing both of hers. "I'm jealous."

"Believe me, they aren't worth what I went through to finally have great tits."

"Can you do me a favor?" I ask, hating to bring it up.

Beth doesn't respond but shoots me her "what is it now" expression.

"When Enzo comes here with me, can you not pull them out?" I asked earlier if she minded if we used her as a case study, and surprisingly, she agreed right away.

"Breastfeeding is nothing to be ashamed of. My baby is eating—"

"It's not that. It's because if I ever do get to second base with him, he's going to wonder why he's with the small-tit sister."

Mae throws a pillow at me but can't stop laughing.

Beth laughs, the poor baby getting a milkshake.

"I already feel inadequate. I have to ask myself, why would he even want to kiss me?"

"Because you're gorgeous," Beth says.

"And wicked smart," Mae adds.

"I'm not a size two though. Doesn't he seem like the

kind of guy who would be with a girl who could walk the catwalk?"

Mae contemplates it. Beth doesn't count because she's my sister, but Mae will tell me the truth. "No one has ever seen him with a woman, so who knows? I think what you should be asking yourself is whether he's worth losing your job for."

Suddenly our lighthearted conversation turns serious, and my biggest insecurities rise up to the surface. Quietly, I say, "I've been used before. In college, there was a guy who acted like he liked me just to coerce me into writing his paper for him."

"Forget that jackass Heath. He was an asshole," Mae says. "He was a selfish prick."

"That's terrible, Annie, but you have to let that go," my sister says.

I helped Enzo get the campaign that will get him partner. It's not out of the realm of possibility that he'd sleep with me to get ideas to benefit himself. Keep me happy and content, distract me, and bam, he's partner, and I'm out on my ass.

It's possible, I guess, but just thinking it feels a little ridiculous.

"Listen." Mae comes to sit beside me on the couch and places her hand on my thigh. "You're so smart and this?" She points at my stomach. "Your gut is going to lead you in the right direction. What's it telling you right now?"

"It tells me that Enzo Mancini is a god in bed."

They laugh, nodding.

"What about his intentions?" Mae asks.

I chew on my lip, thinking it over. Everything between us over the past month has been eye-opening. I never thought he'd be the person I've come to know.

My phone rings on the table, and Mae grabs it. Her eyes shift to Beth before she hands it to me. Lorenzo Mancini flashes on the screen as it vibrates and rings in my hand.

He's never called me, and I wonder if it has something to do with the almost kiss earlier.

"Answer it." Mae nudges me.

I slide my thumb over the screen and bring it to my ear. "Hey."

"Hi, Annie. I'm sorry to bother you, but I just got a call from Blair Peterson, and they want us in Houston tomorrow to talk with the director of the commercial. We get the company jet since it's Coddle, so I'll pick you up at nine tomorrow morning and we'll head to the airport."

My stomach sinks. "Are we flying back tomorrow?"

"Yeah, no need to pack anything. We'll be in late, but we're not staying."

Phew. I release a breath.

Mae and Beth share a look.

"Great. Okay, but I can meet you at the airport."

He's silent for a moment. "No. I'll pick you up."

"It's out of your way," I argue.

"I want to, okay? The car will be there at nine."

He hangs up, and I stare at the phone. I shouldn't be surprised. He never says goodbye. I fall back into the couch.

Mae squeezes my shoulder. "What was that about?"

"I have to go to Houston with him tomorrow." I pick up the pillow and put it over my head.

"Sex in Houston sounds like as good a place as any." Mae laughs, and Beth does too.

I throw the pillow at Mae, but she stands, holding the pillow up to her face.

"I can't fight it anymore, Enzo," she says in a seductive voice.

"Me either, Annie. Let me make sweet love to you for hours," Mae says in a deep voice.

"No. No, Enzo, I'll gladly blow you."

She faces one direction then the next as if she's actually two people.

"I can't wait to eat you out for the whole night. It's my favorite thing in the world to do."

Beth puts a stop to it, throwing a dirty burp cloth at her. "Okay, my kid is in the room."

Mae sinks into the couch, her own laughter entertaining her. Then she turns and looks me square in the eye. "I expect details and none of that I-don't-kiss-and-tell shit."

I say nothing because it sounds easy. A quick trip to Houston and back. But nothing has been easy since Enzo came into my life, especially pretending I don't want him as my own.

CHAPTER EIGHTEEN

Enzo

We sit around the table in Houston. Blair Peterson obviously runs the show here, and I wonder why that information was never given to me when Coddle came looking for a new ad agency. Mr. Jacobson told me my point of contact was Mr. Peterson, and I felt like a fucking fool after the first pitch when I ignored Blair. She hasn't held it against me, but she definitely favors Annie.

"Why don't the two of you do the skit?" Blair waves her finger between us, laughing.

I chuckle. "I think the tape will do the trick."

"Yeah, I was just kidding. I'm sure you guys are eager to get back to New York." The meeting has been quick and easy, and really, the director could've gotten all the information over the phone, but when a client makes a request, we do as they ask. "Enzo, do you mind if I borrow Annie for a few minutes?"

Interesting.

I plaster on a smile. "Not at all. I have a few calls to return."

"Great, we'll be right back. Let's go to my office, Annie." Blair opens the door of the conference room.

Annie shoots me a look as though I'm letting them lead her to the dungeon. She's still a little green when meeting with clients, but she has good instincts and even better ideas. As she grows in this business, she'll become more comfortable with clients. She's way too talented not to.

It could be my dick talking, but she's a hidden gem at Jacobson and Earl. If she hadn't had to cover my assistant's desk that day, would she have stayed hidden?

The fact that I might be working for a misogynist sits in the back of my mind, but it's hard to accept that as truth. Have I really been that blind all these years? Ever since Annie Stewart walked into my office, I feel as if all the signs that she's right are shining in big neon lights.

Fuck, am I a misogynist? I gave my assistants my dry cleaning. Was that demeaning?

My ma raised me to respect women, sure, but do I think of them equally? I like to think I do, but do my actions really represent that?

"Hey." Annie appears in the doorway. "Blair says bye. We're good to go."

I slide out from the table and stuff my phone into my pocket, grabbing my computer bag. "Do you want to tell me what that was about?"

She looks down and shakes her head.

"Is it about the campaign?"

"Um..." She looks me in the eye. "No."

What did Blair want from her then?

Annie turns, and we head toward the elevators. Coddle

owns the entire building and the factory next door. I turn over theories and ideas as to why Blair wanted to see Annie until we're in the elevator, then boom, I piece it all together.

"She offered you a job." I don't ask, I state it as fact. It's the only logical reason why she wouldn't include me in the meeting. Am I always this distracted when Annie's near?

She straightens her back. "I don't want to talk about it."

"You don't want to talk about it? What kind of job did she offer?"

She glances at me with a hint of fear in her eyes, so I hold back my temper. It's not her fault she was offered a position. It's Blair's for trying to steal one of Jacobson's best employees.

"Let it go. I declined," she whispers.

The elevator heads to the bottom floor and ends with a stomach-dropping stop.

She's out before I can say anything more.

We give our badges back to security and slide into the waiting car.

Thanks for arranging our ride right before you tried to underhandedly steal our employee, Blair.

"Airport," I snap at the driver. I push the button for the partition and turn my attention to Annie. "Talk."

She grants me a fleeting look. "No. It has nothing to do with my job at Jacobson and Earl. I don't have to share the details with you."

She's right, but I thought we'd developed a friendship, or at the very least a coworker relationship, since we started working together.

"Please, Enzo, don't tell anyone." Her eyes prick with wetness before she stares out the window.

That "Please, Enzo" doesn't have the same effect it did

weeks ago. This time, I want to murder whoever is making her upset.

Why is she crying after being offered a job? Crap, is it me? I'm so out of my wheelhouse right now.

"I won't."

Silence descends over us and stays as we get out of the limo, walk up the stairway to the Jacobson and Earl jet. We situate ourselves across from one another. The flight attendant asks us if we'd like a drink. Annie kindly declines, and I order a scotch neat. A half hour later, we're up in the air and Annie's head rests on her seat as she stares out the window.

I desperately want to tell her to talk to me. Tell me why she declined. Was it a crappy offer? Why is she so upset about it? Why is she closing me out, and where is the free-spirited girl from Central Park? The girl I almost kissed because she made me forget myself. Instead, I drink my scotch and return emails, sneaking a peek at her once in a while.

Mid-flight, the attendant comes over, picks up my glass, and asks if I'd like another. I decline, and as she walks back to the hidden bar, the plane dips and she loses her balance. The glass falls from her hand, shattering on the floor.

I unclip my seatbelt to help her get up and pick up the shards of glass. Annie moves to unclip hers too, but the flight attendant puts up her hand for Annie to stop and instructs me to go back to my seat.

There's a beeping sound coming from the phone outside the cockpit.

I ignore the flight attendant's warning because I can handle myself. If she falls on this glass, it's bad for all of us.

She answers the phone and I hear it in her voice. Something's not right.

I deposit the shards of glass in the garbage. On my way to pick up more, the plane tips to one side, and I knock my head on the corner of the restroom wall, knocking me on my ass.

"Enzo!" Annie screeches and rushes over to me. She touches my forehead. "You're bleeding." Her fingers are coated with bright red blood.

"Here." The flight attendant hands her some tissues.

"Are you okay?" she asks, staring into my eyes.

Annie's mouth keeps moving, but I can't hear her. The flight attendant nudges our shoulders to get us up. Annie stands, holding out her hand for me, and I follow, but all I can really see is her eyes. The pure soul that lives inside her. No wonder Blair wanted her. Who wouldn't?

We sit down, and Annie continues to hold tissues to my forehead after we strap in.

"We're making an emergency landing," the flight attendant says and steps over the glass to her seat on the other side of the wall from us.

Annie's eyes cloud with worry. If I could form a coherent thought, I'd tell her it's all going to be okay, but my mind is a jumbled mess. The only consistent thought running through my head is how does Annie taste? Why am I willing to ignore the fact that I feel something for a woman for the first time in years? Maybe even ever. She intrigues me, and I know she likes me. At least the way I look. She might still think I'm a prick. No, she said in Central Park she thought I was great.

Without weighing any more shit in my head, my hand covers hers where it's pressing the tissue to my head and I lean forward, my lips hovering over hers.

"What are you doing?" she asks softly.

"Giving us what we both want."

Our lips meet, and it's like nothing I'll ever forget. My stomach dips, my lips tingle, and when she's the one to slide her tongue along the seam of my lips, my dick twitches. I want to unbuckle both of us, drag her into my lap, and kiss her until I'm a breath away from dying.

My hand slides to the back of her head and I deepen our kiss, my tongue seeking hers. Not knowing if she's going to knee me in the balls or not after this, I take the opportunity to do what I've been thinking about for weeks. I suck her bottom lip into my mouth, scraping my teeth against her flesh. Her strangled moan makes me do it a second time. She wraps her hand around my stretched arm, clinging and holding onto it as though she'd protest if I tried to stop the kiss.

The tires of the plane hit the runway, and the plane bounces up and back down. I slow our kiss when I realize we're on the ground.

I just lost control of myself.

We move back a bit and stare into one another's eyes. She blinks then releases my arm and sits back in her seat, so pale it looks as if she's seconds from throwing up.

Perfect. Just the reaction a guy wants.

CHAPTER NINETEEN

Annie

The plane lands, and I look out the window to find we're surrounded by cornfields.

"Where are we?" I ask the attendant.

Enzo unclips his belt, stands but sits back down, holding his head.

"Please sit down, Mr. Mancini, until the pilot says it's okay." The flight attendant stands. "I was told we were landing in Akron."

"Akron?" Enzo says as though it's a foreign city.

"You know, the rubber city," I say.

"Rubber what?"

His sharp tone is not appreciated. He just kissed me so thoroughly, I almost passed out. Out of nowhere, he placed those lips on me, and stupid me, I kissed him back. I'm such an idiot. He thought we were dying, so of course he grabbed the first willing female.

"Tires. Goodyear, Bridgestone..."

He nods with an expression that says, "just be quiet."

"We're going to get you to a medical professional, sir." The flight attendant heads to the front of the cabin and picks up the phone.

"No need. I'm good."

"You're clearly not," I say.

"I am."

Sure, because he kisses me every day as if he needs me more than air. The man is one hundred percent perfect.

"Whatever." I cross my arms.

"What's with the attitude?"

"Nothing. I just want to be home."

"Believe me, so do I," he says with a sneer, as though he wants to be on the other side of the country from me.

It's not my fault we didn't die, and we can't ignore the fact that he kissed me.

I'm giving us what we both want. His words right before the kiss register and tingles explode between my legs. My fingers touch my lips as though I imagined the whole thing.

The plane stops, and the pilot emerges from the cockpit. Thank God, get me on the next plane out of here.

"Sorry about this. We had some technical problems mid-flight. The airport has assured me their best mechanic will be on it first thing in the morning."

"First thing in the morning? Unacceptable," Enzo says.

I turn toward Enzo, wondering where this old version of him emerged from. The one who treats people as if they don't matter.

"Unfortunately, this isn't a major airport, so it is what it is. I have a car on the way to get you, but Nancy told me you hit your head, so we have a doctor coming out before you head to the hotel for the night."

Hotel? I don't even have a toothbrush, let alone anything to sleep in or take off my makeup with. And no clean clothes for tomorrow. The sun is quickly descending, but I should have time to shop somewhere. I'll make certain of it.

"Just sit tight and we'll get this handled as quickly as possible. I can call you in the morning when we're good to go." The pilot nods and disappears back into the cockpit. He's probably used to egomaniacs like Lorenzo Mancini and figures he's going to get out of Dodge before he blows his top.

"Drink?" the flight attendant asks with a smile.

"Sit and relax. No one needs a drink," I say.

"I'll take another scotch," Enzo says right after I finish speaking.

She moves to stand.

"Um, no. You're not drinking."

I've seen scathing looks before, many from Enzo himself, but nothing compares to what's directed my way right now. I'm waiting for little bullets to come pummeling out of his eyes.

"You have a head wound," I state.

He rolls his eyes and faces out the window. Ha. He knows I'm right.

We wait in brewing silence for another twenty minutes before a man with a medical kit comes on the plane.

He smiles at Enzo. "Hi, I'm Dr. Redwood. You're my patient, I assume."

Enzo tightly smiles back then sulks some more. He should be happy. We're one step closer to getting off this plane.

Dr. Redwood examines Enzo while Nancy and I wait. He stares into Enzo's eyes with a flashlight, asking Enzo to do different movements with his eyes. Which he does, begrudgingly.

"I'm going to bandage your wound, but I see no need for stitches. I would, however, be on concussion alert. You could come down to the hospital and I can—"

"No," Enzo cuts him off. "I'm good."

The doctor looks at him then at me. "So, signs to look out for..."

He rattles off all the things, and all I can think is, "Why are you telling me this?" Then I clue in—he thinks I'm the woman in Enzo's life. Sorry, doc.

"Keep him awake for a bit, then you need to wake him every few hours to make sure he's all right. If he gets disoriented or starts talking gibberish, call an ambulance right away." He stands, and I stare at him wide-eyed. "This was it?" He knocks the wall where Enzo hit his head. "Yeah, I'd bet my youngest that you have a mild concussion."

"Thank you so much," Nancy says, seeing him out.

Enzo doesn't so much as thank him. *Jerk.*

I look out the window and see a black town car pull up. "Our ride is here. Let's go."

Enzo moves to stand then sits back down, his fist slamming into the arm of the seat. "Shit."

"Maybe we should go to the hospital?" I offer him a hand.

He waves me off. "I'm not going to the hospital. I'm fine. I played football in high school. I was hit by linemen twice my size. I know what a concussion feels like."

He does make it out of the plane and down the stairs without incident, but I'm still worried.

"Thank you so much, Nancy." I smile at her. "We'll look forward to that phone call tomorrow. Like, really early so I can get away from Mr. Crabby, okay?"

She giggles.

"Annie!" he shouts from where he stands next to the car.

"Thanks again." I walk down the stairs slowly just to annoy him. From the way his jaw is clenched, I'd say I'm successful in my endeavor.

"Take us to the closest hotel," he tells the driver.

"Actually, I need to go to a mall. A big box store at the very least."

Enzo glances at me.

"I need clothes. I have nothing. A toothbrush would be nice."

He mumbles something.

"What?"

"Nothing," he says and doesn't speak the rest of the way.

After a not-so-quick stop at Target—because who comes out of there with only the items they went in for?—we arrive at the hotel.

Enzo slides his card across the counter to the hotel employee. "Two rooms."

"No."

"What?" He looks at me.

The woman behind the counter holds his credit card, intrigue in her features.

"You might have a concussion. The doctor told me the signs to look for. How am I going to do that from a room away?"

"I'm fine. I told you." He nods to the front desk employee.

She moves her hand to swipe the card, but I stop her.

"I'm not calling your mom tomorrow when you don't wake up and saying, 'Well, he told me he was okay.' Do you want me to make that call? Because I'm sure if the roles were reversed, you wouldn't want to make that call to my dad."

His body deflates like a balloon and I worry he's going to fall to the floor. He's tired. That's one sign of a concussion.

"Well, Mother Teresa, what do you suggest we do?"

I look at the front desk employee. "One room please."

The woman smiles and I bet she's thinking, "Yeah, I'd play the concussion card to share a room with him too."

"One room?" Enzo says it as if I asked him to buy me a box of tampons.

"We're adults. I'm sure there're two beds." I whip my head in the front desk girl's direction. "There're two beds, right?"

She nods.

"See. We're good. You sleep in one bed and I sleep in the other. Do you snore?" I wave it off. "It doesn't matter. I bought earplugs at Target just in case."

"Good to know."

The woman sets up our room, and we walk over to the elevators.

"I'm not sure why you want to share a room with me," he murmurs once we're in the small space.

"Because I don't want you to go unconscious and die. Sorry for caring." The door dings and I file out, following the signs to the room. "Are you hungry?"

"No. I just want to lie down."

"Okay, but no shutting your eyes." I wiggle my finger in front of his face, and he blows out an annoyed breath.

I open the door and step into a typical hotel room. Probably not Enzo Mancini's typical hotel room, but there're two beds, it looks clean, and there's room service, so we're good.

As I inspect the sheets, Enzo puts his computer bag on the chair and falls into the other bed on his back, blocking the light from his eyes.

"So you're picking that one?" I ask.

"Appears so. Is that a problem?"

"No. I don't like to sleep by the door, but it's okay." I'm totally joking, but he doesn't have to know that.

"You want me to move?"

"Could we play rock, paper, scissors for it?"

His arm falls off his face, and he props himself up on his elbows to give me the look of death. Like he legit wants me to fall to the floor and die in his presence.

My laugh bubbles up before I can stop it. "I'm sorry."

He crawls off the bed and on to the one closest to the door. "You've been waiting to use that line, haven't you?"

"Maybe." I shrug and go into the bathroom to put my stuff away. "Don't fall asleep on me," I holler from the bathroom.

When he doesn't respond, I peek around the corner. His arm is off his eyes and they're closed. I run over, hop on the bed, and jump on it, but I lose my footing on the comforter, slip, and land right on top of him.

His eyes pop open.

"Oh good." I pat his stubbled cheek. "You need to stay up."

Unfortunately, as I try to slide off him, I realize something else is up.

CHAPTER TWENTY

Enzo

I'm fully aware I'm being an asshole. Should I ask her why she pulled away from the kiss looking repulsed?

Hell yeah.

Am I going to?

Hell no.

I grip her hips and prop her up off my growing erection. "It's a natural response." I roll over because it's not a natural response for me. It's just my body's response to her.

"Sorry, but you have to stay up. I'm going to order us some food." She disappears back into the bathroom.

I'm being punished. I know I am. Otherwise, why on Earth would I be staying in the same hotel room as the woman I want under me, on top of me, next to me, on all fours... shit, the list goes on.

She walks back in, her hair thrown up in a messy bun,

the ridiculous pajamas she bought at Target clinging to her body.

I eye her, sliding up to the headboard so she doesn't pounce on me again. "I really don't understand why you bought those."

She looks down and laughs. "What? They're cute. You could've been Captain America."

I'm not complimenting her, but the way the lounge pants with Wonder Woman logos hug her ass is only making my dick want to point north again. "I told you I'm fine."

She shrugs then grabs the room service menu near the telephone. After she has it in hand, she hops on her bed like a kid in her first hotel room.

"You like this?" I ask.

She smiles. "I do. Hotels are fun."

I admire her child-like attitude. It reminds me of when she was in Central Park. She thinks I have multiple personalities? She should look in the mirror.

"You want to have a look?" She extends the menu to me, but I don't take it.

"You know what I like."

"Sadly, I do. Is it a healthy day or junk food day?" she asks, setting the menu on the bed.

I quirk an eyebrow, looking for further explanation.

"Every Monday, it's salad or a protein and vegetable only. As the week carries on, you request subs, burgers, and fries."

I think about the past week, and damn, she's right. After a Sunday dinner at my parents', I swear to eat healthy all week, but it eventually wanes.

"I get it, the whole Monday morning diet thing, but..." She buries her head in the menu once more.

"But what? Let me guess, you're going to lecture me about all the trans fats I'm consuming?"

"No!" She chuckles. "I'm ordering two appetizers hoping the side Caesar salad will make up for it, but everyone knows that's not healthy. But we're here and I'm going to make the most of it. We should rent a movie too."

"Okay, and then I'll freeze your bra when you fall asleep first."

She smirks, glaring at me from the corner of her eye.

"Blanca, my sister," I answer before she asks how I would know.

"Just so you know, that doesn't actually happen."

I shrug. "Enlighten me as to what does."

"Those are secrets for the vault." She tosses the menu onto my bed. "You pick what you want. I'm off duty now."

Just her saying that makes me want to ask her for another kiss.

I pick up the menu, glance at it, and toss it back to her. "Nachos and a beer."

"Nachos are a go, but no alcohol, Mr. Concussion." She wiggles her finger in front of me.

"I'm fine, I told you."

"And yet you can barely keep your eyes open."

I feign annoyance, but the truth is, if I fall asleep, then the temptation to do anything other than pig out on room service and watch a movie won't be stirring underneath every word we speak to one another. "Fine. Water."

She picks up the phone, orders room service, then snatches the remote off the table between us.

I swing my legs off the bed to grab my computer. "I might as well work."

"When's the last time you just chilled out?" she asks and holds up her hand before I can answer. "Remember, I have access to your schedule. You're always going somewhere, whether it's with your brothers or clients."

I stay seated, realizing she's right. "Well, since Blair Peterson is trying to steal you from under me, I have to stay on my toes."

Her smile fades. "Not from you. From Jacobson and Earl."

"You ready to talk about it?"

She picks at her fingers, her twelve-year-old self vanishing and transforming into a twenty-seven-year-old woman who doesn't want to disappoint anyone. I hope one day she takes what she wants without apology. It's a hard lesson to learn, but one she'll need in this business if she ever wants to succeed.

"I declined the offer. It's no big deal." She shrugs.

"You look like it's a big deal."

Her eyes dart to mine briefly then back down to her lap. "It's just... my future at Jacobson and Earl isn't guaranteed. Sure, they agreed to the new terms, but who's to say I don't sit at the junior ad exec level for ten years?"

"Then take Coddle's offer. Which is...?"

She blows out a breath. "They would bring the advertising in-house. I'd be in charge of coming up with the overall branding in the various ads for each product line."

Fuck. My head rears back. Blair takes no prisoners. How can Annie turn down that opportunity? It's huge. I can't deny I'm slightly jealous. No company I've worked with has asked for me to come on their staff full-time. If Annie goes to Coddle and they pull their advertising in-house, my chances at making partner are shot. "That's... big."

She nods, still concentrating on her hands. "But I can't take it."

"Why?"

She looks at me, those burning embers of what's developing between us there for a moment before they disappear. "Beth just had the baby and I don't want to be away. My dad is in New York."

I nod. I understand how important family is.

Picking up the remote, she presses on the movie section. "What do you want to watch?"

Just like that, the conversation is over. I wish I had a crystal ball and could see that Mr. Jacobson will take care of Annie in the future, but I don't. If I have to go on my gut, I think she might be right in her assessment.

I strip off my jacket and toss it on the chair before stepping out of my shoes and positioning the pillows so I can lean against them on the bed. "No chick flicks."

"Let's rock, paper, scissors for it?" She laughs.

I shoot her my most bored expression, and she falls over on the bed, flailing in laughter.

She's so fucking cute. Will I survive tonight? I'm not so sure.

"What's your choice?" I ask.

She rests the cursor on *Wonder Woman,* raising her eyebrows my way. "I'm kidding," she says before I say anything.

"*A Quiet Place*?" I offer.

"And I won't even make you play me for it."

"I regret ever telling you that. Just FYI, I do win. Often."

"I'm sure you do."

I want to kiss that cocky smirk off her face. "Just play the movie."

She smiles sweetly and presses Play, wiggles under the

blankets, and turns off the lights. "I'll be checking on you. No falling asleep."

A grunt is my only response.

YOU KNOW what's the worst thing you can do with the woman you want but can't have? The same woman you've been jerking off to for weeks? The woman you kissed less than five hours ago and can't wait to kiss again? Watch a movie with zero sound when she's sitting one bed away.

Room service has arrived, and I suggest we watch the movie while we eat, but no, she's decided we should pause it because we'll miss something.

"Are we going to eat in silence since we can't watch the movie?" I ask, needing something as a distraction.

"We could talk," she offers, stabbing her lettuce with her fork.

"About the campaign?" I'm torn because I don't want to talk about the campaign, and I don't want to talk about myself. I'm a pro at this though, so I'll swing the conversation her way. "What's the deal with you and your mom?"

She blanches. "Um... want to talk about past hookups?"

"Those aren't nearly as interesting as your mom."

"I don't believe that. Have you ever had any stalkers?" She picks up her drink.

I snag a nacho chip. "No. Why would a woman stalk me?"

I fail to mention the girl in college who had a hard time realizing we'd hooked up and there wouldn't be anything after.

She looks me over, her pupils dilated. "You're you."

"I take it you consider that a good thing?" *Then why were you repulsed when I kissed you?*

"Oh please. I'm pretty sure you live in a house with mirrors." She bites into her potato skin.

I chuckle. "I do."

She waits for me to say something else, but silence falls over the room.

"What about you?" Time to turn the tables. "How many serious boyfriends have you had?"

She places the potato skin down and sips her Coke. "Why do you assume there were boyfriends? Maybe I just had hookups."

I laugh.

"What?"

"Because you're not the type."

She accepts defeat quickly. "No one worth talking about. Believe me, if we swapped rosters, I'm sure you're more a football team and I'm more of a basketball team."

"Sports analogy. I like it." I don't refute that my list of partners is probably much longer than hers. No way she's willing to sleep with just anyone. Nor should she be. She's damn near perfect. If perfect is beautiful, bossy, and sometimes infuriating.

She only eats half of her food and I accept her leftovers, the nachos not nearly enough to fill me.

"Can we play a game of rock, paper, scissors?" she asks coyly, as though she's shy to ask, but it's something she really wants to do.

I blow out a breath. "Are we playing for something?"

"No. Unless you want to."

"How about questions and answers?" I say.

"What do you mean?"

"If I lose, you get to ask me a question. If I win, I get to ask you a question."

"So this will pretty much be the Enzo Mancini show?" She giggles, jumping off her bed and onto mine, the *Wonder Woman* T-shirt rising up her waist. She's quick to pull it down, and her cheeks flush my favorite apricot color.

"You wish." I push away the room service table, wiping my hands and mouth with a napkin.

"On the count of three."

From her eagerness, I worry she's some kind of pro.

"One."

"Two."

"Three," she says.

She shoots scissors.

I shoot paper.

She uses her fingers to cut my flat palm as if it's paper. Dom, Carm, and I don't do that.

I like it.

"I win." She dances with her upper body and her breasts jiggle.

Holy shit, is she not wearing a bra?

"Shoot." I nod at her.

She stares at the ceiling for a second then levels her gaze on me. "Were you ever hurt by a woman? Is that why you can't commit to anyone?"

"No and no. Should I ask why you'd ask that question?"

She shakes her head. "I always had this suspicion about you. You never brought a woman to the Christmas party. You didn't treat your assistants very nicely."

"So you thought a woman tore my heart out?"

She shrugs. "Yeah."

"And what do you think now?" I down a gulp of my water.

"I don't know." Her mood sobers, and I don't know why. "Again?" she asks, perking up a bit.

"Um, yeah! I haven't gotten to ask a question."

"And you might not." She giggles, bringing her fist to her palm.

"One."

"Two."

"Three," I say this time.

She shoots rock, and I shoot paper.

Her eyes widen. "Are you hustling me?"

"I told you I can win."

She picks up my hand and places it over her fist. I really like this "show how you lose" thing she does.

I pretend to examine her as though I'm trying to think of the worst question to ask her. I could nail her for the mom thing, but that seems unfair. I could inquire more about the Coddle offer, but I really don't want to talk about work tonight. There's only one answer I really want, and since I'm Enzo Mancini and I don't dodge bushes, I jump over them, I ask what I really want to know.

"Why were you disgusted after I kissed you on the plane?"

Her face falters and I wish I was anyone else right now. Someone who wouldn't have had the balls to ask that question. Someone smarter who would've flirted their way into that question. Because it looks as though I won't like the answer.

CHAPTER TWENTY-ONE

Annie

He's going there. I thought I could laugh at how many times he lost. I thought we'd ask our favorite ice cream flavors and maybe how old we were when we lost our virginities. I know I asked about a woman who hurt him and maybe this is in retaliation to that question, but I suddenly wish I'd just turned the movie back on.

"Um..."

He waits, not about to give me an out.

"There wasn't any disgust. I think the better question is, why did you kiss me?"

He shakes his head. "You should've asked that question on your turn."

I move to slide off the bed, needing to not be this close to him when I tell him it was the look of regret in his eyes that made me react.

He lightly clasps my elbow. "We need to address this. I

can't ignore what happened between us if we're going to stay in the same room tonight."

I blow out a breath. "I was anything but repulsed. I was turned on. If we weren't on that plane, things would've gone so much further, but we thought we might be dying. That's all it was. I get it."

He looks as if I slapped him.

"We should probably forget the game. I gotta use the bathroom." He stands and goes into the bathroom.

I push the room service table out the door into the hallway and shut it before nestling back into my bed. The toilet flushes and the tap water runs for a minute before he emerges. He spares me a quick glance and sits on his bed.

I click on the movie without his prompting, because the tension in the room is stifling.

During the movie, all I hear is his legs moving along the sheets and the even cadence of his breathing. I can't concentrate on the small details this movie requires. I want to get out of this bed and join him in his. Ask him why he's mad.

I'm letting him off the hook, which I have to say is big of me, because the man can kiss. He kisses like his personality—a dichotomy between gentle and dictating. His firm lips told me what he wanted, but as our mouths opened, his lips softened, his tongue almost lazy as it explored mine. My stomach lit up with fireflies when his teeth scraped my bottom lip, then he licked and sucked it, soothing any pain he caused.

I'm so screwed.

The credits roll, and I jump up and run to the bathroom. After splashing cold water on my face, I brush my teeth and go to the bathroom. When I emerge, the lights and the television are both off.

I walk by his bed and see his gaze on me. "Just checking that you're not asleep."

"Nope." He climbs out of his bed as I climb into mine.

Our night of fun is slowly turning into a night of uncomfortable silence.

Five minutes later, the bathroom light shines on him leaving the bathroom in just his boxer briefs. My breath hitches. He's kidding me, right? Desire is chased by anger sparking inside me. What kind of game is he playing? Is he trying to tempt me?

"Real nice, Enzo," I sneer then clasp my hand over my mouth. *Shit. That was out loud.*

"What?" He gets into his bed.

Screw this. He says whatever he wants when he wants. He brought up the kiss instead of forgetting it. I'm calling him out.

"You don't see me walking around here in my bra and panties."

"I usually sleep naked. Would you prefer that?"

I flip the covers open and stare at him. Damn, the man is everything I imagined and more.

"See something you like? Want me to pretend the building is under attack so we can make out?"

I slide up to the headboard. "What's that supposed to mean?"

"Whatever you want it to." His fist hits the pillow a few times. He lays his head down then hits the pillow some more. He's as high maintenance with his pillows as he is with his assistants.

"Stop being vague."

"It's not worth it."

He might as well say *you're* not worth it.

"Oh nice. Well, feeling the same over here." I circle my

finger and point at myself. I sound like an idiot, but I don't care.

"That why you were ogling my body a second ago?"

I narrow my eyes, but he can't see me in the dark, so I flick on the light.

My eyes come face to face with his bare chest. Bad idea. Really bad idea.

I clear my throat. "You ogle my body too. Your eyes aren't always on my face."

"I never said they were."

I throw my hands in the air. "Neither did I!"

"But the kiss on the plane was just because we were dying, or so we thought, right?"

I purse my lips, unable to look at him anymore. I flick off the light and throw myself on the bed with my back to him.

The light flicks back on. "No, we're finishing this now."

"Go to bed, Enzo."

"No, *Mom*. I'm not tired because this woman I'm sharing a hotel room with is living in dreamland instead of addressing what's going on in reality."

Off go my covers. I sit up and cross my legs on the bed. "Fine. What do you want to talk about?"

"This attraction between us." He waves his finger between the two of us.

My shoulders fall. Looks like we're doing this. "There's no conclusion to this problem. We work together. You're my boss."

"Technically, Shelby's your boss." His hands grip the mattress while he stares at me.

I try to keep my vision focused on his eyes, but they stray, admiring the ripped muscles in his abdomen and the prominent bulge in his boxer briefs. All my blood flow zeros down in between my legs.

"Eyes up here, Annie," he says, pointing toward his eyes.

"I'd have to be blind to not be attracted to you. It doesn't mean we should act on it."

"I could say the same thing."

"I'm what every woman hates." I throw my hands in the air. "Falling for the boss? I mean, how cliché is that? People will think you're giving me special treatment at work because I give you special treatment in the bedroom. I can just hear all the sexual innuendos in the break room now."

He leaves his bed and comes over to me.

"Nope. Go back to your bed." I slide up toward the headboard as far as I can.

He laughs, and it's nice to not have that tension that was pissing him off moments ago occupying every crevice of the room. Not that I prefer this.

"I would never do that. Nor would I ever expect you to sleep with me. You know that, right? I would never hold your job over your head because of something we did or didn't do outside of work." His features say how serious it is for him to get clarity on that.

I nod because from what I know of Enzo so far, he wouldn't do that.

"Do you think I expected this? Hell, you're everything I usually try to stay away from—everything about you screams trouble to me. I don't do more than one night, yet here I am with you and I already know one taste of you won't satisfy my craving."

"But?"

He slides closer and I don't fight him, allowing his hand to land on my thigh and shoot what feels like a million jolts of electricity up to my core. "I didn't kiss you because I thought I was dying. I knew we were going to land. I kissed you because it's all I've thought about doing for weeks and you were there, and my willpower finally faltered, so I said fuck it."

"We have to think this through." I put my head in my hands. "We're being irrational, acting on lust."

"It's no one's business what happens in this room or outside of Jacobson and Earl." His hand slides up my leg, molding to my hip. "I need you to agree to that before we go any further. I need to know you're in this with me."

I stare into his caramel eyes. I mentally make note to recall this moment when I get fired from Jacobson and Earl, because no matter what way I twist it, this is the stupidest decision I've ever made, but at the same time, I'm owning it.

I slam my lips against his, surprising him, and he loses his balance, falling to his back. And then it's almost as if someone blew a horn and said game on. Frantic hands and lips go to work to see how many inches of skin they can touch.

His hands are firm, sliding under my pajama pants, gripping my ass. A growl rumbles deep in his throat, and he moves my hair away from blocking access to my neck.

I grind along his length, the friction taking me to the point of no return faster than it should. I need to relish tonight. To remember his hands and the path they took. Right now, I'm the seventeen-year-old virgin in the back of Johnny's Civic. Except Enzo isn't Johnny. Not even close.

The night I lost my virginity, I was eager for it to end. To get over the pain my friends had told me I'd experience. Tonight, I desperately want to slow us down because I have no idea what it will be like after this. But slowing down feels nearly impossible because all the tension that's been tightening around us has snapped and neither one of us can control the pace. It's going to be fast and quick and earth-shattering.

He runs his mouth along my breasts, his teeth scraping over my T-shirt and latching on to my nipple. My arms reach behind his head, holding him to me. My hips go into overdrive, and that early crescendo of my orgasm appears.

While I'm lost in my head, his hands venture under my shirt and pull it over my head. Once I'm bared for him, his hands cradle each breast. The smoldering looks he's given me over the past few weeks are nothing compared to right now.

"Damn, you're beautiful." He buries his head in my breasts, kneading them and kissing each one while he grinds his erection into me.

The only barriers are his boxer briefs and my pajama pants, and my orgasm inches closer and closer to the point where I can't control it. I've wanted this man for so long, and he's living up to every fantasy I've envisioned. I slide down his chest, kissing every crevice of his abs.

"Shit, Annie." He bucks when I cup his package over his boxers, looking at him with my best seductive stare. His hands thread through my hair, moving it aside so he has a clear vision of me.

I run my hand under the hem of his boxers and up his leg until his length fills my hand. He runs his thumb over my lips, opening my mouth. I suck on his thumb and twirl my tongue around it, mimicking what I'll do once I get his hard length there. His eyelids slip further and further down the more I tease him.

All of a sudden, he flips me over and his lips devour my breasts, his eyes on me as though my expressions will guide him to make this a night to remember.

"Enzo," I whisper, my eyes falling closed as my head hits the mattress.

"Nope." His hard body runs up the length of mine, the weight of him falling on me as his lips meet mine. The kiss isn't nearly as intense as it was a moment ago, but it's deep and prolonged and rhythmic. He ends it, and I'm clenching to keep my orgasm away. "Eyes open."

I open my eyes, and his cocky arrogant smirk is front and center. My hand runs down his cheek, his stubble softer than I expected. Will I finally get to feel it between my thighs?

Once he's satisfied, I'm going to adhere to his rules. His tongue slides down my neck, through the valley of my breasts, and past my belly button. Sitting up, he hooks his fingers on the sides of my pajama pants and pulls them down my legs, then he situates his face between my thighs.

Yeah, his scruff feels delicious there. I knew it would.

"I found that tattoo you were talking about."

"Jackpot," I say.

"Just remember that I said one taste will never be enough." He licks me, and my head falls to the mattress, my eyes shut.

He stops. I pick up my head, my nerve endings frazzled and crying out for more.

"I told you, eyes open," he says.

I don't even have a sharp reply because I miss him being there and I'll do about anything to have him back. "You should be warned payback will be a bitch."

He chuckles, taking my hand and placing it over my clit. "I expect nothing less. Now let me watch you play with yourself."

If I thought I was on the cusp before, I'm downright ready to scream out now.

CHAPTER TWENTY-TWO

Annie

His eyes no longer watch my face. They're watching my fingers. After a minute, he nudges my hand away, taking over my preferred rhythm himself by using a mixture of his tongue, mouth, and fingers. I lose myself in the sensations he's piling on. His eyes flicker with the same desire that's coursing through my veins.

"Enzo." I buck up off the mattress. "I can't."

"You can," he says, his one large hand gripping my breast, pinching my nipple. "I'm going to make you."

My body is moving so much, I have no idea how he's able to keep me in place. His mouth is so talented. He's the fucking Picasso of oral sex. He's just as talented in the bedroom as he is in the boardroom. *Damn it.* I curse myself for thinking about that now. Especially when all I can think of is my legs spread wide on the conference table with him in a chair in front of me.

He groans, his pace increasing, his fingers probing while he sucks my clit.

I try to fight my impending orgasm to prolong this unforgettable ecstasy, but my ass rises off the bed and he grips my cheeks to keep me in place, burying his entire face in my core.

"Oh, God," I cry out, my toes curling and my fingers gripping the sheets until they ache.

He lets my climax wash over me, gradually decreasing his speed until my back is on the mattress and my eyes struggle to remain open.

Enzo crawls up my body, then his hand splays across the back of my head and he threads his fingers through my hair. He kisses me, and I taste myself on his tongue, only spurring another flutter of desire. The tip of his cock pushes at my opening, waking me from my daze.

I push on his chest. "Condom."

He smiles, kissing my jaw. "Give me a second."

Enzo stands, and I miss the weight of his body immediately. He walks over to his computer bag and produces a strip of condoms. My smile falters. Is he always ready and available to screw whoever is willing?

"You're overthinking. I bought them at Target just in case." He kisses my neck.

How did he even know what I was thinking? Because he reads people so well. It's why he's so great at his job.

"You sure about that?"

"These were bought with the sole intention of using them with you." He sits up on his knees, and I watch him slide it down his thick erection. "But if you'd rather not?"

His hands slide down the outside of my thighs, his touch soft and caring.

He's right. I'm overthinking this.

I sit up, grab the back of his neck, and pull him down on top of me. "We're using them."

I kiss him and he lets his weight fall on me a bit, his tongue pushing into my mouth at the same time as he inches his way inside me. I open my legs wider to accommodate him. No one has filled me the way he does.

"We good?" he asks once he's fully seated inside me.

I bite my lip and nod.

When he circles his hips, easing in and out of me, all my worries from earlier vanish. I can only focus on the multitude of sensations overwhelming my body and the intense look on his face as he takes me in below him. His lips venture to my jaw and ear but always return to my mouth as though he can't go too long without a kiss.

Sweat forms between our skin, our breathing labored the longer we grind together. He places his hands on either side of my head and thrusts as deep as he can. I buck up to meet him, wanting him to hit that same spot over and over.

Our eyes are locked, and somewhere between our moans, the heat building in the small room, and feeling of us becoming one, I lose myself in a hurricane named Enzo. He whirls me around, my thoughts jumbled, and the moment I think I'm on solid ground, he whisks me away again.

"Fuck, Annie." He hammers into me again. "You feel so good. So wet."

I wrap my legs around his waist, and he sinks in deeper.

"You need to come." He struggles to get the words out through his clenched jaw.

Knowing he's hanging on by a thread is enough for me to meet him with every thrust. Sweat drips down on me and my fingers grip his back, pulling at his shoulder blades until he nibbles on my earlobe. The desperation in his strangled breath finishes the job. I'm thrown out into a raging sea when my orgasm surges over me until I'm once again floating in the calm ocean.

How did I not know that sex like this existed?

Enzo pumps into me one more time, a grunt rising from his throat, then he stills.

Once we've regained our breathing, we look at one another. I can't tell what he's thinking. What is he thinking?

"I'll be right back," he says, slipping out of me.

How can that feel like a loss? It shouldn't.

Grabbing my pajama pants and T-shirt, I quickly clothe myself while he's in the bathroom. Once he's out, I hurry into it and lock myself in. Damn it. I wish I could call Mae.

I take care of business then wash my hands. "You got this, Annie. If he's already asleep when you get out there, it's no sweat off your back. You got what you wanted. All you wanted was to sleep with him."

Even I want to point at myself in the mirror and scream liar.

I abandon the whole pep talk and open the door, shutting off the light. The room is black, which means Enzo's asleep. *Don't get upset.*

I head to my bed and slide in. A big hand wraps around my waist. I scream, startled.

Enzo laughs. "Is this a problem?" he asks, moving his hand and sitting up.

"What?"

"Sharing a bed? Did you want me in my own?" I hear a hitch in his voice, and I silently pray he's not doing this out of some misguided effort to make me feel better.

"No. It's fine." I tamp down my excitement because that'll produce an expectation and I can't have any of those with Enzo Mancini.

"Why are you in your pajamas? Those have to go." His

hands fall to my stomach and he pushes my shirt up over my head. Once that's off, he works on my pants.

"I can do it."

"Not quickly enough." He chuckles, kissing my neck.

"You're kind of surprising me right now."

"Why? Because I want to cuddle? It's really just a reason to touch you. Plus I'm a mama's boy, what did you expect?"

I sit up. "Okay, you cannot put those two thoughts together. Touching me and bringing your mom into it."

He chuckles. His hand lands on the back of my neck, bringing me down to him to kiss.

Damn, he really is a great kisser. I press my hand on his chest and tear my lips off him.

"What's the matter now?" he whines.

"We need rules."

"Rules?" He sits up, the sheet falling to his waist.

I turn on the light.

"Lights. Hurt. Eyes."

"Come on, you know we can't very well just sleep together then go with the flow."

Finally I find some agreement in his expression.

"So if we're going to do this again—"

"We're doing it again," he confirms.

I blow out a breath. This new Enzo is surprising. "Well, if we do, nothing happens at work. No inappropriate talk or touches."

He clicks his tongue on the roof of his mouth and shakes his head. "No promises there. That's half the fun. You expect me to be around you all day at work and not cop a feel?"

I shake my head, but he's probably right. "It has to be discreet. No one can know. Not your brothers. Not my sister. Not Mae. No one. This is going to the grave with the two of us."

He chuckles again and cups my breast. "I promise on your mouthwatering tit."

I smack his hand, but I can't deny this playful side of Enzo is fun. And I don't have it in me to be serious. It's been a long day—emotionally and now physically. I'm sure in the morning light, reality will hit, and we'll figure out this new terrain.

So I slide down the bed. He turns off the light. As we fall asleep with his leg wedged between mine and his hand on my breast, I worry about what I've done to jeopardize the future I was making for myself.

"The best day ever was when you had to cover as my assistant," he whispers before kissing my jaw right under my ear.

"That's your concussion talking."

"I don't have one." He tightens his arms. "Just go to sleep."

And at some point, the freaking out over what I've done disappears and the euphoric feeling from Enzo holding me takes over and my eyes drift closed.

CHAPTER TWENTY-THREE

Enzo

"We went through four condoms. You're insatiable."

Annie peeks her head out of the bathroom. "*I* am? I believe it was me mumbling incoherently when you rolled over me at three a.m."

Lazy, middle-of-the-night sex with Annie was amazing. I felt bad waking her up, but I couldn't resist having her when she was all I could feel, smell, and see.

"You didn't have to join me in the shower this morning." I put on my shoe, my phone alerting me to a text. I open my phone. "The plane will be ready in three hours."

She peeks out again. "Three hours?"

"We have two more condoms." I raise an eyebrow.

She emerges from the bathroom, clasping her earrings and wearing the clothes she did yesterday. "I'm surprised you bought the economy-size box. Most men would have bought the three-pack." She sits on the bed across from me, putting on her heels.

"If I'd only bought three, you wouldn't have had any shower sex this morning." I grin.

She blows out a breath and shakes her head, but she's smiling, which puts that warm feeling front and center in my chest.

My phone dings again and I look at it.

Dom: *Who's the guy?*
Carm: *??*
Dom: *For Blanca. Enzo?*

"Fuck," I mumble.

"What's wrong?" She stands.

I ignore my brother's text, wrapping my arms around her middle and dragging her down on the bed. She squeals, and I kiss her neck.

I'm screwed. I realized it last night when Annie threw all the obvious issues on the table and I was okay with them. That's me though—I take what I want, and I want Annie. If I had to guess, she feels differently though. Whereas I feel free, with all that tension gone, it seems as though she's holding back. And I don't like it.

I sit up. "Talk to me. What's up?"

She meets my gaze, and I guess men's intuition isn't too shabby because I nailed it. She's apprehensive. "Nothing."

She stands, but I wrap my arms around her waist and pull her down to my lap. "I can't fix it unless you tell me." I nuzzle her neck.

"You don't have to fix anything. I'm good." She tries to get up, but I don't release my arms. "Enzo..."

"Say please," I say.

"You and your games. Pl—"

I cover her mouth, muffling the rest of the word. "On second thought, you can do that at my apartment tonight. If you say it now, I guarantee our clothes are coming off."

She swings her arm around my neck. "Who said I'm going to your apartment today?"

"Because you don't wanna be away from me." I smile.

She doesn't. She gives me the same look I got after we had sex. She doesn't believe anything I'm saying.

I tuck a loose strand of her dark hair behind her ear. "What's going on?"

She blows out a breath. "This. I don't understand this."

"Let me recap for you. You started as my assistant. We were forced to work together on a campaign. The attraction was immediate. At least for me. We wanted to roll around in the sheets together. Last night we did, and it was fucking phenomenal, so we're going to continue rolling around in the sheets together."

"So we're just fuck buddies?"

I hadn't really thought about that. "No. You're not just some woman I'm going to call for a good time."

"Then what am I?"

"Do we have to classify it? I like you. I *really* like sleeping with you. Can't we go from there?"

"Okay, fine. You're so touchy. Are you always so touchy?" She smiles, changing the subject.

I can't tell her I want to start dating. I mean, I don't date. I'm not going to answer to anyone where I'm going and what I'm doing every second of the day. Though I don't think she'd expect that. She said herself she doesn't want to date anyone until she's established.

"I like to touch *you*. Now, let's make out until we leave for the airport."

Her stomach rumbles.

"On second thought. Breakfast?" I rest my forehead on hers.

"Yeah." Annie gets off my lap, grabs her bag. She looks around the room and some emotion crosses her face, but I can't read what she's thinking.

To my surprise, I find that bothers me. This is new territory for me. Usually I don't care what women are thinking. Was our one night together enough for Annie? Was it enough for me?

I'd be a fool to even think that though. I knew one night wouldn't be enough even before we slept together. Isn't that the entire reason I waited until the need to have her was unbearable before I made my move?

WE EAT breakfast then hop on the plane.

Annie insists on sitting across from me in case the flight attendant says something to our boss about us. We're lucky she didn't see our kiss last night.

Midflight, I text her.

Me: *This is your opportunity to join the mile-high club.*

When her phone vibrates, she picks it up then stares at me as if I'm boring her. I'm already laughing by the time she slides it open and reads the message.

Annie: *Who's to say I'm not already a member?*

That's not what I want to hear. At all.

Me: *Not cool.*

She checks her phone, not looking at me.

Annie: *I told you, we're strictly professional except behind closed doors.*
Me: *Good thing the bathroom has a door.*

She huffs and I chuckle, picking up my scotch now that Annie's letting me drink again.

Annie: *Not going to happen.*
Me: *Come home with me.*
Annie: *No.*
Me: *Would you be more comfortable at your place?*
Annie: *We're spending the night apart.*
Me: *I have the economy box of condoms at my condo.*
Annie: *I'm sure you do.*

Why is she giving me the cold shoulder?

Me: *What gives?*

She looks at me again, and I reach across the aisle for her hand. She narrows her eyes and shakes her head.

Me: *I thought sneaking around would be fun. You could sit by me and I'd discreetly slide my hand up your skirt, slide your panties to the side.*

Fuck, I'm getting a hard-on imagining it.

She reads my text then puts her phone down.

Me: *I'd apply the lightest pressure to your clit. Slow and lazy circles and then I'd dip my finger in, just the tip to test how wet you are. Of course, you'd be soaked, and I'd massage the wetness on your clit.*

Her phone dings. I love that she can't help but read the text. She inhales a deep breath.

Me: *You'd be so close to me, your hands would be on my forearm and your mouth on my shoulder to muffle your enjoyment of my fingers inside you. I'd be rock hard under my slacks and you'd grow even wetter when you saw me straining my pants.*

Ding.

Me: *Just when you least expect it, I'd arch my long fingers inside you, and you'd bite my shoulder in surprise. I'd plunge in and out, your wetness coating my fingers.*

Ding.

She reads it then looks at me with a flush all over her body. It's not only in her cheeks but her chest too. I'm not stopping now.

Me: *You'd clench around my fingers, but I wouldn't relent. You'd murmur how you're almost there. Just when I'm about to open my slacks and plop you right in my lap, you clench around me so hard my knuckles almost break.*

Ding.

Me: *The flight attendant comes out and I slide my fingers out of you. As she asks you if you'd like a drink, my fingers are in my mouth, tasting how delicious you are.*

Ding.

Her head falls back to the headrest and her eyes close. I notice her legs are partly open instead of crossed, as usual.

Annie: *You play so unfair. Payback Mr. Mancini. Payback.*
Me: *What did we discuss about calling me Mr. Mancini? Although now that you can use it in the bedroom, I'm kind of warming up to the idea.*

She laughs and drops her phone into her purse.

I look at my straining cock. *We're in for a long road, buddy. She's a ball-buster for sure.*

CHAPTER TWENTY-FOUR

Annie

I'm officially the weakest woman alive.

"What kind of dressing do you like?" Enzo asks, putting the take-out place on hold.

"Whatever is fine. French."

I tried not to come over tonight. I tried to give him some distance to really think about what he wants because if things go any further between us, I'm bound for heartbreak. I'd rather have it now than later. But after his teasing texts on the plane and advances in the limo, how could I resist? I wanted to come here.

After he finishes on the phone, I say, "Your place is everything I assumed it would be."

"What does that mean?" He hands me a glass of wine by the window.

"It's a bachelor pad. A bunch of electronics and black."

He chuckles. "What's your place like? Colorful?"

"Compared to yours, it's like a coloring book colored by a three-year-old. It's neat, but there're a lot of knick-knacks. Not like you and your perfectly placed sculptures and paintings."

"I hired someone." He shrugs.

"I figured."

I follow him to the couch. Black leather. How original. All of this pulls my wariness to the forefront. I should've never told him I couldn't talk to Beth or Mae. I should've said I need to talk to them, otherwise I'm going to go crazy dissecting every little thing.

It's good that he wanted me to come over tonight, right? Maybe it's all about the sex. We do it well together. More than well. It's like nothing I've ever experienced. The girls Enzo's usually with are probably a lot more experienced than me.

I gulp down the wine, finishing the entire glass.

"Another?" he asks, his fingers circling on my thigh.

"No. I shouldn't if I'm going home after dinner."

He tilts his head. "You said you were staying. We went to your condo and got your stuff."

I made him stay outside while I ran upstairs to change and grab an overnight bag so he wouldn't have to see how small my one-bedroom condo is. "I forgot I have a family brunch, and you have your family dinner on Sunday."

He stares at me as if he's wondering how the hell I know about that.

"Your calendar. It's marked on every Sunday."

He nods.

"Oh, God." Bile rises my throat. This is ridiculous. I've memorized his calendar. Not on purpose but still.

"Annie? Are you okay?"

I stare at his soft brown eyes and ask myself the same question. Truth is, I'm not. "I'm sorry. I can't do this."

He places his wineglass on the table. "Do what?"

I wave my finger between us. "I'd love to be a girl who can just turn it on and off, but I'm not. There's no 'call me when you want to hook up and I'll be waiting' thing for me. I'm a dating kind of girl. I'm not a 'come to my condo, I'll order dinner, and we'll fuck like animals until the morning' girl. I'm sorry." I stand, disappointed it can't be different but I'm at peace with my decision. I circle around before I leave his living room. "I hope this doesn't affect—"

He puts up his hand and I remember how those long fingers felt so amazing inside me. "We've been over this. Your job is secure."

I nod, hurrying to his bedroom to grab my overnight bag. When I come out, his hands are in his hair and he's pacing behind the couch.

"I'll see you Monday," I say, slipping into my shoes.

"Annie?"

I turn.

He stares at me for a moment, and I wish I knew him well enough to read him, but I don't. "Thanks for your honesty. I never would have wanted to hurt you."

"You're welcome."

I lug my bag over my shoulder then walk out the door. I squeeze my eyes shut. *You're doing the right thing. There's no future behind that door. He's told you that himself. He doesn't want anything serious. You're looking at a long line of unanswered texts and phone calls. You'll grow attached and he'll probably be sleeping with other girls when you're not available.*

After forcing myself to take the excruciating steps toward the elevator, I press the down button, glancing back at the empty hallway and closed door. Maybe I'm being stupid. He's always treated me nicely. Maybe I could change him. Make him want those things. *No, a man like Enzo is bound to get bored at some point and want to move on.*

The elevator arrives and I step on, looking one more time at the desolate hallway.

"Bye, Enzo," I whisper, and the doors slide shut.

By the time I reach the lobby, his doorman stands to round the desk. "Miss Stewart?"

"Yes?"

"Mr. Mancini called down. He'd like you to wait."

I laugh. Of course he did. So he can pitch some idea he's brilliantly thought of in the last two minutes about why he and I aren't a terrible idea? He can try to sell me like he does his clients. And I'll fall for it just like they do because he's excellent at his job. Probably convince me I don't want to date him, and before I know it, I'll be half naked in the elevator with my lips on his.

"Please tell Mr. Mancini I'm tired and I had to go." I circle through the doors, ignoring his protest.

Turning right, I walk down the street and flag down my own taxi.

"*Annie*!" Enzo yells from behind me.

I turn in the direction of his building. He's jogging toward me in his bare feet.

I put out my palm before he can get close. "Don't feel bad. This isn't some kind of romance movie. You don't have to come running after me."

"Just shut up and stop being so damn stubborn." His

hands grab each side of my face and he presses his lips to mine. Our tongues glide together, and he strips his mouth from mine. "I'll try, okay? Is that enough? You're not going to be just some girl I hit up when I want to screw. I can't promise you anything, but I promise to explore this. Really explore it."

"But—"

"Stop overthinking everything. You're not that girl for me. You're different."

I place my hands over his on my cheeks. "So you want to date one another?"

"Yes. I'll take you to the movies, to Broadway shows, to dinner. Anywhere you want. I just... I want you."

"The minute you get sick of..."

"You can go." He grabs my bag, shuts the taxi door, and bangs on the roof. He links his hand in mine and we walk back to his condo.

The taxi drives off as my footsteps pause. "Enzo..." I sigh.

"What?"

"Are you doing this just because you want to sleep with me?"

He drops my hand and guides me to the side of the building. "I want to sleep with you right now. Hell, I get hard just thinking about you. Especially after last night. But I ran down here because I want you in my life. And if dating you is the only way I can have you, then I'm going to date you."

"But—"

He puts his fingers to my mouth. "Let me prove it, okay? There's no way I can convince you right now. Just give me time to prove it."

How can I argue? He's right. I could fight and fight, but

the man has surprised me the entire time I've gotten to know him.

I might be ridiculous to believe him, but now that he's laid it on the line, I have to go in with two feet. He's never given me a reason to doubt him.

CHAPTER TWENTY-FIVE

Enzo

I see now why there's a no-fraternization policy in the employee handbook. My concentration has been shit since I slept with Annie. Especially since she wore a tighter-than-normal skirt this morning. Even after Friday at the hotel, Saturday at my house, and all day Sunday, because we both blew off our commitments with the excuse of being sick.

You always hear those stupid cliché love stories about lazy Sunday mornings with breakfast in bed and reading the paper. Well, they're not so stupid after all. We ate bagels, but we didn't share a paper. She read *Adweek* and I read the *Times*. Each on our iPads.

Then at five o'clock, she said she was leaving. I didn't fight her, and she left with a smile.

Like every morning, my eyes fall to her desk outside my

office. She's talking to Mr. Beardsman's new assistant. She smiles and points at the paper between them.

My phone rings.

"Yes," I answer, having seen Elise's, from reception. name on the small screen.

"Hi Mr. Mancini. Both you and Annie were on a call, so I took a message. Our email is down, and Orange Glow is looking for the updated contract."

"I sent it to Annie earlier."

"I don't believe they received anything from her yet. Maybe the email was already down, but they'd like it today."

"Let me see if she already sent it, okay?" I hang up and ring Annie.

"Hello, Mr. Mancini."

"This bullshit with Mr. Mancini." I blow out a breath. She offers no excuse for not saying Enzo. "That contract for Orange Glow, did it go out?"

"No, I don't have a contact for Orange Glow." She looks through the door at me, shaking her head.

Sometimes I wonder why we even bother conversing over the phone. I'm sure I could get plenty of business done with her on my lap and my hand between her legs. I'm an excellent multi-tasker.

"It's lost in cyberspace until email is back up then. It needs to be sent today."

Last time our email went down, it was the entire afternoon. Not sure who we hire in that department, since their only advice when something goes wrong is to reboot.

"Okay, send it to my personal account. astewart730@electromail.com."

I scribble it down. "Perfect."

Going over to my own electromail account, I notice it's

been a long time since I checked it. I have a bunch of emails from the gym and a few restaurants.

I call Elise back. "I'm sending it to her personal email, and she'll be sure to get it to them today."

"Great. I'll let them know. Thank you, Mr. Mancini."

"Welcome." I hang up and attach the contract to Annie before hitting Send.

Scrolling through my emails, I realize it's the only private thing I can do at the office without the dipshits in IT knowing. Then another brilliant idea forms.

To: Annie Stewart (astewart730@electromail.com)
From: Lorenzo Mancini (enzothelegend@electro-mail.com)
Subject: Important Inquiry

Are you wearing panties?

MINIMIZING MY PERSONAL EMAIL ACCOUNT, I wait for her reply. Five minutes go by before my door opens, and Annie stands there.

"A word?" She shuts the door and sits down in front of my desk.

"You're supposed to call first. Don't be thinking just because you suck my dick now you can barge in uninvited." I laugh.

She doesn't. She opens her tablet, showing me the email I wrote to her.

"Oh awesome, never mind about barging in. You want

to show me instead of emailing me back? Want to go into my bathroom?"

She's staring at me as if she's planning the best way to murder me and get away with it.

"What?" I ask when an uncomfortable amount of silence falls over the room.

"You can't send this to me."

"I could reprimand you for checking non-work-related personal emails at work. But I'm feeling nice today." I wink.

She rolls her eyes. "You're incorrigible. You know that, right?"

"You haven't answered the question. You purposely wore that skirt today, didn't you?"

A smile tilts her lips. "No."

I lean forward, putting my arms on my desk. "I want you. Let's go out for lunch. And by that, I mean I'm eating you."

"No," she says, scrawling some notes in her notepad. She probably wants to look as if I'm instructing her to do something for me in case anyone outside my office is watching.

"This whole screwing-your-coworker thing isn't as fun as I thought it was going to be. Whose place are we at tonight? I'll happily to come to yours."

She stands. "If that will be all, I'll leave you to your work."

She walks toward the door, but outside of this office is trouble. She's yet to see it because she glances at me over her shoulder, biting her bottom lip. I should tell her about the spanking she deserves, but I'm too concerned about who's about to storm into my office.

Carm pushes the door open. Annie's steps falter back,

her eyes widening as my brothers walk into my office unannounced.

"Sorry." Carm stops, steadying Annie with his hand on her hip.

Red coats my vision.

"It's okay. Can I help you?" she asks.

"Nah, we're here for him." He lets her go, and her eyes shoot to me.

"Annie, meet my brothers, Carmelo and Dominic." I lean back in my seat. "Usually they're too busy to visit during the day, which is how I like it."

I wait for one of them to enlighten me as to why they're ruining my flirting with my new... girlfriend, I guess.

Whoa, that sounds weird.

"Because Blanca has heard jackshit from you about fixing her up. And Ma had three girls at Sunday dinner yesterday. One for each of us." Dom sits down first, propping his ankle on his knee.

Carm keeps flicking his gaze to Annie.

She shakes her head. "If you need something, Mr. Mancini, let me know." Annie slides out of the room, probably creeped out by Carm.

"Thank you, Annie," I say, but I doubt she heard me. "Can you stop mentally undressing my assistant?"

Carm laughs, sitting next to Dom. "She's hot. You hit that?"

I wasn't prepared for the direct question. "No. I'm not you. I don't drink from the company water cooler."

"Mind if I drink from yours?" He turns to look at Annie, whose ass is facing us as she talks to Jake.

I pull up my email.

To: Annie Stewart (astewart730@electromail.com)
From: Lorenzo Mancini (enzothelegend@electromail.com)
Subject: Turn around

My brother is ogling your ass. Sit. Down.

I MINIMIZE the screen again to make sure my brothers don't look at what I'm doing.

"You lost the bet. It was yours to handle," Dom says.

"Excuse me, I do have a job."

"I think you've been banging some girl and that's why you canceled on Sunday dinner." Dom levels me with an intense stare.

Carm grins at me. "That was your assistant, wasn't it?"

"Enough about Annie!" I yell.

I must've been loud, because Annie turns my way outside the door. I point at her computer. She rolls her eyes and disappears in the direction of the restrooms.

"You're fucking her." Carm chuckles.

"Get a fucking clue." I give him my best "you're insane" look, but these are my brothers. They know me better than anyone.

"We're here for Blanca," Dom tries to get us back on track and I couldn't agree more.

"Technically, she didn't ask for our help," Carm chimes in.

I agree with him, but right now, I'm just thankful he's off Annie.

My computer dings.

"We drove all the way over here. You can at least stop

working for five minutes." Dom blows out an annoyed breath.

I ignore him and sneak a glance at Annie. She's back behind her desk. Good. Then I pull up the email she sent me.

To: Lorenzo Mancini (enzothelegend@electromail.com)
From: Annie Stewart (astewart730@electromail.com)
Subject: RE: Turn Around

You're delusional. He isn't checking me out.
Oh, and FYI, I just took off my panties.

I SWALLOW back my groan and shift in my seat.

"Just give me one second." I put my finger up to Dom.

His nostrils flare like he's about to explode, but some things are more important.

To: Annie Stewart (astewart730@electromail.com)
From: Lorenzo Mancini (enzothelegend@electromail.com)
Subject: Package

Put them in an envelope and bring them in.

IT TAKES every ounce of willpower not to look in her direction.

"Are you done yet?" Dom asks.

"Listen, I can't just find some random guy worthy of dating our sister."

Dom stands and looks out the glass door. He points at Jake. "There's a guy."

"I think he's gay."

"Ask the hottie. She probably knows people." Carm glances at Annie, who's rounding her desk with a brown interoffice envelope in her hand. "Perfect, she's coming in."

She knocks on the glass.

Dom opens the door for her. "Come to save him from us?"

She flashes him her kind smile, that hint of apricot I love so much in her cheeks as she walks across the room. "Here's the item you asked for, Mr. Mancini."

"Perfect. Thanks, Annie." I smile.

"Do you know any available guys?" Dom asks her, crossing his arms. "Our sister needs a new guy in her life, and we don't know anyone we'd set her up with."

Annie glances at me and shakes her head. She's already familiar with our goal, but she can't let them know. She crosses her arms and leans her hip on the edge of my desk. "You're trying to set up your sister?"

My gaze falls to her ass. She's got the best ass and I want so badly to squeeze it. She definitely needs to be punished for wearing that skirt.

"She deserves a nice guy, and it's a bonus if we like him," Dom says.

She looks around the office, much like Dom did. "There's Jake." She glances at me.

I wave off her suggestion. "I told them he's gay."

Small crinkles indent her forehead. "No, he's not."

"He's not?"

"No. He's straight."

"Then there we have it. Let's call him in." Dom claps in a let's-get-this-going motion.

Carm grabs a drink from my mini fridge before putting his feet on the edge of my desk and cracking open the soda.

"Get your feet off my desk," I say, pushing them down.

"You're so touchy today." He sips his drink. "Let's bring the guy in."

"How about I handle it?" Annie offers. "I don't think he's going to agree when her three large brothers are staring down at him."

Dom looks at me, and we both shrug. "True."

"Why don't we double date with them?" Carm says to Annie.

She looks at me, and I inhale. She asked me not to say anything, but I really want to knock my brother out right now for this little fishing expedition.

"That's not a good idea," Annie says sweetly.

"Because you're fucking my brother?"

"Carm, for Christ's sake." I stand, my chair rolling to the window. Anger coats my vision. I cannot believe he said that. What if I wasn't fucking my assistant? Then what?

Dom smacks the back of Carm's head. "Please forgive our younger brother. He's lost all sense of propriety." Dom gives him the lethal look I'm sure has made more than one trader down on Wall Street piss their pants.

To my surprise, Annie giggles. "It's okay. I *am* fucking

your brother." She sounds so cool and calm, even my mouth is hanging open. "But mum's the word, okay?"

Shit. I'm floored.

Dom raises his eyebrows at me.

"So the whole metaphor about the water cooler... you were really talking about water?" Carm asks, circling his finger between Annie and me.

"Carm, piss off." I push a hand through my hair.

Carm laughs. "Is that any way to talk to your brother?"

I shake my head, exasperated.

"This is so interesting." The grin on Carm's face means trouble. "Are you going to come to Sunday dinner this week?"

"Shut it," I say.

"Okay, so you're going to fix Blanca up with that guy? He looks nice. Right?" Thank God for Dom's interruption.

"Jake's very nice and respectable. I've never met Blanca, but I can't imagine a girl not liking Jake."

"Then why is he single?" I ask, a hot poker of jealousy stabbing me in the chest.

"I don't know. It's none of my business," Annie says.

"Thank you, Annie. You've done more for us than Enzo. If you ever need anything, let me know." Dom moves toward the door and turns the handle. The man is constantly on the go.

"Well, there is one thing," Annie says.

Dom stops and shuts the door.

She eyes me, and her smirk says she's going to ask something embarrassing about me. "How often does Enzo lose at rock, paper, scissors?"

My brothers look at one another and laugh.

"Want to watch it live?" Dom steps forward, his fist on his palm.

"I'm not playing." I sound like a petulant four-year-old, but I don't care.

Carm swings his arm around Annie's shoulders. "If you're playing for sexual favors in bed, definitely play rock, paper, scissors. You'll never have to blow him again." He winks my way.

Annie stifles a laugh. "Thanks for the advice."

"Hope to see you at Sunday dinner," Carm says with his most charming smile.

Idiot.

"Let's go, I have to work," Dom booms, done with any chitchat.

"Coming, Daddy," Carm says then swivels around. "Did I steal your line, Annie?" He laughs all the way out of the office.

Hands on my hips, I shake my head. "I can't apologize enough for my brother."

She turns to me. "Don't forget to open your package, Mr. Mancini."

Just like that, I'm hard again.

CHAPTER TWENTY-SIX

Annie

I'm not sure how this whole observation thing at Beth's is going to go. I'm not sure how comfortable she's going to be with Enzo and me observing her every move.

The car drops us off outside their condo.

"What does your brother-in-law do?" Enzo asks, opening the building door for me.

"Something in banking. And Beth has a popular blog that's been getting a lot of traction."

"About what?"

"Budgeting. She does a lot of DIYs and posts on how to stretch a dollar. I can't even imagine what she does to my poor niece to save a few dollars." We step into the lobby and head over to the doorman's desk. "Hey, Ernie."

"Good evening. I heard it's date night." He eyes the both of us.

We look at one another before going to the elevator.

"I thought we were shadowing?" Enzo asks, his hand on the small of my back as we wait.

"I did too."

We step onto the elevator, and as soon as the doors begin to shut, Enzo closes the gap between us. I won't lie—I love that he's so touchy-feely and that he can't go long without kissing me. I've never felt more wanted than I do in his presence. He makes me feel beautiful and sexy.

His arms lock me in the corner, his lips on my neck. "You smell so good."

One hand slides up the back of my shirt. His touch electrifies my skin, and my eyes fall shut.

"I'm going to come all over these tits tonight. I'm going to fuck you until I'm about to come, then I'm gonna pull my dick out and watch my cum stream all over your gorgeous tits." His big palm grabs my breast, and he tweaks my nipple, his mouth covering mine.

Will I ever get enough of him?

Wrapping my hands around his neck, I wind my fingers through his strands and grind myself along him, not getting the friction I need. The elevator doors *ding* open and he extracts himself too fast, as though it's not his first time making out in an elevator, while I'm fumbling to find the floor again.

When I finally right myself and look up, there stands Sam, eyes wide. *Shit.*

"I must be so sleep-deprived I'm seeing things." He walks toward their condo.

"Sam," I say sweetly, shooting my best pissed-off look at Enzo for seducing me in the elevator.

Sam opens the condo door. "Honey, guess who I found while taking out the garbage?"

We follow him in, and I slip off my shoes. Sure enough, if Sam's nice jeans and non-stained shirt wasn't a tip-off, my sister's full face of makeup and curled hair is.

She hands me Cecilia. "I just fed her. We'll be back after dinner. The instructions are on the counter." She points, and I turn to see a piece of paper on the counter.

"Beth? We were supposed to be shadowing you guys." I look at Enzo, who's turning green.

"You're her aunt, you wouldn't do anything to harm her." She kisses my cheek then the top of Cecilia's head. "I need this, Annie."

I give her a small nod, and they rush out the door before I can object anyway.

"Why didn't you stop them?" Enzo asks.

"Because it all happened so fast."

The minute the door shuts, it's like Cecilia knows, and she wails in my arms. I rock and sway and bounce. Nothing helps.

"I'm going to change her." This I can do.

As I'm changing her diaper, I gain the self-confidence to get through tonight. What's the difference between this and when I watch Cecilia while Beth's sleeping most Saturdays? Nothing. Except she's usually down the hall. But that's okay. We can do this.

I pick her back up and she cries again. Beth said she just ate, so I'll try to burp her. Maybe she's gassy.

Enzo sits on a breakfast stool as though he's about a minute away from fleeing and leaving me here by myself. I notice he hasn't taken off his shoes yet.

I bounce her, patting her lightly on the back as she rests on my shoulder.

"She's getting a weird look," Enzo chimes in from his nosebleed seats.

"Like what?"

"Like Carm does when he's about to throw up."

I stop all movement. A huge belch comes out of her, followed by a trickle of something warm down my back.

"Oh fuck!" Enzo gags.

I circle around to find her throw-up on the floor. Enzo runs to the sink, continuing to dry heave.

"Man up, Enzo."

"I'm not made for this." His shoulders still rise and fall.

"You're going to have to take her. I have to clean up."

He crosses his arms, resting his body by the sink just in case. "I don't know how to hold a baby. Want me to call my ma?"

"No. Come here and I'll put her in your arms."

"I don't want to break her. Your sister will definitely cut off my balls and put them in a blender if I break her baby."

My patience has grown thin. I get that this isn't Enzo's gig, but he needs to suck it up. "Please, Enzo?"

"No. Don't use those two words right now." He shakes his head like a disappointed ten-year-old.

"What is wrong with saying 'please, Enzo'?"

"You know I like that in the bedroom, and now the next time you say it to me, I'm going to be thinking about throw up all over your back instead of you begging to come." He chokes again.

For heaven's sake. I spot her swing and figure she can sit in there while I clean up. When I place her down, she screams as I latch the straps.

"Read the instructions Beth left." I hear him pick up the paper. "It says don't put her in the swing. She hates the swing."

I glare at him, and he points at the writing on the letter.

Enzo's worried about my sister, but it might be me cutting off his balls and putting them in the blender.

"It says she likes the bouncy. What's a bouncy?" he asks.

"Why don't you help me find it?"

He walks around as though there're bombs on the floor, tiptoeing around everything. I spot the bouncy chair and put her in it. She instantly calms.

"Thank God," I say, then head to the kitchen to grab the paper towels and cleaning supplies. I'm more annoyed by Enzo than anything Cecilia's done. "Can you at least sit on the couch and watch her?"

He sits on the edge of the sofa, staring at the baby. Her eyes are shut, but her face is still flushed from crying.

"I have to go change. Want to strip this off me?" I joke.

He chokes again.

"What will you do when you have kids of your own?" I ask, shaking my head.

"Easy, I don't plan on having any."

I back-step from down the hall. "What?"

"The way tonight's going, I'm not sure kids are for me."

"Just watch her." I point at Cecilia and head back down the hall.

Digging through Beth's drawers, I find a sweatshirt that says, "I just married him." The woman needs to do laundry. I was stuck in Akron, Ohio, this past Saturday. Sam couldn't have taken over for me?

Cecilia cries again as I'm wetting my hair to try to get the throw-up out. I understand the whole mom ponytail now. I secure my hair up on top of my head with Beth's holder then spray some perfume on me so I don't smell like barf. After grabbing my shirt and a bunch of their clothes, I throw them into their small washer and start it.

Cecilia continues to cry, and I growl out of frustration. "*Pick her up*!"

"I don't know how to do that."

I stomp down the hall, glare at him, and swiftly pick her up, but instead of holding her, I place her in his arms. "This is what we're here for. I'm not doing all the work. We're a team."

His eyes widen as one hand cradles her head and the other holds her butt.

Not having time to deal with his immature attitude, I head to the kitchen and start cleaning all the bottles and dishes for Beth and Sam. A second later, I realize Cecilia isn't crying.

I finish the bottles, fill the dishwasher, and start it. When I walk over to the couch, Enzo's holding Cecilia to his chest, but he still looks incredibly awkward. He's staring at her as though she's talking to him, but her eyes are shut.

"Here." I take her from him. "Slide onto the couch."

He does.

"Open your arms. I'm going to cradle her in them."

He does. I place her in his arms and prop a pillow under the one that isn't on the armrest. Beth showed me that trick after I thought my arm would fall off. I flip on the television.

"Can you turn up the volume?" he asks.

"Nope. This is the setting for when she's in the room."

He rolls his eyes. "Nice sweatshirt by the way."

"Want me to sit next to you?"

"Is that a trick question?" Just like that, the Enzo I know—the flirty and fun-loving one—returns.

I go over the notes for tonight. Beth wrote down clear instructions about bath time, but I'd be lying if I said I wasn't terrified. A slippery and slimy baby sounds like a challenge.

"She has to take a bath," I say to Enzo.

He tries to hand her to me.

"There's no Annie in team," I say and put my hands up in front of me.

He laughs. "She's cute, you know. She scrunches up her nose right before she releases a deadly fart. And a second ago, her hand wrapped around my finger."

I slide closer to see her and lay my head on his shoulder, staring at my niece. "She's the cutest baby ever born."

"I'm sure you were cute."

I fight a smile, but it escapes anyway. "Look at you sweet- talking me."

"I owe you after the asshole I was earlier." He turns to me. "I'm sorry."

I nod. "Thanks for that. Are you ready for the bath?"

He shakes his head and I laugh, picking her up. Immediately he stretches his arms over his head and to the side. "How much does she weigh?"

"Twelve pounds, I think."

"Why do my arms feel like Jell-O?" he asks, continuing to stretch them as he follows me to the bathroom.

"Okay, we need that baby bath." I point at the pink plastic thing in the tub of their second bathroom.

He picks it up and puts it on the counter.

"Grab the temperature thing." I flip on the water. "Beth says it needs to be at one hundred degrees. I'm going to undress her."

"You're leaving me responsible for the water?" His fearful look makes me laugh.

"I trust you."

Once I undress Cecilia, I come back to the bathroom, place her in the baby bath, and she opens her eyes, smiling.

She loves the water. Thank God. Using the washcloth, I try to bathe her the same way I witnessed Beth do.

"I'm going to hold her up, and you're going to get her back," I say to Enzo, who's watching from behind me, not really participating.

"Thanks for taking one for the team. She's slippery, and though I'm a pro at handling wet things, this is something entirely different."

"Okay, no sexual innuendos in front of the baby."

He takes the washcloth from my hands and washes her back and the back of her head.

We finish quickly. Picking her up under her arms, I lift her out of the bath. Enzo holds his hands under mine in case she slips. God love him.

I gently place her on the towel and wrap her up before carrying her into the bedroom.

Enzo waltzes in moments later with our instructions. "We have to turn this on." He flicks on this circle thing that projects stars and animals onto the ceiling. "We have to make sure everything is out of the crib." He looks over the edge as I dress her in a pair of giraffe pajamas. "We have to turn on the monitor." He flicks on another gadget that lights up.

I kiss her forehead. "Time for bed," I whisper.

Her eyes are already shutting as I place her in the crib.

"We're done."

"According to this."

I lean into his chest as we watch Cecilia fall asleep, my own eyes drooping with exhaustion.

A minute later, we tiptoe out of the room and Enzo falls onto the couch, so I join him. We lie there for five minutes before his hands slide under the hem of my sweatshirt. Just as he cops a feel, Cecilia screams.

"So much for bedtime." I look back at a spent Enzo. "Still gonna come all over my tits tonight?"

He peeks one eye open . "Raincheck?"

I laugh while walking back down the hall. Yeah, we've got lots of time to make that happen.

CHAPTER TWENTY-SEVEN

Enzo

The Coddle bath time presentation goes smoother than the diaper one. Blair said she's swamped and didn't even ask us for an actual presentation, just to send over the video, which they loved.

"Mr. Jacobson will see you now," Mindy, his assistant, says.

"Thanks."

I walk in and shut the door, hoping this is when he'll give me the news about my partnership.

"Enzo." Mr. Jacobson pours himself a scotch, holding up his glass to offer me one.

"Of course," I say.

Instead of sitting at his desk, he guides us to his couch and chair with a view of Manhattan that makes my view look like a back alley. "You know, I was the one who hired you. I saw your resume. Saw what you did as an apprentice.

Benny said you were a hotshot and that your ego would get in your way."

Good thing poor Benny Earl passed. May he rest in peace.

"But I told him your ego was what would make you great." He smiles and sits in the chair across from me. "And years later, here we are, talking about a partnership."

I nod, sipping my scotch, and place the glass on the table. I need my A-plus game here. "I can't thank you enough for every opportunity."

He nods. "You know I don't listen to rumors. I hear them, but I learned a long time ago not to listen."

I shift in my seat in an attempt to ease some of my discomfort.

"We've all had our indiscretions." He sets his drink on the table between us and leans forward. "It's hard when all these young women are walking around flaunting what they've got, fishing to find themselves a rich husband."

I slide to the back of the couch, any words lodged in my throat.

"You and Annie Stewart are getting along well. After your long run of assistants, I'm curious what makes her so easy to work with."

Shit. He knows. I open my mouth to speak, but I don't get the opportunity.

"What I'm asking is are you going to bat to try to get her promoted because of a relationship the two of you have after hours?"

"No." I don't stop to even think about it. She deserves the promotion whether or not she's sleeping with me. "She's good, Mr. Jacobson, one of the best I've worked with."

He takes a sip of his scotch and sets it down. "I see where the advantage might come in to have her on board to handle the female products. She saved our ass on the diaper thing. Motherly instincts, I suppose." He chuckles.

I don't agree . I'm finally realizing that I'm working for a class-A asshole.

"I think she'll benefit Jacobson and Earl overall," I say because I have nothing to add to his sexist talk.

He mulls that over for a minute. "I guess we could promote her to junior ad exec. What could it hurt? It'll make her happy and avoid a sexual discrimination issue for a while."

"Sir—"

"But we'll wait until after we're done with Coddle. I heard you're on to tampons. Good luck on that one. Why don't you let her lead it? I want to see what she has without your input."

"You want to give her the tampon pitch all to herself?"

"Well no, she's too green to let her have at it with no oversight."

I could argue that she's not, but I don't say anything.

"Guide her. Oversee it. Makes sure whatever she's got lives up to the standard we've set here."

"Okay." I sip my drink, wondering if there's more to discuss, like, I don't know, me becoming partner.

He sips his drink for a second, staring off into space, and I wonder for a second if the old man died on me.

"As far as you go..."

I want to rub my hands together. Here's the good part.

"I know we've talked about the possibility of you making partner. As you can imagine, this is a hard decision for me to make. Benny and I were partners from the get-go. I've tried to keep things going with the same vision he and I originally had for the company, and I can't deny that the idea of you as a partner scares me a bit."

"Why would I scare you?" I slide to the edge of my seat.

"You're young. You're going to want change. Teddy Beardsman, now there's a guy who understands the rules to play by."

I rewind his words, trying to bring clarity to them. Is he fucking kidding me? Beardsman? That hack?

I inhale a deep breath to try to cage in my anger. "With all due respect, Mr. Jacobson, I bring in double the clients Teddy does. Not only in number but in revenue."

He holds his hand up in a placating gesture. "I know, I know, but you and this Annie Stewart thing has me wondering if…" He leans forward. "If Jacobson and Earl is eventually going to have a daycare for working mothers who will be out once a month 'sick.'" He puts the word sick in air quotes.

It doesn't take a genius to read between the lines. He's afraid I'll promote women and change the culture of the office.

"I'm getting older, and I don't want to be here all day. But it's a bigger decision than just making you partner because you bring in the most revenue. I have to pick someone Benny and I would've agreed on, and like I said, he always thought you were too cocky."

My arrogance is what makes me so great at my job. I don't second-guess decisions. I trust my gut, get excited about my idea, which in turn makes clients believe in me and my vision for their campaigns. I've given this company my entire twenties and into my thirties. I have no life other than work and now he's decided that maybe I'm not the right fit? "Mr. Jacobson—"

He holds up his hand to stop me, and I clench my fists. "Just relax, Enzo. I'm not making any final decision right now. I just figured you were wondering where this is all going. I know you're probably the best candidate. Teddy's always off for some kid's activity." He rolls his eyes. "You're my bachelor, no-strings kind of guy. You could very well bring Jacobson and Earl to the next level."

Finally he's talking sense.

"But I have to weed through it all. I really called you in here to talk about Annie Stewart. Like I said, rumors are flying because you're finally getting along with a woman you work with, and in my experience, that usually has nothing to do with actual work."

If my ma had raised me differently, I'd punch him and not care if I broke every bone in his face. I don't understand men like this. I know there's a generation gap, but saying I'm only getting along with Annie because he thinks we're having an affair? The fact that we are in a sexual relationship aside, I have respect for her work. That's why we work well together. But that seems to be a foreign concept to him.

"I assure you, sir, Annie Stewart has a bright future and you don't want to pass her up. I say that based on her work performance alone." I down the rest of my scotch and set the glass on the table a little harder than necessary.

He nods. "Okay then. Well, good luck, and I'll have an answer on the partnership at the same time as I do for Miss Stewart and the junior ad exec position. A couple weeks max."

I refrain from arguing that he said he'd promote her after we landed two more products for Coddle. I can't be the prince who swoops in every time, no matter how much I want to be. "Thank you, Mr. Jacobson."

I shake his hand and leave his office feeling as if he just shoved a massive stick up my ass.

"Have a nice day, Enzo," Mindy says.

"Thanks. You too." I walk out of his corner office area and down the hall to mine.

Annie isn't there, which is probably a good thing. I need to work off all this pent-up energy, and if she were around, I might try to seduce her into letting me bang her in my office with the blinds drawn. Actually, that's exactly what I'm going to do.

I sit in my office and draw the blinds. Who the hell cares? Mr. Zilroy does it every damn day between one and two. I won't be napping though.

To: Annie Stewart (astewart730@electromail.com)
From: Lorenzo Mancini (enzothelegend@electro-mail.com)
Subject: Not a Request

I need to see you in my office ASAP.

I SEND her the email since it's our go-to communication at work. We're off the radar of the IT guys and she doesn't have to have her cell phone out all the time.

With the blinds drawn, I won't see when she returns to her desk, so I focus on the Orange Glow account while I wait for her. But the entire time I try to work, the conversation with Mr. Jacobson runs through my head. What a sexist prick. I mean, not only his feelings about Annie but in relation to me. Even if there was a daycare, who cares? I bet there would be fewer absences and more productive workers.

There's a knock on my door.

"Come in."

Annie walks in. "Why are the blinds drawn? Whatever you're thinking, it's not gonna happen."

I lock the door using the button under my desk.

"Enzo..." Her tone is one of warning.

I walk across the room, pull her into my chest, and bring my lips to hers. As always, her fight wanes because she wants me as much as I want her.

My hands run up her back, but I rest my forehead on hers. "Am I a misogynist?"

"What?" She places her hands on my cheeks.

"Before you got to know me, did you think I was a misogynist?"

Her face softens as if she wants to let me down lightly. "I didn't really know. I mean, you were Lorenzo Mancini, the asshole who kept expecting unrealistic things from his assistant. I didn't think you were a misogynist per se."

"But?"

"You know the advertising game. It's a man's world."

I break apart from her and head over to the couch. She follows.

"Yeah, but..."

"Enzo, you're a man, so maybe you don't see things as blatantly as a woman might. But I never saw you purposely knock a woman down. Other than the whole dry cleaning thing, you never did anything degrading. Except for the blinds being shut right now and the rumors that are bound to swirl." She raises her eyebrows.

"I really want to be inside you right now." I squeeze her knee.

"Is this about the meeting with Mr. Jacobson? Did it not go well? Did he say anything about the partnership?"

She hammers me with all these questions, but I can't tell her the shitty things her boss thinks. But she should know so she can go somewhere else. She could go to Coddle.

The selfish part of me doesn't want that to happen. I like her. I like spending time with her. Hell, I like working with her and seeing her in action. And I *really* like fucking her. Her strict rule of only one sleepover during the week isn't the best, but if she takes the Coddle job, she'll move to Houston.

"The tampon ad is yours," I spit it out.

"What?"

I nod. "I'm here to guide you, but truth is, you don't need me. It's yours."

"Enzo." Her hand covers her heart. Then the excitement in her eyes fade. "Wait. Is this because I'm a woman?"

I run my thumb over her cheek. "You do know the product."

She nods, but she knows why it's hers. She also won't make waves because it's the first account she's had to herself.

"I'm sure Blair will love it." I roll my eyes.

"Stop being so sour toward her. It's not her fault I'm awesome and she wanted to snatch me up out of your grip."

I grip her hips and pull her onto my lap. "She has no idea the fight she'll get."

She smiles but says nothing.

"I'll work on the condom ad while you're doing the tampon one. After you present, you can hop on the condom one and help finish it up. Before we know it, you'll be a junior ad exec and I'll be partner."

Her head dips, and I capture her lips with a kiss I'm hoping convinces the both of us.

CHAPTER TWENTY-EIGHT

Annie

"What do you mean he wants to set me up with his sister?" Jake pops a fry into his mouth.

"She's super pretty, he showed me a picture. And if you don't want to go alone, he's offered for the two of us to tag along."

"Oh really, a double date?" Mae puts her chin in her palm.

I throw a fry at her. "Stop it."

She's been making references throughout our lunch about Enzo and me. The rumor train has arrived at Jacobson and Earl, and Enzo's stunt of closing the blinds the other day only made it stop for a prolonged layover.

My phone dings with an email. "I swear, I think you'll like her. Hold up one sec while I check my messages."

To: Annie Stewart (astewart730@electromail.com)
From: Lorenzo Mancini (enzothelegend@electro-mail.com)
Subject: Lunch order

You.

I ROLL MY EYES, but Mae catches it.

"What's that look for? Who is it?" she asks.

I place my phone on the table, face down. "Just Enzo's lunch order."

"Oh, let me guess. You on his desk?" Mae rolls her eyes, but they pop back in place, pointed right at me.

Yeah, not much getting past her. If she didn't work at Jacobson and Earl, I'd tell her everything, but if everyone finds out about the fraternization, I'll never get that promotion.

Jake, God bless him, continues as if he hasn't noticed Mae's focus. "I'm not sure, Annie, I mean what if... the stakes are high if I go on a date with her."

I put up my hand. "Hold on."

Me: *Send me a pic of Blanca.*

Three dots appear.

Enzo: *Did you get my email? I'm starving for my lunch.*

I shake my head.

Me: *Pic?*

Enzo: *You want a dick pic? Sure thing sweetie.*

Me: *Unless you want me to show Mae and Jake your dick, I suggest one of Blanca.*

Enzo: *You're no fun.*

Enzo: *Pic attached.*

I enlarge it and put it in front of Jake. His eyes widen, then Mae steals the phone.

"Okay, I'm in," Jake says.

"You'd be an idiot not to be." Mae hands me back my phone.

"Great. Do you want to go alone?" I ask.

"I really don't want to go with Enzo."

I laugh. "Okay, so...?"

"I'll go alone. I'm not twelve."

Phew. I didn't know how I would survive dinner with Enzo. The man would be sending me texts and probably fingering me under the table. One day I won't be like a shiny new toy for him to play with. That thought makes me sad, so I push it away.

"Great. I'll let him know."

Me: *Jake says it a go. How do you want this to happen? Are you going to call your sister?*

Enzo: *I'm bothered that my texts and emails are being filled with setting my sister up. Go to the bathroom and send me a pic of your tits.*

"There's that damn smirk again. Are you dating someone?" Mae reaches to grab my phone, but I slide back the chair, knocking into the man behind me.

"I'm so sorry."

His wife gives me a dirty look while handing him a napkin for the spoonful of soup all over his shirt. I shoot Mae a look like "look what you made me do."

"It's okay," the older gentleman says.

I pluck the napkin Jake is about to use and hand it to the man, along with my own.

"Was that not mine?" Jake pretends to look around as if he's missing something.

"Thank you, dear. Accidents happen," the man says.

His wife's scowl indents further, so I back off and sit back down.

"My napkin?" Jake says.

"Sorry, it was an emergency." I stand up to head to the counter and grab him a handful of napkins.

On my way back, I spot Mae glancing across the table at my phone, which I accidentally left face up, as the screen lights up.

It happens like it's in slow motion—me trying to get back to the table while a crowd of people walk toward me. I say excuse me, slide past the strangers, unable to reach the table fast enough. Mae's eyes widen in shock. She's probably staring at a picture of Enzo's dick. My only saving grace is that Jake still looks clueless. Until he leans forward to drink his Coke.

"Excuse me." I dance to the right then to the left with a man who seems to feel just as awkward as I do with us being unable to get by one another.

When I finally reach the table, I drop the stack of napkins, but I'm too late. They're both gaping at me.

"It's true?" Mae's tone holds a hint of judgment.

I slump into my chair, pushing my sandwich to the middle of the table because I won't be finishing it now.

My phone vibrates with text after text. Damn Enzo and his inability to have any patience. I pick up my phone to see exactly what they saw.

Enzo: *I'm still waiting.*
Enzo: *Don't worry, I'll close the blinds when I'm eating "lunch".*
Enzo: *FYI... I'm calling bullshit on the once a week thing. I'm coming over tonight.*
Enzo: *Your silence will only resort in me having to use my best teasing practices tonight.*

Well, at least they didn't see his dick. Though Mae would have appreciated it because it's a beautiful thing. I was never a lover of the male anatomy until Enzo, but his manhood is like a work of art. That I know what it feels like when he fills me probably adds to my admiration.

Mind out of the gutter, Annie.

Back to Operation "Make my friends keep their mouths shut."

I lean forward with my hands splayed across the table. "You can't tell anyone."

Mae smiles. She's enjoying this too much. "So your gut led you there?"

"Yeah."

She throws a fry at me. "Why didn't you tell me?"

I sulk in my chair, looking at Jake from the corner of my eye. "Because I have no idea where it's going. And hello, I'm sleeping with the boss while trying to get promoted. I'm officially the stupidest person in the world and a disgrace to all women."

"That's a tad dramatic," Mae says, crossing her arms. She eyes Jake. "You're pretty quiet."

He shrugs. "I figured it out the day the blinds were shut."

"What? No, you didn't." I sit up straighter in my chair.

He wipes his hands on the napkins I brought him. "You came out and the button on your blouse was undone and your cheeks were flushed. You'd just been stranded for a night on the way back from Texas. It's really not that hard to figure out."

"Do you think badly of me?" I cringe, waiting for his answer.

He sips his drink and places it back on the table without a glance my way. "No, but I don't see it ending well for you. I think you're going to be the one on the sidewalk with a box, not him."

I blow out a breath. That's my worst fear, but Enzo hasn't given me any special treatment at work.

My phone vibrates again, but I don't pick it up.

"You better read it. I'll be living through you until this whole affair ends." Mae chuckles.

I lean back in my seat, her words soaking in. Affair and end. My friends don't see a possibility that this thing with Enzo could go the distance. The thought shouldn't bother me. He told me he'd try, and he is.

I push away Mae and Jake's negative thoughts. They know the Enzo I did from before, not the Enzo I know now.

I OPEN the door to my condo. Enzo's big body makes my apartment feel even smaller.

"It's colorful, like you said."

"You're the one who insisted on coming." I grab the pizza from his hands, and he follows me into the kitchen.

"It's you. It suits your personality." He looks around every nook and cranny.

"That's what happens when you decorate it yourself." I smile and he mocks offense.

We both know he doesn't care.

My galley kitchen isn't anything to rave about. There's barely enough room for the two of us to be in here together. I grab the six-pack of beer from him and put it in the fridge.

He picks up a picture frame from my entry table. Beth, my dad, and me when I was in high school. "Beautiful as always."

He knows how to make someone feel special.

"No mom?" he asks.

"She was already out of my life by then." I put the pizza on the table and a beer on either side before sitting on the couch. I pat the spot next to me. "Stop prying."

"Hey, it's my first time here and I haven't even seen the bedroom yet." He ventures down the shortest hallway ever.

I follow because him being in my condo feels weird. I keep thinking there's something embarrassing I forgot to put away.

He's already exploring my bedroom, his eyes scouring every surface. The room is so small there really isn't any space for extras.

"Where the magic happens?" He points at the bed with his usual smirk.

"No magic has ever happened on that bed except for me and my toys." I cross my arms with a smug grin and lean against the door frame.

"Toys?" He opens the drawer next to my bed.

"Might as well give up, you'll never find them."

He stops searching and walks over to me. "Can I play with your toys too?" His lips fall to my shoulder before his mouth travels up to mine. "I promise to treat them with respect."

I laugh, but he swivels me around, guiding me to the bed.

"What about dinner?" I ask.

"I'm more in the mood for something else."

I fall back onto the mattress and bounce up. Enzo bends down and slides my box out from under the bed. Damn him.

"How did you know?"

"When are you going to realize I'm brilliant?" He flashes a smile that makes me want to strip before he sets the box on the nightstand. He pulls the lid from the top and pulls out my favorite vibrator. "Ladies' choice?" He turns it on as though it's not his first time using one.

I face-palm myself. Of course, it's not his first time. "That's the Unicorn Cock."

He rests it on his palm, testing out the four speeds and two pulses. His hands fall to my inner thighs and he pushes my legging-clad thighs apart then puts the vibrator right between my legs. My head falls back. I love the sensation of having it on my clit without me being the one guiding it.

"We need to get you naked so I can watch you use it."

He helps me get unclothed, then it's my turn to help him. I sit naked on the edge of the bed and unbutton his jeans, pushing them down his legs. I stare up at him while I rub his rigid length through his boxers. His fingers thread through my hair in a way that feels possessive and at the same time loving. He's clearly struggling to not push my mouth to him.

"I want to watch," he says in a thick voice laced with need. He steps out of his jeans and boxer briefs and strips off his shirt, revealing more of his perfect body. He nods toward the head of the bed. "Go on."

I crawl up and situate myself, propped with pillows behind me, my legs partly open. Enzo sits on the bottom half of the bed, his hand already tugging his cock. He picks up the vibrator, turns it to level one, and hands it to me.

I flush from embarrassment but somehow, I'm not uncomfortable when I bring the toy to my nipple. My greedy gaze lands on Enzo as his fist runs up and down his cock languidly like he wants us to take our time.

I trail the vibrator over to my other nipple, the sensation only more intense with Enzo watching. My eyes close briefly and I struggle to watch him because he's growing harder and making noises. I move it down my stomach, teasing myself by slowly putting it between my legs then moving it before I can come.

"Jesus, you're so damn beautiful," he says and his pace increases.

I wouldn't have thought watching him jerk off would turn me on but let me tell you—it is *such* a turn-on.

Our eyes lock and I slide the tip of the vibrator down to my slit, bucking from pleasure. Enzo's eyes hood and he slides up the bed. He grabs my breast, his thumb and forefinger twisting my nipple.

"I tried to just watch, but I gotta touch."

The way he tells me exactly what he's thinking turns up the notch on my impending ecstasy. I arch my back, welcoming him, but the longer the vibrator is on my clit, the closer I am to climaxing.

"I don't want to come before you. Get inside me," I beg.

He stares at my body writhing on the bed. I can't contain the desire flooding every vein in my body.

"Please, Enzo," I say the two words that are his undoing.

His hand leaves my breast, and he rips open the condom from his pants that he abandoned on the floor. He situates himself at my center, holds his dick, and guides it into me. I watch from below, positioning the vibrator on my clit again. Enzo increases the speed two more levels and my walls clench the minute he's fully inside me.

"Fuck," he says, stilling for a moment.

"Oh... Enzo," I say, my hands anchoring to his shoulders as our hips lock the vibrator between our bodies.

"Shit." He keeps swearing, moving in and out of me.

There's no sweetness to the way he's hammering into me, and I don't want whispered words and slow circles. This is the animalistic side of a man who is going to take what he wants. And he wants me. So much he's unable to contain himself.

"You're so wet... and that vibrating." The words mindlessly leave his lips.

Just as I feel the two of us losing control, he looks down at me and that's it. That's all it takes before I explode. Whether it's the smoldering desire laced in his eyes or what I swear is hidden underneath that look, I unravel.

He reaches between us and changes the speed to level one before pumping into me a few more times and coming himself.

Falling on top of me, he kisses my forehead. "Damn, I never thought I'd enjoy this thing." He pulls it out from between us, shuts it off, and places it to the side.

"Aren't you happy I like to share?" My hands slide through his sweaty hair.

"We'll be adding to this collection." His head falls into the crook of my neck and he kisses me. "Let's just fall asleep like this."

I wrap my arms around his neck, holding him.

Yeah, we're in trouble.

CHAPTER TWENTY-NINE

Enzo

"She's going to see us," Carm says, peeking out from behind a fake bush placed in between the bar and restaurant.

"He pulled out her chair, so that's good," Dom says. "Gentlemanly."

I drink my beer, pulling up my email on my phone.

To: Annie Stewart (astewart730@electromail.com)
From: Lorenzo Mancini (enzothelegend@electromail.com)
Subject: Bored

I'm bored and I want to come over. Come being the most important word in that sentence. ;)

I KNOW she's on her computer because she told me, for the first weekend night since we've been together, that we're not meeting tonight. The tampon pitch is next week, and she needs to concentrate. Hence why I'm here with my brothers, spying on Blanca's date with Jake.

I'm usually a convincing guy, but Blanca was suspicious when I told her I had a great coworker to set her up with. She's not stupid. She knows what we're trying to do. But she agreed anyway, which goes to prove that she does want to find someone.

My phone vibrates.

To: Lorenzo Mancini (enzothelegend@electro-mail.com)
From: Annie Stewart (astewart730@electro-mail.com)
Subject: Family time

I thought you were going out with your brothers for some quality time? Don't call me later for a booty call when you're drunk.

I PRESS REPLY.

To: Annie Stewart (astewart730@electromail.com)

From: Lorenzo Mancini (enzothelegend@electromail.com)
Subject: Booty Call Benefits?

If I were a lesser man, I might ask what the point of having a girlfriend is if you can't booty call her. I own that booty! Truth is that I really want to slide into bed with you tonight.

Xo,
Enzo

I PLACE MY PHONE DOWN. Carm is playing peek-a-boo through the bushes, and Dom's ordering food. Does the guy ever let himself get hungry?

To: Lorenzo Mancini (enzothelegend@electromail.com)
From: Annie Stewart (astewart730@electromail.com)
Subject: In that case...

If you own my booty, that means your dick is mine. I'm shocked you used the word girlfriend. How hard was that to type? Should I send the paramedics? BTW - I'm thinking it's not my bed you want to slide into.

I LAUGH.

Dom hands the menu to the waitress, who's practically tongue-tied while waiting on him. "What's so funny? Texting your *assistant*? Don't say I didn't warn you when this all blows up in your face."

I hit Reply, ignoring my brother's advice.

To: Annie Stewart (astewart730@electromail.com)
From: Lorenzo Mancini (enzothelegend@electromail.com)
Subject: My Honey Bun

I'm not even addressing the girlfriend remark.
Which brings up the question... any pet names you want me to call you?
Also, you caught me. What I want is to slide into your honey pot. What's a guy have to do to make that happen?

Dying from blue balls,
Enzo

"SHIT. WE MAY HAVE BEEN SPOTTED." Carm picks up a menu and hides behind it.

Dom stands and leers over the bushes. "They're talking and the waitress just brought over wine."

"Why are we spying? I mean, he's a good guy... I think. Annie endorses him, so he must be." I sip my beer, waiting for her to reply to my last email.

To: Lorenzo Mancini (enzothelegend@electro-mail.com)
From: Annie Stewart (astewart730@electro-mail.com)
Subject: My Shy Guy

Get it? Like when someone calls the fat guy tiny? As far as honey bun… No, but you can dip your finger in my honey pot anytime. Except tonight. :P

Need to finish work,
Your ___________

"PUT THE PHONE DOWN," Dom says.

Carm looks over my shoulder. "You're emailing her? What a waste. Join us in the future where there's sexting. You don't even need complete sentences. An emoji of an eggplant, a peach, and a champagne bottle says it all." Carm smiles, snagging a piece of the complimentary bread while I roll my eyes at him. "Speaking of ancient times, how's that whole permanent hook-up going, Dom?"

I'll be amazed if Dom manages to pull that off without any drama. Annie wanted no part of anything like that, but lately, I feel as if I'm the one who's more attached. Which sucks on nights like this, when she's put the palm out on sleepovers. Not only does it suck, but it's unsettling. It's getting hard to picture my life without Annie in it.

I reply as Dom tells Carm how awesome it still is. He's heading over to her place after she's done clubbing.

You're telling me a regular hook-up is getting more action than I am tonight? I don't think so.

To: Annie Stewart (astewart730@electromail.com)
From: Lorenzo Mancini (enzothelegend@electromail.com)
Subject: Sweet pea, Cuddle muffin, Snuggie woogems

There are some choices. ^^^ Pick one. As for shy guy. Hell no. I don't do that reverse meaning bullshit. Here's a list of suggestions for you to select from: Captain, champ, tiger, stud, hunk, sexy... daddy?

Put me out of my misery,
Enzo

I SET down my phone and sip my beer.

"She doesn't even care. She's the one kicking me out or leaving my place right after. It's literally just sex and it's fucking awesome." I catch the tail end of Dom's description. "No cuddling. No chick flicks. No chick food. It's like a dream, really. That's exactly why that"—he points toward where Jake and Blanca are—"has to work out, because I am not letting Mama force me into some relationship."

I sip my beer and rehash Dom's words. Annie hasn't made me watch a chick flick... or wait, yeah, she did. Somehow lying naked in bed with her while watching Ryan Reynolds pour his heart out isn't that bad though. Chick food? No way. Annie's diet is worse than mine. Oh, but she did that whole bet about who could refrain from fried foods longer the other day. Cuddling? I don't care. I'll take it. Annie's ass cheeks are my cock's favorite place to rest.

"Hello!" Carm waves his hand in front of my face. "Daydreaming about Dom's situation? I know. How do I find myself one of those?"

Dom smiles as if he's Zeus.

"Seriously?" Annie's voice sounds from behind us, so I turn around.

"Hey," I say, my mood improving.

She puts her hands on her hips. "Why are you three here?"

I pick up my phone and realize it's been a while since she sent her last message. I stand and wrap my arm around her waist, my lips going to hers. It's a little unsettling how happy I am to have her here.

She lets me give her a chaste kiss, but when I try to deepen it, she shifts her body toward my brothers.

"Shit. Denied!" Carm calls, and the people at the next table glare at us.

"Well?" she asks with her hip cocked.

This demanding side of Annie is turning me on. So much we might have to make a pit stop in the bathroom before I follow her home like a lost puppy dog.

I pull out my stool, and she sits down.

The waitress narrows her eyes at Annie as she puts Dom's food in front of him. Fried pickles and tilapia with green beans. There's no rhyme or reason to the shit he orders.

"Interesting," she says, staring at his food.

"Don't mind our big brother, he's like an ogre." Carm leans forward on the table.

Dom looks at him like he does right before he's about to put him in a headlock.

"Far from an ogre," Annie says with a chuckle.

Jealousy weighs heavy in my stomach.

Annie holds up her finger to the waitress, who reluctantly stops. "Can I get whatever they're having?"

She nods and walks away.

"Don't take it personally, apparently only Dom gets a smile tonight. She has no personality." Carm flashes his bright white smile.

I knock him with my hand. "Slide over to the other stool."

"No. You go over there."

The only open chair is next to Dom. I'm not sitting next to Dom instead of Annie. He's delusional.

"Go." I nudge again.

"No... unless." A gleam lights up his eyes before he holds his fist to his palm. "Play for it?"

"I'm not playing rock, paper, scissors to sit next to my girlfriend."

The table quiets and Dom and Carm stare at me.

"Girlfriend?" Carm asks Annie more than me.

"I know, and he didn't even choke the word out." Annie pats me on the back like a proud parent.

"Well, on this special occasion, I'm going to give you a pass at losing," Carm says as he moves next to Dom.

I slide my stool as close to Annie as I can.

"So tell us about this little revelation?" Dom motions between Annie and me.

I shake my head. This isn't a conversation to have in front of Annie. These two won't understand it. Hell, Carm is jealous because Dom gets to have sex with a girl who throws him out a minute after he comes.

"How did you know we were here?" I change the subject.

"Jake texted me. Do you know how nervous you three are making him?"

"He's not sixteen," Dom says.

"You're her brothers. He can't be himself with you watching his every move."

The waitress slides Annie's beer onto the table without a smile or a word to any of us.

"She's friendly," Annie murmurs but directs her attention back to us. "How would you feel if the roles were reversed?"

Dom wipes his mouth and hands, staring at her for a moment, then me, then back to her. I want to tell him to bite his tongue before he opens his mouth.

"Well, we don't have to worry about that because you're his girlfriend now. You can come to Sunday dinner and we're all off the hook."

I slide my finger across my throat. Annie will not be coming to dinner for a long time. Ma would get her hopes up and I'm already struggling to figure all this out.

"Um..." Annie looks at me with wide eyes.

I really hope I'm not about to piss her off when I say what I'm about to. "Annie's not coming to Sunday dinner yet."

Her lips tip down for a moment, but she nods in agreement.

Carm leans back with his beer as though he's enjoying the show.

"Why not?" Dom asks.

"Mind your own fucking business," I say.

He picks up his fork and digs into his tilapia. "It was just a question."

"And you know what Ma says, Enzo. 'Don't be impolite. Answer the questions that are asked of you.'" Carm imitates our ma with a high-pitched voice.

"You know what? You assholes can stay here and spy on Blanca. We're leaving."

"Oh, don't be such a sour puss," Dom says. "Let's all play to see if Annie comes to Sunday dinner."

He and Carm put their fists on their palms.

"Grow the fuck up," I say.

"Do I get to play?" Annie props her fist on her palm, already ready whether they say yes or no.

"Then it's going to end up in a tie...." Carm chimes in with a polite answer meaning no.

"I'll play for us. Since we're a duo now." She smirks.

My dick twitches at her sarcasm. I'm not usually a guy who likes a woman to fight his wars, but this is damn sexy. She can bet that we're leaving after this showdown and I *will* be spending the night.

Dom and Carm look at one another as if there are rules and silently asking if the other one is okay with it.

"This isn't the Super Bowl, dipshits," I say.

"Fine," Dom says.

Carm blows out a breath.

"I win, and I don't have to go to Sunday dinner. I lose, and I'm there." Annie's confidence is inspiring, but my gut churns.

I'm not in control. Annie might not understand how important this is. I'll recite the word girlfriend a million times, but Sunday dinner? Nope.

"One," Dom says.

"Two," Carm says.

"Three," Annie says, and I almost close my eyes.

Dom shoots paper.

Carm shoots paper.

I look at Annie, peeking through one eye.

Annie shoots scissors.

She uses her two fingers to chomp at Dom and Carm's hands. They look at her as if she's an alien.

I laugh. "Suckers!" I slide the bar stool from the table. "We're out."

Dom and Carm stare at one another as if they were hustled, shaking their heads.

"Nice seeing you guys." Annie waves. "Better luck next time."

Her cocky arrogance diminishes the last of my willpower.

"I'm not even going to make it to your apartment," I say into her ear from behind while we walk toward the exit.

"I figured." She stops at the hostess table, and the woman there lifts a bag from behind the counter. "I packed a bag."

I smash my lips to hers and force her to walk backward all the way out the doors to the street. "You're amazing."

"I know, but you can say it again." She giggles and I open a cab door for her.

I'd follow that sound to my grave.

Fuck, I'm in… deep.

How the hell did that happen?

CHAPTER THIRTY

Annie

"I'm so nervous." I pace Enzo's office.

"You'll do great. I love the campaign." He leans back at his desk, his fingers steepled in front of him.

"You know nothing about tampons."

"I like the direct approach you took. It's honest, which is different than anything out there right now."

"Different isn't always good." I fall back onto his couch, picking up my notes and sketch pad. Enzo gave me little direction on the campaign, letting me carry it through all the way to the end.

He rounds his desk before sitting next to me. His hand lands on my knee. I pick it up and move it back to his side.

"We're at the office," I remind him.

Not that I hold it against him. It's hard not to cross the line when outside of this building, we're constantly touching and kissing. I'm actually impressed with us, but I don't think Mr. Jacobson is going to grade on a curve for our willpower if we're caught.

"Remember when I told you no excuses months ago?"

I nod.

"You're going to go in that room with your shoulders back, head high like this is the best idea and you are the ass they need to kiss for delivering it to them." He taps my sketchpad. "This is a great campaign. I can't relate, but that's okay, because it will speak to women. The testing group raved about the approach and laughed at the truthfulness of it."

"But Coddle has wanted heartfelt for all their other products."

He picks up the sketchbook, puts it on the table, and grabs my hands, squeezing harder when I try to retract them. "Relax. There's nothing heartwarming about a woman sticking cotton up her vagina." He tips his forehead to mine. "It's a fact of life."

I nod. He's right. Why can't I have an ounce of his arrogance?

"Listen, if it makes you feel better, I threw up before my first pitch. Twice." He holds up his fingers. "But you've got me, and I'm your biggest cheerleader. I'll be there, and if that doubt creeps in, look at me and think, he's the most talented guy in the world, he's a legend in advertising, and he thinks it's a knock-out-of-the-park pitch."

I laugh, wanting to be in his arms.

As though he reads my mind, he stands. "I have to go to the bathroom." He walks into his small bathroom and leaves the door ajar.

I look out his door like an idiot. Everyone is busy on their computers. Following him, I shut the door behind me, and he opens his arms. I step into his embrace and feel all his words of encouragement in the strength of his shoulders and arms.

He rubs my back and kisses the top of my head. "You're going to do great. I promise. You were made for this."

I nod into his shirt, drawing back before I leave a makeup stain. "You want to hear something funny? Well, not funny, but..."

"If it means getting your mind off the campaign, I'm all ears."

"My first day at work here, I walked into the bathroom and you were in there."

He laughs and kisses my forehead. "I know."

"You know? Why didn't you say anything?"

He uses his body to cage me against the wall. "It's not every day a gorgeous girl follows me into the bathroom and stares like she's going to watch me pee. You remember that sort of thing." His hands rub my hips.

"Why not say anything before now?"

"I'm sure it was embarrassing, and you've come so far from that girl who didn't know what to say."

My head falls to his chest, and he kisses the top of my head again.

"You didn't even know my name before I started working with you."

"I knew you though. What can I say? I should pay more attention to details, but my mind has been on the partnership since I was hired here. It's like a tunnel from the elevator to my office. But just because I didn't know your name doesn't mean I didn't notice you." He puts his finger under my chin and raises my head so my eyes meet his.

I smile. The man could sell hay to a farmer, but I'll take it because today I need every piece of self-confidence.

He checks his watch. "It's showtime."

I inhale deeply and nod.

He opens the door, squeezing my hand one last time before I have to act as if I haven't been falling for him for weeks.

A HALF HOUR LATER, we're all seated around the table —Blair and Mr. Peterson sitting closest to me, and Mr. Jacobson and Enzo at the end of the table with Billy to their left. Mr. Jacobson leans over and says something to Enzo, whose jaw clenches for a moment before he smiles. He sits up straighter and his smile only widens when he catches me watching.

"I want to thank you again for joining us today. When it came to your sanitary products, the approach you've taken so far has been the one most companies in your industry take. 'Look, no leaks!' Ignoring the realities of what it's like to have your period. Even if a woman feels totally confident she's not going to have an embarrassing leak, she still doesn't want to go out riding her bike, or dancing the night away, or any one of the hundreds of activities I've seen women do while wearing white pants in commercials over the years.

"Just the word period can make a man uncomfortable. So why would you want to bring that word into an ad campaign? I think there's a way to get across what's happening—at least to the gender using the sanitary products. Women. When I show you this campaign, I don't want you to think how you're feeling about it, but how a woman would feel. Obviously, Blair, you're good."

Blair laughs and smiles, hopefully meaning she's receptive to changing their approach.

"I'll show you the tape, then I'll talk about the case study and answer any questions you have."

Enzo stands and turns off the lights, and I smile at him in appreciation. He winks and my already-anxious stomach flips.

The ad plays. A woman is on screen in a cycling class, working out vigorously, sweating and panting. A man walks in the room and talks about having your period and how nothing can stop a woman. The camera slowly moves to show another woman barely moving the pedals, hunched over her machine.

From there, the ad continues, showing a woman getting ready to go dancing in a short white skirt and tank top, running out of her house to a car full of her friends. The scene flips to another girl lying on the couch in oversized black sweatpants and a sweatshirt with a bowl of ice cream in her lap, yelling at her significant other to grab the heating pad.

A scene of a woman dining in a five-star restaurant with a hot guy morphs to one of a woman sorting through her laundry and tossing a couple pairs of panties in the garbage.

As the ad draws to a close, a slogan lands on the page. "We're there for you when your life is on pause for three to seven days."

Enzo, being a champ, turns the lights back on slowly. Billy pats himself on the back for a job well done, which eases the pressure of wondering about Blair's thoughts.

I pick up the handout to talk about the case study, but Blair doesn't turn the page.

"It's chancy," she says.

I nod. "It is."

I glance at Enzo, who beams and nods, silently acknowledging that it's going well.

"But I like it. I can relate, and I'm sure most women can too," Blair says.

"If you look at the study, you'd be surprised how many women enjoyed the realism."

She shakes her head. "I don't need to see any of that. I go with my gut and I love it. Dad?"

Our heads all turn toward Mr. Peterson.

"I doubt your dad has an opinion on what is clearly a woman thing," Mr. Jacobson says.

Blair glances at me as though she's waiting to judge my reaction to my boss.

I smile, masking my distaste. I'm sure Mr. Peterson does have an opinion.

"I've seen a period take down my wife more than once. If you think period is a bad word, try menopause. If I could have traded places with my poor wife, I would have."

Blair touches her dad's hand with a smile.

"I love it. It's chancy, but I like playing the odds and being different once in a while. Great job, Annie." He puts out his hand, and I shake it.

Relief drains all the tension out of my body.

Mr. Jacobson stands. "Good job, Enzo and Annie."

Enzo cocks his head at Mr. Jacobson. "It was all Annie."

Blair's head turns from Enzo to me, and a mask of clarity falls over her features.

"I know she had to do the heavy lifting, but don't think I don't know that you guided her along." Mr. Jacobson slaps Enzo's back, and Enzo's mouth is ajar, but no words come out. "Let's go to lunch and celebrate."

"Actually, we have to catch a plane back to Texas. We have a tournament to get to." Blair catches her dad's eye, and they smile.

"Yeah, my granddaughter told me she's going to hit a

home run for me tonight." Mr. Peterson winks at me, and I smile.

Mr. Jacobson lingers by the door. "She plays softball?"

"Yeah."

"That's cute when they dress like baseball players in pink."

Blair's eyes cut to her dad's. I'm pretty sure smoke is blowing out of his ears.

"Actually, they wipe the field with the baseball players, and they wear black," Mr. Peterson says.

Enzo is surprisingly quiet. I'd expect him to be interjecting and playing nice.

"Of course there're good softball teams, but there isn't really a future for them."

I desperately want to tell Mr. Jacobson to leave. He's going to be the one to ruin this account for us. Can the man not read a room?

"With all due respect, many baseball players don't have a future either," Blair chimes in. "And if we wanted to go into reasons why women's sports aren't as big as men's, we could be here all day."

"I didn't mean any offense. Guess I'm just old school."

I look blankly at Enzo, and he closes his eyes. This is getting worse.

"Annie, is there any way you can show me the sketches you did for this before we leave? I want to make sure I see your complete vision."

"Um... sure... I'll be right back." I step forward to slip out.

Enzo shoots me a look to say he knows what Blair wants and it's not the sketches.

Blair follows me out. "I'll just go with you. Save us some time."

"They're in Enzo's office," I say and try not to slow my footsteps, but when we reach his office, I have no choice but to stop and let her catch up.

She follows me in and shuts the door. "Annie, you gotta see the writing on the wall here. That campaign is brilliant, and I know Enzo Mancini had no part of it. That was written and directed by a female."

I nod.

"You heard Mr. Jacobson's sexist remarks. You have to jump ship. And I'm hoping you jump to mine."

I sit on the couch, picking up the sketchbook, but I know she doesn't want it. "I told you, I can't."

"Because you and Enzo are screwing around?"

My head whips in her direction. "What? No."

She sits next to me, clasping her hands in her lap. "I saw the looks between the two of you. They weren't of the way-to-go-coworker variety. They were the you-rock-the-bedroom-and-the-boardroom type. I'm not judging you."

Sure feels like she is.

"I'm merely suggesting the Enzo is directly under Mr. Jacobson, so he knows what kind of man he is and yet he's willing to work for him. What does that say? I promise if you stay here, you're going nowhere."

I blow out a breath.

"Your talent will be wasted, and you'll never thrive if you stay here."

I want to bury my head in my hands and admit defeat.

She pats my leg like a mom would and stands. "Just think about it. But I can tell you one thing, I'm not letting a man like Mr. Jacobson profit from our company forever."

"Blair..." I sigh.

She turns around, her hand on the door handle. "Don't worry, it wouldn't be immediate. Please, this is your future.

Think hard about it." She raises her eyebrows and opens the door, where Enzo's already waiting to come in.

"Blair," he says and nods.

"Enzo."

After she leaves, he walks in and shuts the door. "Should I even guess?"

"We both know she wasn't here for the sketches." I bite my lower lip.

Is Blair right? Am I going to end up with nothing at the end of all this?

CHAPTER THIRTY-ONE

Enzo

It's been three weeks since Annie secured the tampon deal from Coddle. Surprisingly, Mr. Jacobson did promote her to junior ad exec, which makes me feel a hell of a lot better that she won't be moving halfway across the country. Though they haven't found a replacement to act as my assistant yet.

"Don't you find it funny that not one interviewee has come in? They could get you a temp if they wanted," Annie says to me while I'm in the bathroom.

I'm thankful I'm not in front of her because my face would give away what I think is happening—they're purposely dragging their feet. "Did you ask Shelby?"

She blows out a breath so loudly, I hear her over the running water. "Yeah, and she says they're trying, but your assistant needs certain qualifications."

I walk back into my bedroom, reluctant to join her.

After the way Mr. Jacobson acted in front of the Petersons, I'm surprised we still hold the account. I can't help but think there must have been signs of his sexist line of thinking before now. Did I just never notice?

"I am hard to please." I fall into bed next to her.

Lazy Sundays with the two of us in bed until noon are fast becoming my favorite thing. I can't believe this is what I tried for so many years to avoid.

"I should get going so you can go to dinner." She picks up her sketchpad and slides her legs over the edge of the bed.

"I canceled. Said I was sick." I snag her waist and pull her toward me, quickly shifting her so she's straddling me. I kiss her neck while my hands slide up the hem of her tank top. "I love when you're not wearing a bra."

Her arms wrap around my head and her fingers play with the hair at the back of my head. Seriously, I was an idiot. This is so much better than lounging around by myself on Sunday until dinner.

"You'd keep me naked all day if you could."

I look at her and latch on to a nipple. "You know me so well," I say against her skin before pulling the fabric over her head.

"We really need to talk about this condom ad, and I think you should go to your family dinner. What will your mom think?" The way her back is arching says she won't need any convincing to stay where she is.

"First of all, let's try the condoms out. You know, so we're better able to write a campaign. Second, my mom thinks I'm sick in bed." I flip her over and she squeals.

"You're going to fall off that favorite son list you like to brag about."

I laugh and busy myself with pulling her shorts down

her long, thin legs. Her excuses fall away with a moan as I kiss my way up between her legs.

"It's my turn," she says, sliding up on the bed and away from my mouth.

"You're denying me a taste?"

She giggles, her hand cupping the bulge in my pajama pants. "You've had a lot of tastes. I'm simply taking my turn."

Her palm applies just the right amount of pressure over the thin material. Her eyes are on me while her tongue slides along her lips. I leave one hand behind my head, propping me up enough to watch her, while my dick twitches as she pulls down the front of my pants. Like a spring, my cock pops out.

She wraps her hand around the base and twists up and down, her bare tits running along my balls. Watching this woman tease me is pure ecstasy—she's amazing and beautiful and intelligent and everything I didn't know I wanted.

Sure, I've had women who want to please, but Annie's eyes seduce me. She's searching for the telltale signs that I'm enjoying it, doing everything she's mentally cataloged over our months together to pull out the reaction she wants.

Like when her tongue first touches the tip of my dick and I squirm.

Or when she slides her tongue around the top like an ice cream cone and my fingers thread through her hair, gripping the strands, anticipating the moment when she deep throats me.

The way she stops blowing me, teasing me while she runs her tits over my dick, her hands sliding across my stomach.

And like now, when she's found the perfect rhythm and she peeks up to make sure I'm looking at her. I wind her long hair around my fist, securing it out of the way so I have the perfect view of her bobbing up and down my cock.

I swear every blow job before Annie was an act of obligation, but with Annie, I don't lie back and let her blow me. I'm already imagining the ways to return the pleasure.

Watching my cock fall in and out of her mouth, I don't direct her. She sets the pace. She fondles my balls when they tighten and the tip of my cock hits the back of her throat, and it's game over for me.

"I'm coming, baby," I say before biting my bottom lip.

Like always, she doesn't move, and I fill her mouth.

She rises up my body and I kiss her, tasting myself, and turn her over, my dick already perking back up. I grip her tits while I cast open-mouth kisses along her flesh. She wiggles, getting comfortable on the bed, her legs already preparing to go over my shoulders when a knock sounds on my door.

"Ignore it," I mutter.

Since I have a doorman, I have no idea who it could be.

"Enzo," she says, sliding up the bed.

The knock sounds again. And again.

"There's something wrong," she says, hopping off the bed and grabbing her clothes.

"Ugh." I rise from the bed, grab my pajama pants, and step into them. "Jesus, hold on," I holler.

The knocking doesn't stop, and I pull the door open without looking through the peephole.

Carm barrels in. "Fuck, answer your phone." He bends at the waist, heaving for breath. "I'm not made to run up that many stairs. Your elevator was taking too long. You owe me for this, fucker." He pants and points at me.

"For what, and why aren't you at Ma's?"

Annie stands in the entrance of the hallway.

"Hey, Annie," he says, still bent over and gasping.

"I think you should actually use the treadmill instead of picking up girls at the gym," I say, shutting the door.

"Hi, Carmelo. I'll be back." She disappears down the hall.

Which I'm happy about since her tits with no bra were there for Carm to admire.

"Nice ass," he says.

I roll my eyes. "If you weren't my brother, I'd beat the shit out of you."

"I'm not sure how you expect me to not notice. Just because she's yours doesn't mean she's not fucking hot. It's unnatural not to notice a hot woman. Just take that she-devil for-sale-by-owner chick. She's hot. I beat off to her last night. But I fucking hate her. You can't explain attraction."

I roll my eyes again. "Why are you here interrupting my Sunday again?"

A smirk I'm too familiar with wraps around his face as though he's a millisecond from cracking up. "Sunday dinner is happening here." He smacks my back like *way to go*.

See what happens when you miss too many Sunday dinners?

"What?"

"Yep, I sprinted over here to give you a heads-up, but Ma is going to be knocking on that door in..." He waits a second and a knock happens at the door as if we're in some television show. "Well, now." That shit-eating grin mars his face again.

"But I have Annie here."

He laughs. "I noticed. But hey, I tried to warn you. Which you've yet to thank me for."

Annie comes back out in a sweatshirt. My sweatshirt. My NYU sweatshirt. Damn if I don't love seeing her in my clothes, but I do not need my parents seeing her in my clothes.

I glance at Carm. A knock sounds on the door again.

"Who else is here? You better answer it." Annie sits on the couch, pulling a blanket over her lap.

I love that she's comfortable with my brother, but damn, I don't know how she's going to feel around everyone else. I can't very well kick her out to avoid having her meet the rest of my family.

"Annie..." I approach her, but the knock sounds once more.

"Enzo, get the door." She turns her attention to Carm. "Why were you knocking like there was a fire?"

Carm laughs. Like bent over in a fit of laughter laughs. I can't blame him. If roles were reversed, I'd be doing the exact same thing.

"I need you to go into my bedroom."

"Why?" she asks.

I should have known she wouldn't just take my direction without arguing. "Because my ma is on the other side of that door."

Her face pales and she flings the blanket off her lap. "What? Tell me you have a fire escape."

Carm sits on the couch, putting his feet up on my coffee table and resting his hands behind his head. "This is so fun to watch."

"No, you're coming to Sunday dinner, and I'm fairly sure you don't want to meet Ma in my old sweatshirt and a pair of pajama shorts."

"Ugh. You couldn't have called?" she says to Carm.

He holds up his hands. "I tried. You two were obviously too busy fucking. Next time, answer your phone."

She narrows her eyes and runs down the hall.

Another knock.

I blow out a breath and head to the door.

"That was ridiculously long. Were you sleeping?" Ma asks. I take the tray of food from her, and she touches my forehead. "No fever."

"No."

I put the tray in my kitchen, and Ma spots Carm on the couch. "Carmelo Mancini, I know you are not sitting there while your poor father is trying to bring up five trays of food." She thumbs toward the door, and he jumps from his seat.

"I might as well just give up my gym membership," he mumbles as he passes by.

"Now you, go put a shirt on. You'll catch a cold."

I look down. Shit. I'm a mess, and I can't believe Ma can't tell what I've been up to all morning. "Yeah, well..."

I debate in my head if I should come clean now or just surprise her with Annie. I could ask Annie to stay in my bedroom, but Ma tends to clean my condo when she comes, which means she'll end up in that room at some point. I have no choice but to tell her about Annie.

"Now, don't go getting your hopes up, okay? I don't want to hear anything about marriage or babies or love coming out of your mouth."

She takes the silver top off the tray of bread. "What are you rambling on about?"

"I have a woman here."

Her eyes light up and she flings her arms around my body. "Who? What's her name? Do I know her?"

So much for not overreacting. "No. You don't know her, but did you hear me, Ma? No marriage and baby talk."

She smacks my chest. "I won't embarrass you. Is it serious?" She leans closer to me. "Is she Italian?"

I don't even know, but I'm going to go with no, Annie is not Italian. "Please stop. I'm not even sure she's going to want to come out of my bedroom."

She ties her apron around her middle and smiles at me. "I'll go make her welcome."

She turns, but I guide her back to the kitchen. "No. You're not going in there."

"Are you ashamed of me? Is that why you won't bring her to Sunday dinner?"

I run my fingers through my hair. "I didn't bring her because we're not there yet."

"Have you met her family?"

I hadn't anticipated that question. Shit. "Yeah, but it was under different circumstances."

Her face falls, and she turns her back to me, opening cabinets, searching for something.

"Ma..."

"You're embarrassed of us. I get that we have accents and sometimes we might not know a word here or there, but we are your parents. Have your brothers met her?"

Damn it.

"Only because they came to the office," I say, without thinking. Now she'll realize I work with her.

"So it's not serious, but you've met her family and she's met your brothers. What about Blanca?"

Thank God Annie hasn't met my sister in person. "No, not Blanca."

"I don't understand. Why are you hiding her?"

I blow out a breath, really wishing Carm and my dad would hurry the hell up here. I need a distraction. "I'm not hiding her. It's just you want us all to get married and you know I don't bring women home."

"I know. And just so you know, I would never force you to marry someone before you were ready."

I nod, although her recent depression is like a guilt trip for all her kids. Does she not realize that? "You're going to meet her today, but just don't get any hopes. She's just a woman I'm dating."

"Fine." Her voice is curt, and my shoulders sag.

How did today go from a blissful orgasm-filled Sunday to 'strap me to the train tracks because I'm about to be railroaded'?

CHAPTER THIRTY-TWO

Annie

I'm in Enzo's shower, scrubbing the sex smell off me when he steps in behind me, wraps his arms around my waist, and kisses my shoulder. I scream and jump, but he holds me firm.

"Unless the condo is empty, you better get out of this shower right now."

He laughs. "I have to get clean too."

I circle in his arms, but he kisses me so hard, my back presses to the tiled wall. His tongue slides into my mouth, and for a moment, everything outside of the steam-filled shower disappears. But the fear of his family being out in the living room soon surfaces as his hand lands between my legs, opening my thighs.

I push him back. "You're crazy. You stay there. I'm going to finish rinsing my body, then you can have the shower to yourself."

He laughs.

How can he laugh? I'm sure he doesn't want me to meet his family. It seems like a big step for him. One he's not ready for.

"What's the plan? Am I staying holed up in the bedroom or are you sneaking me out?"

He sits on the ledge of the shower, staring at me with those flirtatious eyes. "You're meeting the family."

My stomach drops. "No, I'm not."

"Well, it's only Ma and Pa and Blanca. You know Dom and Carm already. Since it's here, you don't have to worry about meeting any aunts and uncles."

"Yippee?"

"I get that neither of us planned for this, but here we are. Let's just roll with it."

I rinse off and step out, purposely keeping my back to him. Mostly because I might throw up at any minute. Meet his parents? When it wasn't like he wanted me to meet them, it's a forced meeting and Enzo had no choice?

I pull my hair back into a bun then open my cosmetic bag to apply my makeup. "So they're, like, outside the door?"

"Yep."

"And you're showering, why? Shouldn't you be out there entertaining them?"

Through his clear glass shower door, I see suds falling out of his hair, down his sculpted body, and to the floor of the shower.

"My mom knows my kitchen, and my brothers and dad will watch the game. Dom and Blanca probably won't be here for a bit anyway."

My hand falls to my stomach with the thought of being

here all day. I hoist myself onto the countertop and apply my foundation. "I feel like I should go."

The water turns off, and he stands in the shower, water dripping down his body. I follow one droplet as it falls through the ripples of his abs. Damn, sometimes I still can't believe I get to have sex with this man whenever I want.

"Too late for you to go."

"I could say a quick hello, stay for a half hour, and say I have somewhere to be." I continue distracting myself with my makeup routine.

"Ma isn't going to let you go. We have no choice but to face this."

I stare at him through the mirror. He's busy drying himself off and tying the towel around his waist.

"Are you okay with this?" I ask the question I really want an answer to.

He shrugs, unhooking the towel that's wrapped around my chest. "There you go. I like you better naked."

I grab the towel, feeling modest due to the fact that his parents are only twenty feet away. "Answer my question."

He grabs his toothbrush and brushes his teeth, staring at me until he speaks around his toothbrush. "It's fine. Not something I thought either of us was ready for, but whatever, it's fine."

Fine. The word people use when they really mean it's not, but they have no choice. That's what fine means.

He spits and I finish doing my makeup before jumping down from the counter to get dressed. It's going to be a ponytail day. Hopefully Mama Mancini doesn't judge me too much.

Enzo follows me into his bedroom. The television from the living room is blaring so loudly, I can almost hear the commentators of the baseball game.

"My dad's preferred volume," Enzo says, putting on a fresh pair of boxer briefs before stepping into athletic pants.

I shrug on my own panties and jeans. "Great. What about the condom ad?"

He's been taking the lead on it, but I offered a few suggestions he said we'd talk over today. I can't help but think he believes he knows more about condoms than I do. Just because he's used them on hundreds of women doesn't mean he knows how to sell them better than me.

Okay, I don't want to think about how many women he's used them on.

"Tonight." He throws on a shirt and walks over to kiss me. "The pitch is in two weeks. We have time."

"Not if we don't want to act out a skit again."

He laughs. "That was fun, but we'll meet with Billy tomorrow to discuss."

He sits on the edge of his messed-up bed. The sheets are wrinkled, the comforter a mess in the middle.

After throwing on a V-neck T-shirt that's plain and boring, I stare at myself in his dresser mirror. This sucks. Here I am looking like an over-age college student, and I have to meet his parents for the first time.

"Come sit on Daddy," he says.

"Ew... I'm not joking, stop with that."

He laughs again, patting his leg.

I sit on his leg and wrap my arms around his neck. "What's up, shy guy?"

He narrows his eyes, his fingers finding the bare patch of skin between the waist of my jeans and my shirt. His finger trails a path across my skin, igniting a rupture of goose bumps. "We talked about that."

"And we talked about daddy."

"Touché."

"We need to get out there. Carm's probably telling my mom we're having sex."

"Probably."

"Before we do, I want you to know something... this might not have been what I was expecting today, but you're important to me, Annie, and in a way, I'm happy to introduce you to my family. So don't try to leave or run away." He waits for me to say something.

"Okay," I say softly.

"Plus, this is just like a long intermission for our Sunday fun day." He gets me on my back, and his body covers mine. "You look gorgeous."

His mouth descends on mine, and for a few moments, I'm lost in Hurricane Enzo.

He gets up, holds out his hand for me, and pulls me up off the bed. I follow him as he opens the door.

Carm is sitting on the couch, no shoes on, legs crossed on the coffee table. A smirk lands on his face as soon as we enter from the hallway. His dad is concentrating on the television, so I'm not sure he sees us. If I wanted to know where the boys got their height, it's their dad. He's an older version of them with a more weathered look. I figure it's from working with his hands more than his sons ever will.

Enzo's hand wraps around mine. "Ma. Pa. This is Annie Stewart. This is my ma Anna and my dad Giuseppe."

He fails to say girlfriend, and I wonder what that means, if anything.

His mom turns around in the kitchen, places down a ladle, and wipes her hands on her apron while walking over to us. I have about three inches on her, so when she hugs me, her face smashes in between my breasts.

Oh joy.

IT'S easy to see the dynamic in this household. Enzo joined Carm and his dad on the couch minutes after my introduction. I guess I should've assumed Enzo is a sports nut since every time I turn on his television, it's on ESPN.

His mom works in the kitchen, shifting her attention between boiling pots and chopping and mixing. This is ridiculous. Please tell me they aren't all going to sit in there until she says dinner is ready?

"Would you like some help?" I ask, peeking over the breakfast bar since I don't want to intrude on her obvious routine.

She looks up, smiles, and waves me in. "You can be in charge of salad."

She places the knife in my hand and my other hand on the lettuce, showing me how to cut it. Oh man, this is her entire gig. Those men *are* going to sit on those couches the entire day.

She stirs a few sauces then watches me. Maybe I shouldn't have offered. "So, Annie, how old are you?"

"Twenty-seven."

"Did you graduate college?"

"I did."

She pats me on the back in a 'good job' gesture. "You like my Enzo?"

I look over toward the couch. He's laughing with Carm, his smile infectious. With his long legs stretched out in front of him, he's relaxed with a pop in his hand. He's sexy, that's for sure. But there's so much more to him, and although I'm kind of pissed he lets his mom make a family dinner all by herself, that doesn't change the rush I get when he enters a room. I've known for a few weeks that I'm falling. Even after convincing myself that this relationship is going to go nowhere, I've lost control. I've even suspended the one-night-a-week rule.

"I do," I say with a smile.

She runs her hand down my upper arm a few times, clearly happy with my answer. "He's a good man. An honest man. I know all my boys love their bachelor life, but once they get a taste of a woman who can take care of them, they'll change."

I smile again, not wanting to upset her.

A knock lands on the door, and she leaves to answer it. God forbid Enzo gets up. He doesn't even look to see who it is.

In barrels Dom and a cute brunette, razzing him about something. Blanca. I recognize her from her date with Jake. Dom stops in his tracks when he sees me in the kitchen, then glances at Enzo. Blanca hugs her mom hello, smirking when she sees me over her mom's shoulder.

"Well, I haven't met you, but I'm pretty sure I know who you are." Blanca sits across from me on the breakfast bar stool, putting her elbow on the counter and leaning her chin on her palm. "Annie?"

"Blanca?"

"Nice to meet you," we say in unison then laugh.

"I'll be right back," she says, sliding off the stool. She moves over to her dad and kisses the top of his head. Then she stands in front of the television and points at Carm, Enzo, and Dom. "Idiot, idiot, idiot. Trying to marry me off." She rounds the back of the couch, her hand slapping the back of each of their heads.

I love her already.

She puts on an apron from a box Anna, Enzo's mom, brought in, secures it around her waist, and gets to work. As

I finish the salad, Mama Mancini layers a lasagna and Blanca boils the pasta.

"Is this the way it is all the time?" I ask. "Them on the couch and you two working in the kitchen?"

Blanca glances at her mom and nods. I'm not sure if it's a sensitive subject or not and I don't want to overstep on my first dinner, but I think Blanca and I are on the same page.

Having some time while the lasagna cooks, Blanca and I find ourselves at the kitchen table with a glass of wine.

"Tell me about Jake? What did you think?"

"Shh." She places her finger to her lips, eyeing her mom.

"Oh, sorry," I say.

"He's nice," she says in a low voice.

I know what that means. I decide to drop it since I don't want to put her in a bad position.

It's like the boys have a radar that we're all done preparing the food—either that or the game is over—because all three of her brothers come over and sit down with us. Enzo's hand lands on my thigh and I slide it away only to have him laugh and try again.

The man is incorrigible.

CHAPTER THIRTY-THREE

Enzo

When I introduced Annie to my parents, it went pretty much how I thought it would. Ma hugged her and my dad shook her hand. Dad went back to watching the game and my ma went to work in the kitchen. I expected more of an inquisition from my ma to be honest.

"So you're at the family dinner?" Dom says, leaning back in his chair, sipping his beer. His shit-eating grin annoys the crap out of me. "Carm, this deserved a phone call. Please tell me you took a picture when you told him Ma was coming."

"You're out of luck," I say.

"I, for one, think it's great. Consider yourself lucky I didn't follow you two on your first date." Dom laughs.

I glance at Annie and she looks back at me. Well... shit.

"What are those looks for?" Blanca asks.

"Nothing," I respond.

But Carm's a smart guy and clues in immediately. "If I didn't know better, I'd say they just realized they've never been on a date."

"We go out." I'm hoping I'm not the only one between the two of us who just figured it out.

"Work keeps us busy," Annie says, but her eyes are cast down.

Dom chuckles then clears his throat when I shoot him the death glare.

"Work can be crazy. Let's talk about the redheaded she-devil. She's insane. Did I tell you what she did?" Carm, being an expert on changing topics in the middle of a conversation, directs the conversation toward him.

"I think you like her," Blanca says then looks at Annie. "Carm's a real estate agent."

"Broker," he corrects.

She smiles sweetly as if she's humoring him. "Sorry. Broker."

"Yeah, I've seen the billboards."

I can tell that Annie's trying not to laugh.

Carm smacks the table. "Yes! And what did you think? Did it make you want to buy or sell with me?"

Annie laughs and the tension of us not really having been on a date dissipates. Carm's my favorite brother today.

"Not really. It made me want to get laid though," she said.

I stare blankly at her then cover my heart and fall back into the chair.

"I'm just speaking the truth." She places her hand on my thigh and leans forward, her tits pressing against my arm. "It means that some brilliant advertising guy came up with the campaign."

I slide my hand to the back of her neck. Those bedroom

eyes she's giving me unglue any reserve I have about kissing her in front of everyone. I pull her mouth to mine, but she turns and my lips land on her cheek at the last second.

"Oh, so sweet," Ma coos from behind us.

That straightens me out pretty quickly. Dom almost spits out his beer.

"Back to the redheaded she-devil." Carm pulls the conversation back his way.

"Yeah, back to my point," Blanca says. "That woman doesn't have to be half naked to get clients, so Carm's jealous of her, but we all know he's just pissed because she's giving his usual flirty advances the cold shoulder. Of course she's public enemy number one." Blanca puts her hand on her brother's arm and rubs. "It's okay, there're other fish in the sea." She says it as though she's talking to a baby, and the entire table laughs.

Annie looks at Blanca as if she's in love with her and not me. "Hate sex is probably pretty good."

"Annie?" my ma calls from the kitchen. "Can you help me in here?"

Blanca moves to stand and shoo Annie down, but Ma must give her a look because she sits back down. "You're being called, lucky lady."

Annie leaves, and I hate that I miss her. It's ridiculous. She's literally fifteen feet from me.

Blanca sets her gaze on me. "I think it's bachelor game over for someone."

Carm and Dom lean in.

I shake my head. "I don't think so."

"Please, you're canceling Sunday dinners for her. I called it the first time I saw them together." Dom puts his hands up as if it's no contest who the winner is.

Carm tilts his head. "The problem is, will he admit it?"

"You guys are a bunch of dipshits." I head to the kitchen to grab a beer and throw away my empty one.

Mom is teaching Annie how to roll a meatball.

"She's really good with her hands, Ma," I say with a wink.

Annie's eyes narrow and Ma shakes her head, understanding the sexual innuendo.

Who's teaching her that crap?

Watching Annie in my world is an eye-opener, because I always thought I'd never want to introduce anyone to my family. But with Annie, it's the opposite. I kind of like her everywhere in my world.

"HOW DOES your mom have the energy for that?" Annie lies down on the opposite side of the couch from me. "I mean, prepping, cooking, cleaning. She must sleep for three days straight afterward."

"She likes to take care of us," I say.

Annie bolts up to her knees and stares at me.

"What?"

She points at me. "You boys need to help her."

I put up my hands. "Her and Blanca do it. I'm not messing with tradition."

"You're going to help her next Sunday."

I grab her finger and pull her down to me. "Only if you come. Wanna see my childhood home?"

She stares into my eyes and places her hand on my cheek. "Are you sure about that, bachelor boy?"

"Completely." I pull her in for a kiss.

The kiss grows out of control, and soon she's straddling

me and grinding along my growing bulge. I'm never going to get enough of this woman.

When my hands slide up her stomach, she jumps off me. "Condom campaign."

I groan. She's kidding me, right? She wonders why we haven't been on a date. We're both workaholics.

"Tomorrow," I say.

But I don't need to hear the word no to figure out she's not going to relent.

"Okay, give me your ad." I lean back on my sofa, relaxed, and full from my ma's food.

"Hold on." She scrambles off the couch and down the hall, running back seconds later with her sketchpad. "So." She gets comfortable on the couch next to me, her legs crossed and back straight. "I'm thinking we start with a couple. We show their wedding rings as they're in their bedroom, trying to be quiet. Maybe the camera shoots to a baby whimpering in a crib—with a Coddle diaper on, of course. The parents stop when they hear the baby on the monitor. The baby quiets and they start going at it again until the wife puts her hand on the husband's chest to stop him and says, 'Condom.'

"The husband is really nonchalant, like, 'Oh, it's okay,' but the wife insists. The ad fades, but we show they grabbed a condom and right after they're finished, they're panting on their backs and the baby cries. Maybe the couple rock, paper, scissors to see who goes to the baby and the dad loses." She flashes me a smile as if I'm the dad. "Then the next day, the dad comes home, unpacking groceries with an economy-sized box of condoms, and the wife laughs. I'm not sure of the wording, but maybe we could go along the same lines as the tampon one... 'Let us protect you until you're ready.'" Her hands run in a straight line in front of her as if the words are appearing there. "That's not a good line, but I'm sure we can think of one."

I sit there. It's not a bad ad. I see the appeal to parents, but they aren't the ones buying condoms. Single guys are. Single girls are. "It's good, but I think we should look at the demographics of who buys condoms."

Her shoulders round into themselves. She's going to take this personally instead of as creative criticism. I've been doing this for years, and although I think she's wicked talented, my experience trumps everything else.

"I think our campaign should be directed toward single men," I say.

She gawks. "What about single women?"

I run my hand through my hair. This is going to end with me on the couch and her in my bed. Or her at her house and me at mine. It's going to end with me not getting laid tonight.

"Single women don't buy condoms."

"That's not true." She's getting heated. Her cheeks are flushing and she's fidgeting.

"Listen, I have the info at the office. Let's table this until tomorrow. We'll meet with Billy—"

She stands. "Your mind is made up."

"No, it isn't. I told you I like your idea, but let's be real for a moment. A married couple with a small baby is not buying a bulk box of condoms. Single men—straight men, gay men—are."

She throws her hands in the air. "What about single women? The gay women… er… I mean. *Ugh.* You know what I mean."

I grab her hands and guide her to sit down. "Don't lose your cool over this. We're sparring, throwing ideas out there.

I'm not saying you're wrong. I'm simply saying we need to look at the facts so that our ad gets them the most business."

She nods, but I bet if I placed my hand over her heart, it'd be beating faster than when we fuck. She's new to this. I remember kicking and hitting things when I was a newbie and they didn't like my ideas. You take it personally and have a hard time seeing the other side.

"Why don't you straddle me again and we can have the night I was hoping for?" I pat my leg.

"Ugh." She stands.

"Remember earlier when you said a hate fuck could be fun? I'm down to give it a try."

She spins on her heel and heads down the hall. "You're just like Mr. Jacobson."

Yeah, I can't let that fly. I follow her, and I'm about to enter the room when she slams my bedroom door in my face. I open it right back up and find her packing her overnight bag like I expected.

"Don't you dare compare me to him."

She rolls her eyes. "You want to gear the ad toward men and won't even listen to my reasoning."

"Because men buy condoms. When is the last time you bought condoms?"

"I have three in my purse."

I throw my hands in the air. "Okay, bad example."

She puts her hands on her hips and hammers me with a pissed-off expression.

"Come on. I don't want to argue about this. If this is going to work, we need to keep work at work and home at home." I step forward, hoping the brush in her hand doesn't nail me in the eye.

Her shoulders slump. "I'm just trying to give Mr.

Jacobson a reason to actually hire your assistant so I can be a full-fledged junior ad exec."

I bring her to my chest, hugging her because I worry as much as she does that she might never get that man's respect. I don't want her to move to Texas, but at this point in her life, it might be the best option for her. But as selfish as it is, I can't find it in me to voice my concerns for her future at work. I… well, I can't see living without her at this point. It has to work out for her at Jacobson and Earl. I vow to do everything in my power to make sure it does.

"We good?" I kiss the top of her head.

"Billy gets the tie-breaker vote," she mumbles.

My girl's a fighter and will never throw in the white towel. I would never expect her to. But I worry our work relationship is going to ruin whatever we're building outside of Jacobson and Earl.

CHAPTER THIRTY-FOUR

Annie

Well, mostly because Billy put his hands over his ears and kept repeating, "Mom and Dad, stop fighting," the decision was made to give Blair and her father three ads to choose from. It's not unheard of, and both Enzo and I felt strongly about our ideas, so we threw in a third, so it won't seem like a "he says, she says" deal.

Weeks after being promoted, I'm still bringing Enzo his coffee, although I fear I'm doing it more because I'm his girlfriend than his assistant. He's taken the initiative and learned a lot over the past few weeks , but I'm still stationed in the open floor plan, working in an assistant cubicle, and there hasn't been one interview to replace me. It's not hard to see where the priorities land around here.

Enzo walks in with a dry cleaning bag, and through the plastic, I see my blue blouse and the black dress I dropped off last week. He hangs it up outside his bathroom door when I follow him into his office.

"Did you pick up my dry cleaning?" I ask.

He smiles like "yeah, I'm the best boyfriend ever, see how the tables have turned?" "I was getting my own."

Today of all days I needed this, and I want to wrap my arms around his stomach and kiss him senseless.

"Copies for the presentation?" I ask, searching his desk for last minute to-dos for our pitch today.

"Done. Jake helped me out."

I look at him as if he just saved my cat from a tree. Except I don't have a cat, but he can still be the hot firefighter climbing the ladder in this fantasy.

"I'm pretty good at this boyfriend thing." He smiles, but it doesn't completely reach his eyes, which seems odd. Lately, other than arguing about the condom ad, we've been sitting on a big happy cloud in blue skies with the sun streaming down on us.

Billy walks in without knocking. "Here's the tape." He places the flash drive on Enzo's desk.

"Thanks, Billy."

I run over to snag it. "I can't wait to see it after the final touches."

Enzo grabs it before I can and holds it above his head as if they're about to play a game of keep away.

"Wait until the pitch. It's more fun," Enzo says.

Since we're still supposed to be professional, I'm not about to sprinkle him with kisses. I'm already nervous about seeing Blair after turning down another offer a few weeks ago. I thought she'd strip the account away, but I have a feeling her father is keeping them with Jacobson and Earl.

"Well, I'm going to make sure catering will be delivered

on time." I spin on my heels and walk out of the room, nervous and excited for what the afternoon holds.

I KNOCK on Enzo's door. He's on the phone but waves me in. We've barely talked today, and I haven't received one flirtatious email from him. Something feels off, but I can't put my finger on it.

What could it possibly be? He picked up my dry cleaning and he made copies himself. Would a man do that if he was going to break up with you?

He hangs up his call.

"Are you ready? They'll be here in five," I say.

He stands and grabs his suit jacket.

"Should we go to the bathroom for a pep talk?" I joke, trying to ease this weird tension between us today.

He smiles. I'm totally making more of this than there is. We're good. We're fine. Maybe the pressure of us disagreeing about this ad is making things awkward.

"Let's go." He holds open the door, and I walk through and down the hall to the conference room. Right before I step into the room, he murmurs, "What did I say about that skirt?"

"I do like to tease you," I say, flipping on the lights.

Enzo places the brochures on the table and sets up the flash drive to play on the big screen. The fruit-and-nut tray is already on the table, so I unwrap it and grab waters out of the fridge.

Mr. Jacobson arrives before the Petersons. He eyes me, and I smile though I really want to ask him when I'll actually get the perks of a junior ad executive, like maybe a more private cubicle and not having to answer Enzo's calls.

"Looks great," he says, digging for a handful of nuts. "You two have really been working well together."

I smile again.

"Yeah, we make a good team," Enzo says, his head buried in his computer.

Mr. Jacobson leans against the ledge by the window. He's studying me, and a cold shiver skitters up my spine.

"Annie, the Petersons are here," Elise announces from the conference room speaker.

"I'll be back."

I leave, wishing I could run down the hall because I can feel Mr. Jacobson's eyes on me. He's not checking out my ass or anything, but if feels as if he's assessing me with two question marks in his eyes.

When I reach the lobby, I spot our guests. "Blair. Mr. Peterson."

Blair tucks her phone into her purse, and Mr. Peterson knocks his fist on the reception desk as a goodbye to Elise.

Sliding her arm through mine, Blair leans in close. "Any more thoughts about my offer?"

"You're relentless." I laugh because I need this interaction to be lighthearted.

"I always know what I want, and I'm not sure I can stand another meeting with Mr. Jacobson. My dad said he won't bring ads in-house unless it's someone we know is talented. Which means until I secure you, we're here." A disgusted expression crosses her face.

"Well, as long as I'm here, you're in good hands." I pat her arm.

We're at the conference room in no time. Enzo's ready with an outstretched hand, but his tighter-than-normal smile says how much he might not care for Blair, what with her consistent desire to snag me away. Billy walks in, says his hellos, and we all sit around the table.

We decided ahead of time that Enzo would make the pitch since he's the senior ad exec, so Billy and I sit at the far end of the table, next to Mr. Jacobson.

"Thanks for coming today," Enzo says. "This will be our fourth product campaign, and I truly believe it's a no-brainer. In the ad packet, there's a lot of data about who your consumer is when it comes to condoms. I don't think it's a surprise that it's men. Single men." His gaze shoots to mine briefly.

My stomach drops, and I feel nauseated with apprehension.

Blair puts on her reading glasses. She and her dad open the pages and read them over, nodding.

"Let's show you what we came up with, then we'll discuss after." Enzo steps to the side and clicks on his computer.

Billy slides his chair over and turns off the lights since he's closest.

The ad plays. Enzo's ad comes on the screen first, the one showing guys in different scenarios. A heterosexual male dancing in a club. Two homosexual males on a date. A heterosexual male walking a woman to her door. The slogan, *Play Safe*, lands in big letters on the screen.

I'm not saying it's a crappy ad. It's a good ad. There's no refuting Enzo's talent and I understand his thinking about targeting single males. But Coddle is a family company.

Enzo hits end on the video and the screen goes black.

Billy looks at me but rolls his chair over to turn on the lights.

"I do think something like this is the way to go. It speaks to your target audience," Enzo says.

Blair rests the arm of her glasses at her lips, swiveling her chair toward me then back toward Enzo. "Do you have anything else?"

Enzo shoves his hands in his pockets, rocking back on his heels. "We're confident in this approach."

She nods.

Her dad smiles. "Men do make up the majority of our purchases."

I seethe. That's the only ad he's showing? I look at Billy, but his blank expression says he had no idea Enzo was going to go rogue on us either.

Enzo purposely isn't letting his gaze land on me.

That son of a bitch.

Well, not really. I've met his mom and she's really nice. But still. Asshole.

"Yeah, I think it works. Great job, guys." Blair slides out her chair. "Can we talk about some of the other products while we're here?"

Seriously? That's it?

"Excuse me," I say, standing.

I flee from the conference room. I cannot sit there with the bullshit he's going to spew at them. I head to the bathroom, my stomach revolting, and almost throw up my entire turkey club from lunch. How could I have been so stupid? I trusted him, and he didn't present my idea after we agreed to let the client make the decision. He says he sees me as his equal but in practice that's not true.

I stand straight and leave the stall. Screw him.

Heading to my desk, I spot Enzo walking toward his office. Our paths will cross. I have no choice but to walk right into him if I'm going to my desk.

He's eyeing me. I'm sure he thinks he can grovel and flash me that smirk and I'll melt into his arms. Not this time. This time, Enzo Mancini is *not* going to get what he wants.

Turning right, I look at Jake, who perks up in his chair.

"Miss Stewart, can I see you?" Enzo opens his office door.

I smack on a fake smile. "Sure thing, Mr. Mancini."

Once I'm in the office, he shuts the blinds.

"*No*! Open them."

He blows out a breath. "Don't get bent out of shape because of us. It was a business decision. That's all."

"We agreed. Three campaigns. You only presented yours."

"Because it was the best one." He shrugs out of his suit jacket.

I have no idea where the Petersons are at this point and I don't care. "We agreed!"

He rolls up the sleeves of his shirt. "I'm the senior ad exec. The final decision is up to me." He's cool and calm, seemingly unaffected. "Selling to guys was the right way to go for the client."

"You purposely lied to me."

Before Enzo can respond, Billy walks in and shuts the door. Obviously, the blinds didn't deter him. "You guys better shut the fuck up. The Petersons are still in the conference room. I don't do the people. That's your job. I'm the behind-the-scenes guy, so someone better get their ass back in there."

I've never heard Billy be so authoritative.

"I guess the senior ad exec should do it." I cross my arms and jut out my hip.

"What the hell happened? I thought we were pitching three?" Billy asks the same question I did.

"Mr. Senior Ad Executive decided not to but failed to mention it to us."

Billy raises his hands. "Well, the client loved it, so let's put it aside. All that matters is that Coddle is signing."

"Exactly." Enzo holds his hand out toward Billy like "listen to the man, he knows what he's saying."

I spear Enzo with a scathing look. "You betrayed me."

"I didn't betray you. This is business. That's all."

Billy looks between the two of us. "Shit, are you serious? You guys actually slept together?" From the sound of his voice, you'd think he's four and we just revealed Santa Claus isn't real.

"Billy, give us a moment," Enzo says, his eyes still locked with mine.

He wants a staring contest? Fine. He'll lose at that childhood game just like rock, paper, scissors.

"Things were so great. Why did you have to go and sleep together?" Billy whines but leaves the office.

Once the door is shut, Enzo breaks the distance, but I step back and put my hand on his chest.

"Do not take this personally."

"Why didn't you tell me?"

"Because of this." He gestures to me.

"Are you sure it's not because I'm a woman?"

"What?" His face twists. I know it's incredibly unfair of me to pin him with that, but the Enzo who bulldozed his idea down our clients' throats isn't the one I've come to know. "How could you even think that?"

"Mr. Jacobson, did he tell you to hit a home run for the guys?"

He steps back and shoves his hands into his pockets. "You're kidding me. You need to stop thinking every little thing is some sexist move a guy is making to get ahead of a woman."

"Then cut off your dick and see how well-respected you are. Here I am, still sitting outside your office weeks after getting a promotion, getting you coffee and answering your phone calls. Would that have happened to Jake?" I cross my arms.

Enzo blows out a breath. "I get that, but it's out of my control. I pitched the ad that was the best for the client."

"You stand by your decision?"

His back straightens, and that's all I really need to know.

"Fine. I'm out for the afternoon. You can handle them on your own since you know what's best. I'm just the measly assistant who should feel lucky to play with the big boys, right?"

His head falls back so he's staring at the ceiling in frustration. "For the love of Christ, Annie."

I leave and shut the door. All eyes are on me, and small groups of coworkers are huddled together, gossiping.

Game over, everyone. The gossip train is moving on to another station because it's done here at Jacobson and Earl, just like Enzo and me.

CHAPTER THIRTY-FIVE

Enzo

After working to get myself under control for a few minutes, I leave my suit jacket in the office and head back to the conference room, noting that Annie's desk is closed up. Instinctively, I glance at Jake, who gives me a look of disgust.

Why do these people not understand business?

The conference room is empty, so I assume the Petersons are gone. I find Mr. Jacobson walking back from reception.

"A word," he says.

I follow the man to his office. Mindy peeks up from her computer for a moment as we pass. Does the entire office know what just went down?

"Shut the door," he says, pouring himself a glass of scotch.

He doesn't offer me one, nor do I want one. I'll be high-tailing it to Annie at some point to grovel.

"Sit down," he commands, and I sit in the same seat from weeks earlier. "I assume the rumors are true."

"No. It was a case of creative disagreement. That's all."

He sits down, sips his scotch, and releases a breath. "I know you think I'm senile, but I've been in business a long time. I've seen a lot of work romances come and go. You and Miss Stewart are in a relationship, and you pissed her off during that meeting. Something didn't go the way she wanted?"

I don't confirm or deny his statement.

His eyes find mine over the rim of his glass. "So you were having a sexual relationship with an employee under you?"

"Technically, Shelby was her boss."

He shakes his head. "You're the senior ad exec. She's an assistant."

"You mean junior ad exec," I clarify.

He shrugs like "think what you will." My blood boils. I knew this was all a game to him.

"Anyway." He sets down his scotch and extends his hand to me. "Welcome to Jacobson, Earl, and Mancini. The partnership is yours."

Damn, I never thought this day would come. But my elation quickly diminishes when I realize why I'm getting this partnership.

He smiles, clearly oblivious to my discomfort. "Pour yourself a glass of scotch. We'll celebrate."

I mindlessly wander to his bar and pour myself a scotch. I wish I could just take the partnership and not care. Men in my situation have done it before. Be selfish and take what you've worked your ass off for your entire career. Still, I need to make sure I'm crystal clear on his reasons for finally giving me the partnership. "So what changed your mind?"

"The fact that you didn't let Miss Stewart's sexual power over you override your good sense on this campaign. Here I thought you might've fallen for her, what with you pushing for her to be promoted to a junior ad exec and using her ideas for the Coddle campaigns." He laughs as though I'd only been doing it because she sucked me off after hours, not because she had some good ideas.

I set my drink on the table. "She's talented. My new assistant needs to be hired so Annie can concentrate on her ad campaigns."

"Look at you. She doesn't even have her own campaigns. I think I'm going to leave Coddle with you. She can start off with some magazine and newspaper ads. You know, the smaller accounts."

My heart wrenches. Would I have presented Annie's condom ad to Coddle if it was the better of the two? If roles were reversed and she came up with the male campaign and I went with the family planning line? Would I have seen it her way with the demographics? I sure hope I would have. The decision was hard, and yeah, I didn't tell her beforehand because I didn't want to deal with the fight. The fight that inevitably came and almost in front of a client.

But Mr. Jacobson's belief that I don't value her opinion, or her ideas is way off base. He's going to take her off the Coddle account after she won them over with the tampon ad and her approach for the diapers.

"I think she needs to stay on Coddle with me." I sit back down on the couch.

He shakes his head. "No, she doesn't. You have it from here. Not to mention, you're no longer a couple, so I assume she'll quit. Don't worry, we'll make it uncomfortable enough for her to quit so no sexual harassment case can be filed." The way he says it makes me think he's familiar with this tactic and he's seen success from it.

"It was a mutual thing between us. You don't have to worry about her filing."

He laughs. "I never thought you were so naive. She'll file. You screwed her over. Her panties are in a bunch and one of her feminist friends will convince her to file."

Seriously, how can I just now be seeing how horrible this man is?

"With all due respect, Mr. Jacobson, that's not Annie."

"Annie?" He shakes his head. "I think you have fallen for her."

I have. I know I have. If I didn't care about her, I would've told her before the meeting about the change. I purposely held back the information so we could live in our bubble for one more day. This is probably why people say no work relationships. If she'd been just an assistant to me, I wouldn't have cared what she thought or what her reaction might be. But I didn't want to hurt her and going the nice route to try to convince her I had the better idea didn't pan out.

The last thing I'm doing is telling that to this jerk though. He has no concept of caring for someone other than himself.

"Who do you see taking my place?" I ask, changing the subject.

"I think that Jake fellow. He's been sitting under Zilroy for almost two years. He's the best candidate."

"You're going to make Jake an ad exec and give him my office?"

"Not your office, but he could be an ad exec." He sips his scotch.

He's got to be fucking kidding me. Jake hasn't worked a campaign of this magnitude. The job should be Annie's. The fact he's keeping me around and pushing Annie to the curb tells me all I need to know about this man and this company.

My hands are clenched on my knees and I inhale a deep breath before standing. "Mr. Jacobson, this kills me, but I can't accept the partnership. Actually, I'm turning in my notice."

His eyes widen. "What? Is this about her?"

I hold out my hand, but he doesn't shake it, nor does he move as if he's going to. "It is, but it's more about the way I want to do business. I've told you many times how talented Annie is, but you'd let her rot in an assistant role rather than let her contribute to your company and help it thrive. Your small-minded theory that men rule the world and women are here to please us is old school at best. At worst, it's discriminatory and misogynistic. I can't work for a company that would deliberately keep someone down and promote people who didn't deserve it based on their sex or something else they can't control. Good luck, sir, and I do thank you for the opportunity you've given me with this company."

"Enzo," he calls as I'm about to leave his office. "You do understand what you're giving up? All because you allowed a woman to get under your skin? There are others out there. She's not the only woman in New York. Think about it, son."

I turn toward him. "I'm not your son. In fact, I'd be embarrassed if I was. And you're wrong, sir. She *is* the only woman in New York. The only woman for me. If you think that's the only reason I'm walking out on this job, then you might as well close up shop, because times have changed, and you'll never continue to succeed with your thinking."

I open the door and shut it behind me.

"Mindy," I say with a nod.

"Enzo." She types away on her computer.

I head to my office to pack up my shit, the realization quickly surfacing that I have no idea what the hell I'm going to do now.

CHAPTER THIRTY-SIX

Annie

"Explain it to me again." Beth's rocking Cecilia and can't hear me over the soothing machine. Seriously, didn't our parents survive without all these newfound gadgets? Are they really necessary?

"He didn't even present my idea." I rock myself on the floor of Cecilia's room, my arms around my knees.

"I thought things were good. Why didn't he tell you?"

"You tell me."

She walks to the crib, lays Cecilia down, then signals for me to leave. "You know what I really think?"

We walk toward the family room and I fall into her couch. "I don't know, do I? Are you on his side?"

She hits me to sit up and give her room. I crawl into the corner of the couch, chewing on my nails. "I'm always on your side, even when you're wrong. Let me ask you a question. Why are you so mad?"

I throw my hands in the air. Has she not been listening to me for the past hour? "He lied to me."

"He omitted."

"Same thing."

"Not entirely. If you weren't banging him, would you have expected him to go with your ad idea?"

I narrow my eyes. "Where are you going with this?"

"Just answer the question."

"Yes, I would have. We agreed to show three ads."

"And I agree he should've told you, but I want you to think about why you're really mad because I think..." Her mouth twists in a way that says she doesn't want to actually tell me, but I've cornered her.

"Oh my God, just say it."

"I think you were waiting for him to disappoint you." She stands and heads to the kitchen as though she's afraid of what I'll do.

I follow her anyway. "Why would I do that? He's been great. I know it might be hard for you to believe, but he's been all over me. He wants to spend more time together than I do."

She digs a bag of chips out of the pantry. "You mean more time than you're willing to *agree* to."

The audacity of this woman. "What, did he pay you to act like this toward me? Point the finger my way? I know he has a way of buttering people up, but you're my blood. My sister." My voice is rising.

"Shh, you'll wake Cecilia." She hands me a Diet Coke, and we both head back to the couch. "Let's face it. You've always had this I'm-not-good-enough chip on your shoulder. I get that Mom leaving affected us differently, but you hold it like a badge of honor that you've kept Enzo at arm's length."

"I was guarding my heart. He was a manwhore before me."

"Was he though? We don't really know if he was. He might not have wanted a relationship, but you don't know if he used women. The fact that he's torn his shirt open and let his heart fall out for you doesn't really align with that theory."

I look at the pop can in my hands and back at her. "I guess I thought you'd be on my side here."

Her shoulders slump. "I am. I'm always on your side, but I think you've pushed your issues with Mom away for so long, it's affecting your current relationship. So she woke up one day and realized she didn't want to be a mother. Newsflash, she probably never wanted to be one but found herself in an unhappy life with Dad and two daughters. Was leaving us shitty? Hell yeah. I can't imagine ever leaving Cecilia. But she left us with Dad, the kindest, most loving man who raised us well." She slides over and places her hand on my thigh.

I don't know why Beth has to bring up something so crappy when I'm already drowning in betrayal from the man I was... whatever. "This thing with Enzo has nothing to do with Mom."

"Why did you come up with that rule for how many weeknights you could spend together?"

"Because it was all new and..." Tears well up in my eyes and I swallow them back.

"It's me. I'm your sister. You can trust me." She squeezes my knee.

I glance at her, and the wall of tears topples over. "I was afraid he'd get sick of me and leave."

Beth's lips tip down. She knew. Of course she did. She knows me better than I know myself sometimes.

"You're wonderful. I hate that you don't think so. That you think Enzo wouldn't see how beautiful you are inside and out and how lucky he'd be to have you." She grabs a box of Kleenex from the sofa table behind us and puts it in my lap.

I take one and run it under my eyes. "I'm not that bad. It's just... I didn't want him to get sick of me."

"And maybe you kind of liked the way he fawned and pushed to see you?"

It was nice—his can-never-get-enough-of-you attitude. No one had ever made me feel the way he did. Like I was his and he could spend every second of every day with me and never tire of it. That he never wanted to leave me... meaning he never would.

A strangled cry leaves my throat. "Oh my God, you're right. I'm messed up. I was transferring my feelings of not being good enough for Mom onto Enzo." I pick up a throw pillow and put it over my head.

"You're not messed up. Look at how much you hate her. She hurt you and that's why you have those strong feelings." Beth puts her arms around my shoulders.

"You hate her too."

She shrugs. "Not as much as you. I tamp down my expectations. I'm not going to be upset if she doesn't want a relationship with Cecilia or me. That's her loss. When she's older, if she has regrets, she'll have to live with them. She made her bed."

"You're like a therapist's dream and I'm a basket case. How did we come out of the same situation so differently?"

She laughs. "I guess I'm just the better sister."

I knock her with my shoulder, and we laugh.

"But Enzo?" She doesn't stop with her psych analysis. "I get why you're mad. What he did wasn't right, but I think you both let the out-of-work relationship affect your work relationship. You need to talk to him."

I nod, but I honestly have no plan at this point.

My phone dings in my purse, and Beth grabs the phone and hands it to me. "Call him."

I hold it in my hands, and it dings again.

Jake's name flashes on the screen.

Jake: *Enzo just quit. What the hell happened today?*

I LEAVE Beth's and arrive at Enzo's condo. The sun is dipping below the horizon and the summer nights are becoming chilly, but his lobby is toasty warm.

"Hi, Jeb," I say, before stepping into the elevator.

"Miss Stewart." The doorman nods. "He just returned."

"Thank you."

My stomach rumbles with emotions as the elevator rises up to Enzo's floor. His hallway is quiet, as it usually is, and I knock on his door. I've done this hundreds of times, but I can't help but worry this is the last time I'll ever be here.

Enzo opens the door, his shirt unbuttoned and his tie loose around his neck.

"Annie," he says, thick emotion coating every syllable of my name.

"Can I come in?"

He slides to the side, opening the door more.

"Jake messaged me. You can't quit." I leave my jacket on and my purse hangs from my shoulder.

"I can, and I did. It's done." He heads into his kitchen. "Do you want something to drink?"

I'm not sure what I thought would happen right now,

but this awkward tension between us sucks. I rehearsed my speech on the way over, so I might as well get it out. "About today..."

He shuts his fridge door and puts his fingers against my mouth. "It's on me. I'm sorry. I should've told you beforehand. It was wrong of me. I'm really sorry."

My shoulders fall and I stare into his eyes. How easy would it be to forgive him and move on?

"I can't say I'm not upset. You should've told me, and I still think we should have presented all three ad campaigns, but I see where I probably took it more personally because of our relationship." I step away from him because I'll never be able to do this with him so close.

"We'll have to agree to disagree on presenting all three ideas."

"Your apology doesn't hold any weight?" The anger from before resurfaces. Maybe it's too early to be here discussing this. I should've gone home.

"I apologize for not telling you I made the decision ahead of time, but not for pitching the best idea." He crosses his arms.

"*Okay...*" I draw out the word, annoyance wrapping around me like barbed wire. I hope he doesn't veer close to me again. He's liable to end up cut by my sharp edges right now.

"Look, I have the final say. I'm—was—the senior ad exec, and I did what I thought was best for the client."

I inhale a deep, calming breath, not wanting to devolve into the same argument we had earlier. We're not going to agree on this. "I don't want you to quit. If anything, you should be partner."

"Mr. Jacobson offered me the partnership. I declined it. I don't want to work for that company, and Annie..." He lightly grasps my hand. "You need to leave. You'll never get where you should be if you stay there."

I stare at him, waiting for more information.

After a few seconds, he continues. "There's no future for you at Jacobson and Earl. I didn't want you to go to Houston to work for Blair, but I should've told you my suspicions sooner. Mr. Jacobson is a sexist asshole who will keep you down."

I pull my hand away from his. "What do you mean you should have told me sooner?"

He blows out a breath and runs his fingers through his hair. "I like what we have. I didn't want you to leave and move to Houston." His voice loses the edge of arrogance it had earlier. Now, it's full of regret.

"Enzo, what exactly are you saying?"

"I had a meeting with him weeks ago and got the feeling then that he might not be on board with promoting you. I knew they were dragging their feet on making you a junior ad exec, but I didn't know the half of it until today. That's why I quit. I won't work for a man like that."

I stumble back a step. "After I blew any future at Coddle? That's when you decide to tell me? Was this whole thing a ploy? Only present your ad, I get mad and storm out, we fight in your office. All to make me look unprofessional so she doesn't want me? So you can win?"

"What? No. I just wanted to keep you with me. I'm sorry." His eyes plead for me to understand.

I shake my head. "My life isn't a game. If you truly cared for me, you would've told me I was being used. Hell, I came up with the entire tampon ad myself and you let me. You let that company profit from me, knowing they didn't value me."

I stomp over to his door and start to swing it open, but his palm slams it shut above my head.

His big body cages me between him and the door. "I'm starting my own company. Come with me. We'll be partners."

If it were yesterday, I'd have jumped in his arms and said let's do it. But too much has happened now. "I'm not sure we should work together," I say to the door.

His mouth lowers to my ear. "I love you. I know my actions are far from showing that right now, and I get I was being selfish, but you're the first woman to ever make me feel whole. I can't bear to lose you."

I close my eyes, a lone tear falling. "I'm not a pawn that you win by outplaying someone else. I'm not sure you understand what love is."

I open the door and he slams it shut again, neither of us moving.

"Don't do this. Don't throw away what we have."

"I need some space," I whisper.

This time when I open the door, he steps back, allowing me to walk through. I feel his eyes on me as I walk down the hall, and when I turn around in the elevator, he stands in the hallway, watching me while the doors of the elevator shut between us.

It feels so final that I collapse to the floor and sob.

CHAPTER THIRTY-SEVEN

Enzo

I flag the waitress down while jotting notes about my latest prospect into my notebook. "Another."

"You look like shit." Carm runs the back of his hand down my beard. "Bonus points on that fucking beard though."

"He's in denial. Thinks changing his look will make him forget." Dom piles a forkful of lobster mac and cheese into his mouth.

"If I don't grab these clients quick, Jacobson will act faster, and they have a helluva lot more resources than I'm offering." My phone dings with a voicemail, and I pick it up to listen.

"I think it's great that you went out on your own, but you need to get your shit together," Carm says.

I shake my head, telling him to be quiet. Blair from Coddle is more important than his whining. I've been fishing for Coddle to follow me, though I assumed they would pull their marketing in-house after Annie reached out to Blair. I've put out some feelers to see if she took the job, but since she apparently hasn't contacted Blair since D-day, I asked for a meeting.

Shit. The message is just from the dry cleaners, letting me know the clothes I dropped off weeks ago are still there, waiting to be picked up. I hit End on the call.

"How many clients do you have now?" Dom asks, clearly only caring about me shoving it to Jacobson and Earl.

"Five, but if I can get Coddle, that's huge."

Carm slaps my back. "Way to distract yourself from the real problem at hand."

"Let it go," Dom says to Carm.

"What? He told her he loved her, and she walked out on him. How easy would it be for you to let it go?"

They've clearly been talking behind my back.

"We're not chicks. We don't talk feelings." Carm pushes away his own plate, sipping his beer. "You're Enzo Mancini, man. Come out with me, and I'll help you forget all about Annie."

Just hearing her name is enough to make me want to drown myself in another bottle of scotch. I don't quite remember the first night after I told her I loved her, and she walked out on me.

My brothers can't understand that I have to distract myself because her power is too strong. They don't know how it feels to have sex with someone you care about. How being with the same person time and time again brings benefits one-night stands don't.

Well, I guess Dom might get that, but something tells me a woman who throws your clothes at you the minute she comes is not a girl who wants to give you maximum pleasure with a blow job.

They don't understand how lazy Sundays are the fucking best. And that after you leave work, there's a pit of exhilaration in your stomach because you get to spend time with her. How waiting to hear what comes out of her mouth next, even if she razzes you, has you on pins and needles.

"Let's just call a spade a spade. You're lovesick. So take five minutes away from building your empire and deal with it," Dom says.

"You're crazy. Forget her. Though I did enjoy her. She plays a killer game of rock, paper, scissors." Carm crosses his arms and stares across the table at me.

"There you go. Let's play to see if you go after her."

I throw my napkin at Dom. I'm drawing the line there.

"Seriously, talk to us. What's going on in that head of yours?" Dom asks.

Carm leans his arms on the table, apparently intrigued to hear my answer.

I shrug. I don't really have anything to say. For the first time in my life, I have no idea what the fuck to do. "She's mad and I don't blame her."

"Make her forgive you," Carm says. "I'm charming. I'll go with you. She won't be able to turn you down."

I shake my head at his stupidity. Definitely not in the mood today.

"If you want her back so much, win her over. You're Enzo Mancini, for fuck's sake. Pick yourself up and fight for her." Carm's voice rises, and the people beside us shift their attention our way.

I'm drowning myself in work to keep from thinking of her. I'm well aware I want her in my bed and in my kitchen and by my side every minute of every day.

"What if she says no?" My voice cracks because the idea guts me. I told the woman I love her—the only woman I've ever uttered those words to—and she walked out.

"Okay, I'm giving this to you straight. I've been nice enough up until now." Dom puts down his fork, which means he's serious. "You love her. I know it sucks, but it happens to men every damn day. Don't tell Ma, but I pray every night and you know what I pray for? I pray *not* to fall in love. I don't want some woman leading me around by the balls. But it's like catching the flu—you caught it, so you need to grin and bear it. This working twenty-four seven isn't masking your depressed eyes. You already look like a lovesick puppy dog. Like all she'd need to do is waltz in here, attach a leash to your neck, and you'd wag your tail, happy she took you back."

"This is a pep talk?" I ask.

"What I'm saying is that I saw you at your condo with her. I knew it was over then. You were a goner and off the market. Own it and do something to keep it. Carm's right, you're being a weasel. Embrace your love for her and win her back. That's how you get your man card back." He picks up his fork to dig back into his meal.

Carm laughs. "Hey, odds were that it had to happen to one of us and looks like it's you. Sorry, not sorry." He slaps my back.

I sit up straighter, pushing my beer aside. I slide off the stool to go do something, anything, when I run right into a girl from Jacobson and Earl.

"Hey..." I say, trying to remember her name.

"Mae," she deadpans, not impressed that I couldn't place her.

"Sure, nice seeing you. Take care." I give her a half smile and push past her.

"Things aren't the same at Jacobson and Earl without you and Annie," she says as I pass.

I stop in my tracks and turn back to her. I remember her now, outside talking to Annie and smelling the flowers. She was in the copy room too.

Wait, did she say without me *and* Annie?

She did it. She took control of her future, which makes her so much sexier than she already was. The new information wraps around me, and a proud feeling warms my chest because I know she'll make it big somewhere.

"Where is she?" I ask.

She smiles. "Who?"

"Hello, introductions, Enzo," Carm interrupts, but I put out my palm.

"Annie. You're her friend, right?"

"I am, and I'm sorry, but she'd be mad if I gave you that information." She's acting coy as though she's trying to see how far I'll push. Is she here on purpose or is it an accident that we've run into each other?

"I know where she lives."

Mae shrugs. "She's not there."

"Beth's?"

"Hey, I'm Carm, his brother." Carm puts his hand out to her.

She shakes it.

"I know you want to tell me. So come on."

"I was having lunch with her, and she had to leave to talk to the head of Coddle."

"Coddle?" Finally. She made her move. I'm not even that upset that it means losing what would've put my new company on the map.

"Yeah, but she's turning down the offer because she fell in love with some guy and she doesn't want to ruin his new company or some shit like that." She tilts her head and raises her eyebrows, questioning what I'm going to do to fix this.

"She's declining their job offer because..."

"Yeah. I told her she was stupid and that Coddle probably won't even pick you." She's smug. I like that she sought me out because we're on the same page—Annie needs to take the Coddle position.

"How did you know where to find me?" I ask.

She rolls her eyes. "Please. I had to listen to her go on and on through our entire lunch about how she knew where you had lunch on Thursdays, and it would be so easy to go there and see you."

A small smile tilts my lips. "Where is she now?"

"Lancaster's. They had a layover, so she was running over there."

I turn to run out of the restaurant but head back. "Thank you."

"Go!" Her eyes widen.

"Have a seat," Carm says as I run out to hail a cab.

Lunchtime in Manhattan isn't the easiest time to get to Lancaster's. A cab pulls up to the curb after a minute and I debate walking, looking at the bumper-to-bumper traffic on the street. Instead, I head down the subway stairs. I can't even remember the last time I rode the subway. It's been so long that I have to check the routes to make sure I'll end up where I need to be.

Standing in the underground train, I hold the silver pole and pick up my phone to call her. She doesn't answer. Probably because it's me.

The train stops and a swarm of kids file in, laughing and jumping. Two adults try to rein them in, putting them on available seats. One kid stares at me. I smile, and he flips me off. What the hell? He's, like, six.

I look away. Finally, a lifetime of screaming later, it's my stop. The doors open and I fly out and up the stairs. Lancaster's is across the street, but I don't bother with the crosswalk. I jet across the street, dodging a taxi that should have had me as a hood ornament.

Safely on the other side, I open the doors of the restaurant.

"Can I help you?" the hostess asks as my eyes scour the room.

"No. I'm good."

Blair sees me first, signaling Annie to turn around. She swivels in her chair and I'm not sure what look I expected, but the one on her face isn't what I was hoping for, that's for sure.

CHAPTER THIRTY-EIGHT

Annie

Blair nudges me and nods at the door behind me. I turn to look and find Enzo walking right toward us. There's a sheen of sweat along his forehead and he's heaving for a breath, but he's here.

Why is he here?

I stand and place my hand on his chest. His heart beats against my palm.

"Not now," I say.

"Whatever she told you, she's wrong," he says to Blair.

I jut out my hip. "I am?"

"Take me off the table. I don't want the Coddle account, so..."

Blair leans back and smiles.

"Take the job, Annie. You deserve it." For the first time since he arrived, he pins me with his caramel eyes, and it takes me a minute to get my footing.

"But—"

"No. How many times have I told you to take what's yours? Take what you deserve. Everything that went down is bullshit. We're talking about your career, and the best place for you to be is with Coddle."

I look away. "It would be your biggest account. You quit because of me."

"I quit because Mr. Jacobson isn't a man I feel comfortable working for. Maybe I ignored the earlier signs because I was blind to it. Maybe I only saw it because I fell in love with you and I was pissed at the way he was treating you. I can't say for sure, but you're not to blame."

"But—"

"Stop with the buts." He puts his finger under my chin. "I'm so sorry. I never wanted to hurt you, and I should've presented all three ads. I told you I would, and I went back on that."

"No, you were right. You were the senior ad exec."

I shake my head, and he shakes his. "We should have talked about it."

"That I agree with. I think the line between business and personal did blur," I whisper, stealing a glance at Blair.

"I also should've told you my suspicions about Mr. Jacobson instead of letting my fear of losing you get in the way of my better judgment." He inhales a deep breath. "I won't let my selfishness get in the way of what's best for you again. Take the job." He steps closer.

He's so warm, and all I want to do is step into him and tell him how much I missed him.

"It's not just you, Enzo. It's leaving New York. Beth, my dad..."

"I could go with you. I'm not Beth, your dad, or Cecilia, but you'd have me. I love you and I want to put this behind us." He lays his hand on my cheek. "What we had? Not everyone gets that."

My chest fills with joy and I feel as if I could float away like a balloon. I nod and smile. "I miss you."

"My heart has ached every day we've been apart."

"But you can't come to Houston with me. Your business would never thrive there like it will here," I say. "Plus, I'd be taking you away from your family."

"You're more than enough for me. Take the job, and if you'll have me, let's move to Houston." He steps closer, his chest pressed to mine.

A tear slips down my cheek. "Really?"

"Yeah."

My hand covers his on my cheek. I've missed his touch. "You'd move to Houston for me? Restart your company there?"

He nods. "One hundred percent."

"All because you love me?" A lump lodges in my throat.

"I love you so much. I mean... I'd love for you to stay in New York and work for me here, but I can't afford you."

I'm shocked and touched that he trusts and values me enough—a newbie who can't offer him any clients—to even offer that.

He continues. "I need a creative director but Coddle will give you everything you've ever wanted. You'd be established and secure and we could settle down in Houston."

He remembers. He remembers the reason why I didn't want a boyfriend until I could stand on my own two feet. And he's right, Coddle's salary would offer me the benefits and salary to be independent, but at the same time, I'd be limiting my creativity. Being able to only work with Coddle brands sounds a bit boring for the long term.

The sound of a throat clearing interrupts us. I'd forgotten we were in the middle of a restaurant.

We turn to Blair as she stands from the table. "I'm going to leave you two to hash this out." She touches my shoulder and squeezes. "Call me when you have an answer."

"Thanks, Blair."

"I'm just glad no one will be with Jacobson and Earl." She chuckles and leaves the restaurant.

"So..." I say, my eyes casting to the table, and we sit.

"We're good? You forgive me?" he asks, sliding his chair closer.

If we weren't in public, I'd jump in his lap. "Do you forgive me? I'm sorry for always keeping you at arm's length, but I was afraid you'd wake up one morning and realize that you'd had enough of me."

He crinkles his forehead. "Don't you understand? You're everything to me. These past two weeks without you, I've thrown myself into work, so I didn't have to face the reality that I'd lost you. I was trying to get every client so the company would be big enough for you to come work with me and still have the independence you want." His gaze falls to the floor. "One day it will, but for now, you're going to Coddle, and I'll build us an empire."

I place my finger under his chin and bring it up so his eyes meet mine. "How about we build that empire together?"

I never wanted to move to Houston to work for Coddle. The money was hard to pass up, but I don't want to leave my family and have a niece who barely knows me. I understand what I'm sacrificing, but I believe in myself and I believe in Enzo.

I believe in us.

"What? No. Annie. No." He shakes his head.

"Yes." I place my hands on his cheeks. "I want to work for you."

He's silent, and I can't help but think he's going to turn me down and force me to go to Coddle. Well, if he does, he'll have a fight on his hands.

"We'll be equals." He grabs my hands and brings them down to his lap.

"We won't be equals. You're the owner. Just don't surprise me again."

"You said you love surprises," he says with a laugh.

"Yeah, flowers and candies and parties."

He leans toward me. "Done."

"Come on." I stand. "Take me home."

"Gladly." He takes my hand, and we walk out of the restaurant onto the busy Manhattan sidewalk. "I only have one condition with the new company. No rock, paper, scissors to see who does what."

I laugh, and he's quick to maneuver my back to the brick wall, his lips millimeters from mine.

"And here I thought I had the advantage," I say.

"Oh, you have the advantage."

I wind my arms around his neck. "I love you, Mr. Mancini."

"Didn't I warn you about using that outside of the bedroom?"

"You're my boss now, I have to show respect."

He rolls his eyes. "Please, we both know who's the boss."

I laugh, but his mouth falls to mine and my sounds quickly turn into a moan, as they always do.

EPILOGUE

Enzo

Nine Months Later

I'm sitting in my office. Sure, the view isn't what it was at Jacobson and Earl. It's better.

Annie walks into her office directly across from mine, taking off her rain jacket. She's wearing a skirt. *The* skirt that shows off her ass to perfection.

Luckily, Blair didn't hold it against us that Annie didn't take the job. Coddle got out of the Jacobson and Earl contract and hopped on board with us.

Annie glances at her desk, then her smile lights up the room.

Our office is small, and we don't have a ton of employees, but it's ours. We dictate how things go. Annie thinks that I'm the boss, but she has equal say in everything because one day this will be hers too. There's no way I'm ever letting her go.

"Funny thing, babe, you must've dropped your dry

cleaning ticket on my desk." She leans against my doorframe and holds the slip to her lips. Her pink lips that I'd love to have wrapped around my dick right now.

"I have no idea how that happened."

She walks in and grabs the remote off my desk, shutting the blinds to my office.

"I thought there was no shutting the blinds?" I lean back in my seat, sliding my chair out from my desk so she can do with me what she wants.

"You know what I think happened?" She saunters over to me. "I think you wanted to get a rise out of me. You wanted some angry make-up sex."

"Who, me? Nah," I mock offense.

She knows me well. Angry sex is right up there with lazy Sunday morning sex.

She stands between my desk and me then turns around and bends at the waist. "So what's on your agenda today?" She looks down at my calendar.

My hand cups her ass. "You for the next hour."

She sits on my lap sideways, putting her arms around my neck. "Miss me this morning?"

"Desperately. I think it should be mandatory that out-of-town meetings are done together. Our bed was cold and lonely without you last night."

Yeah, we live together now too. She moved in with me and rented her condo out. Life doesn't get much better than this.

"I'm on board with that."

"Good, now seal it with a kiss." My hand snakes behind her neck to bring her lips to mine.

While our tongues languidly tangle, she slides her hand between my legs and rubs my growing length. "I bet he missed me the most last night."

My cock twitches in her hand.

"On second thought, let's just take today off." I stand us up.

She laughs. I love that sound. "If we took off every day we were horny, we'd never make this company a success."

I lift her by the waist and plop her onto my desk. My hands glide up her inner thighs, parting them to make room for me. Her skirt slides up her legs to her waist, and my hands cup her breasts, finding her taut nipples beneath the silky fabric of her blouse.

Yeah, I might have to be real cliché and screw her right here on my desk.

"Motherfucker!" Carm barges in my office and freezes. "Fuck, you two, come on. You live together. You work together. How on Earth have you not gotten enough of each other yet?" he whines like a two-year-old.

Did I mention that our new office is in the same building as Carm's brokerage? Yeah, it sucks ass, but whatever, he negotiated a killer deal on the rent.

Annie slides off the desk, straightening her skirt, while Carm sits in the chair across from me. I missed her so badly last night I almost say screw it and kick him out, but I can tell that something has him really worked up.

"Thanks for ruining my fun afternoon," Annie says pointedly.

"Yeah, yeah, I have bigger problems than feeling guilty that you didn't get your ten orgasms today."

"Jealous?' she asks, her eyebrows lifted.

Yeah, she's fucking fantastic, right?

"The red-haired she-devil is pissing me off. She just stole a client from me in the elevator on the way up to my office."

Annie purses her lips. "Sounds like some brotherly

advice is needed. I have to go change my appointment with my therapist anyway. Good luck, Carm." She touches my back, kisses my cheek, then saunters out of the room, opening the blinds again before she goes.

Annie's in therapy to work through some of the issues her mom stepping out of her life caused. It's done her a lot of good, and every week, she seems to make progress. I'm not holding my breath for the two of them to have a relationship, but if my girl's happy, so am I.

I watch her go with longing, my dick unhappy with my decision to hear my brother out instead of being balls-deep in the woman I love.

"Don't ever barge into my office again," I say, sitting down.

"You two are worse than bunnies. Seriously, it's gross."

I ignore his juvenile attitude. "Why is the she-devil in the building?"

"Get this... she moved into the office across the hall from mine."

I laugh.

Carm looks at me like 'what the fuck?'

I laugh harder. "Sorry, but man, this is gonna be fun to watch. Why would she do that?"

He throws his hands in the air. "Have all the orgasms made you brain-dead? She's obviously trying to steal all my clients."

"I don't think so."

"You know what? I'm going down there to give her a piece of my mind." He stands and stomps out of my office.

I ignore my brother's tantrum over the first woman who will challenge him. Picking up the phone, I hit Annie's extension, and her eyes find mine from across the hall when she picks up.

"Come back over and let's finish what we started."

"You come here," she says and wiggles her finger at me. "Please, Enzo?"

I hang up the phone and walk out of my office right into hers. I shut the blinds and properly show her how much I missed her.

You can't turn a lady down when she says please.

The End

COCKAMAMIE UNICORN RAMBLINGS

What a ride, huh? Wait until you get your hands on Carm and Dom's stories. Piper is completely gaga over Carm's book and just wait until you read the epilogue!

We were in the middle of writing our Blue Collar Brothers series when we realized how much love our readers were giving our three Italian brothers and their family unit. And somewhere between Crushing on the Cop and Engaged to the EMT, we realized, we didn't want it to end. Piper came up with idea for White Collar Cousins and Rayne instantly loved it. Later we realized that the word cousins didn't make sense unless you read Blue Collar Brothers, so we changed the series name to White Collar Brothers. Piper LOVES alliteration and is still bummed about it. LOL We were thrilled that we had a reason to give you even more Italian brothers who love their Mama but hadn't met those special women to settle down with.

But we wanted our WCB to be a little different... We're both huge fans of alphaholes and wanted our WCB to have more of an edge to them than their Chicago cousins. It's romcom so our guy can't be a complete a-hole to our heroine because he can't have some huge dark secret as to why he's so mean. The way Enzo morphed and transformed from a hard ass, all business man to a guy who would do anything for Annie. Guys, all we have to say is wait until you see them as a couple in Carm's book, Dirty Filthy Enemy. Sigh.

We both had a blast writing Enzo and Annie's story. The banter between brothers. Both of their families and the different dynamics. We couldn't get enough.

There isn't much else to say except this was just the start of these brothers and in case you were wondering Carm and Dom's book will have some Bianco brother cameos! Don't worry!

None of this is possible without our amazing team! We had a newcomer on this one that we absolutely LOVED!

Wander Aguiar for an amazing photo

Jacob Cooley for modeling being our muse for Enzo Manzini

Shari Ryan from Mad Hat Covers (newbie!)

Cassie from Joy Editing

Ellie from Love N Books

Shawna from Behind the Writer

Dani Sanchez and the Wildfire Marketing gang

All the bloggers who carve out time to read and review our books.

All our early ARC readers

And of course, all our unicorns. <3

ABOUT PIPER & RAYNE

Piper Rayne, or Piper and Rayne, whichever you prefer because we're not one author, we're two. Yep, you get two USA Today Bestselling authors for the price of one. Our goal is to bring you romance stories that have "Heart-warming Humor With a Side of Sizzle" (okay...you caught us, that's our tagline). A little about us... We both have kindle's full of one-clickable books. We're both married to husbands who drive us to drink. We're both chauffeurs to our kids. Most of all, we love hot heroes and quirky heroines that make us laugh, and we hope you do, too.

www.piperrayne.com
Amazon
Goodreads
Facebook
Instagram
Pinterest
Bookbub

ALSO BY PIPER RAYNE

White Collar Brothers

Sexy Filthy Boss

Dirty Flirty Enemy

Wild Steamy Hook-up

The Rooftop Crew

My Bestie's Ex

A Royal Mistake

The Rival Roomies

Our Star-Crossed Kiss

The Do-Over

A Co-Workers Crush

Hockey Hotties

My Lucky #13

The Trouble with #9

Faking it with #41

Sneaking around with #34

Second Shot with #76

Offside with #55

Kingsmen Football Stars

You had your chance, Lee Burrows

You can't kiss the Nanny, Brady Banks

Over my Brother's Dead Body, Chase Andrews

The Baileys

Lessons from a One-Night Stand

Advice from a Jilted Bride

Birth of a Baby Daddy

Operation Bailey Wedding (Novella)

Falling for My Brother's Best Friend

Demise of a Self-Centered Playboy

Confessions of a Naughty Nanny

Operation Bailey Babies (Novella)

Secrets of the World's Worst Matchmaker

Winning My Best Friend's Girl

Rules for Dating your Ex

Operation Bailey Birthday (Novella)

The Greenes

My Beautiful Neighbor

My Almost Ex

My Vegas Groom

The Greene Family Summer Bash

My Sister's Flirty Friend

My Unexpected Surprise

My Famous Frenemy

The Greene Family Vacation

My Scorned Best Friend

My Fake Fiancé

My Brother's Forbidden Friend

The Modern Love World

Charmed by the Bartender

Hooked by the Boxer

Mad about the Banker

The Single Dad's Club

Real Deal

Dirty Talker

Sexy Beast

Hollywood Hearts

Mister Mom

Animal Attraction

Domestic Bliss

Bedroom Games

Cold as Ice

On Thin Ice

Break the Ice

Box Set

Charity Case

Manic Monday

Afternoon Delight

Happy Hour

Blue Collar Brothers

Flirting with Fire

Crushing on the Cop

Engaged to the EMT

Printed in Great Britain
by Amazon

21395268R00192